ANGEL FLIGHT

a novel

HooYAH!

by

R. D. KARDON

Angel Flight
First Edition
Copyright © 2020 R. D. Kardon
All rights reserved. Printed in the United States of America.
For information, address Acorn Publishing, LLC,
3943 Irvine Blvd. Ste. 218, Irvine, CA 92602.

Cover design by Damonza
Damonza.com

Interior formatted by Debra Cranfield Kennedy

ISBN—Hardcover 978-1-947392-99-1
ISBN—Paperback 978-1-947392-98-4

To SP

Also by R. D. Kardon

Flygirl

Damaged people damage people

—Marianne Williamson

CHRISTINE

Testing . . . testing. Okay, it's recording.

Erik, my love,

I can't find the Glock.

It's been in the safe since I first got diagnosed. Every now and then, I'd take it out, release the safety, and stick the cool muzzle in my mouth.

Practice.

After you left last night, I kissed you again in my mind and went to the safe.

But the gun was gone.

I waited too long.

Do you know?

PART I:
THE CREW

February 2000

Exeter, Illinois

One

STRIPS OF PURPLE and gold stratus clouds stacked in an infinite sky led Captain Tris Miles home. Low rays of sun sketched the horizon outside the cockpit window, and behind her a swollen wall of snow buried the east coast.

She raised her arms above her head and closed her eyes. The left seat of the twin turboprop Royal 350 had molded to the curves of her body over time and held her like a hug. In the right seat a few feet away, her co-pilot Bruce Burkey had the controls. When her eyes opened a few seconds later, he'd configured the airplane for a graceful descent into Exeter International.

Bruce's perfect approach ended in a soft landing. Tris took command and taxied to the ramp. After the ground crew guided the airplane safely into the Westin Charter Company hangar, Tris hopped off the airplane to finalize post-flight paperwork.

Long after he should have left for home, she found Bruce in the Royal's passenger cabin, crossing the safety belts and lifting errant crumbs from the seats with exacting fingertips. Stooped over in the

11

not-quite-five-foot-tall cabin, his lanky wide-shouldered build, deep-set eyes, and scraggly blond hair gave him the haunted look that had earned him the nickname Lurch.

"You know, the company hires people to do that," she reminded her first officer. Westin Charter's cleaning service brought the airplane's interior back to showroom condition between flights.

Bruce bent over further to pick a couple of lint balls off of the worn carpeting, then moistened his finger to rub a smudge from one of the armrests.

"Bruce, go home. The cleaning crew will be in tomorrow."

He frowned. "You know I'll do a better job."

Bruce surveyed the small but well-appointed six-seat compartment, shook his head, and grabbed the bag of trash he'd already collected.

"And anyhow, if I'd left it, you know you'd just have cleaned it yourself," he said.

Tris had to laugh. "Probably."

Bruce followed her down the plane's air stairs. "Hey, great job this morning getting into Teterboro. First rate." His remark bore not a trace of sycophancy. Tris had flown the early morning leg into the busiest business airport in the country and landed in New Jersey during a driving winter storm that had packed Runway One with snow.

"Our passengers had no idea how difficult that landing was. And you just slid it onto the runway." He tapped his bottom lip with an index finger. "That's the trick. You make it look easy."

"Team effort," she replied. "Hey. You know what they say," Tris began their favorite bad-weather joke, born one morning when they had to dig the Royal out of a snowbank. "The crew—"

Bruce chuckled. "That shovels together . . ."

"Stays together," they finished simultaneously.

Tris had hired Bruce herself, picking him from a horde of anxious, aggressive instructors for the coveted co-pilot job at Westin. And he hadn't faltered, not once, had never been anything but a loyal, exemplary employee from his first day. He was meticulous about the airplane's condition from nose to tail. This conscientious attention to detail was a crucial characteristic of an airplane captain, which he very much wanted to be.

Tris glanced at the clock on the hangar wall. She needed to change her clothes and hit the road in a hurry to make it to the cemetery before it closed.

"Want me to get a jump on the next trip, Cap? Get the aircraft ready for Lemaster?" He asked, although he leaned toward the exit door, the extended handle of his overnight bag tilted forward, backpack over his shoulder, right hand in his pocket clinking his keys and loose change together. She'd noticed he habitually kept his fingers moving, like Captain Queeg in *The Caine Mutiny*.

"Nah. I want you to head home. How long until the baby's here?"

Bruce grinned. "Two months. Heather's gotten really big."

"I'll see for myself in a couple weeks at your party."

"Yup. We're really glad you can make it. So, I'll head out, okay?" Bruce gave a little wave when she nodded, and was gone.

Outside, the day continued its slow march toward night. The cemetery officially locked its gates at sunset. She'd snuck through a hole in the fence once before and learned the hard way that the footing around the graves was treacherous in the dark.

Adjacent to the hangar was a room that doubled as a flight-planning area and passenger waiting lounge. Walking in, Tris noted the ripped carpet, the old map of the City of Exeter that hung crooked on a wall, and the papers peeking out of drawers in the rusty file cabinet. It was a far cry from the clean, modern Tetrix flight department offices. But the dingy atmosphere was a fair trade to Tris—she was valued here, not undermined—respected, not bullied.

Westin Charter shared office space with Westin Flight School. The hum of flight instructors and their students discussing last-minute details, and the squeal of tires from a nearby fuel truck rushing to its next airplane, almost drowned out the sound of someone calling her name.

"Hello?" she called over her shoulder.

"Tris?" The husky voice with its strong British accent belonged to Phyllida, the company's part-time dispatcher. It was a mystery how Tris could have walked right by without noticing her teased beehive hairstyle, purple "jumper," as she'd say, and bright pink leggings. In contrast, Tris—her baggy uniform draped over her slim five-foot-seven frame, light brown hair lying flat against her head—looked frumpy indeed.

"Hey Phyll. What's up?"

"Tris, I'm so sorry. I know you were looking forward to some peace and quiet, but I'm afraid Woody needs you to come in for a chat." More than anyone, Phyll knew how exhausting Tris's schedule was. But Tris was the company's only captain, and more important, Woody's confidante. If he needed her, she'd be there.

"Hey, mind if I change while we talk?" Tris headed to the ladies' room and Phyll followed, folder in hand. "Do you know what about?"

"Of course, my dear. It seems we've been asked to do an angel flight, bring someone down here from Northeast Canada. Let me see . . ." her voice trailed off. "Oh right. Here it is. My goodness, I can't pronounce the name of the place. I-Q-A . . ."

"Iqaluit. I've heard of it."

"Brilliant! Well, yes, so, tomorrow at 10:00 a.m.?"

"Of course. I'll be here."

"Cheers, then." Phyll walked away, her high-heeled boots quiet as they crossed the carpeted floor.

"Wait," Tris called after her. "Do you know how we got this trip?" Companies that flew prestigious "angel flights," transporting critically ill passengers from remote areas to big cities to get specialized medical attention, donated the plane and crew, so the trips were huge money losers. Compensation, such as it was, came through earned respect and attention from industry peers. Flying one could hoist Westin's reputation above all other small charter operations at the airport.

"Not quite sure. The Chief Pilot of another company on the field called Woody today. I don't recall the gentleman's name."

On her way out, Tris mentally ticked off the names of the other flight departments at Exeter who could have offered Westin Charter this trip, those that might have an office in Iqaluit.

Please let it be anyone but him, any company but them.

Her uniform shirt and pants carefully folded over her arm, Tris checked her watch again and walked briskly toward the car. There wasn't time to worry about it now.

Today was Bron's birthday, and he was waiting.

Two

TRIS MADE HERSELF comfortable in one of two cracked leather armchairs that sat side by side in the Westin Charter passenger waiting area. She pulled her sweater down to the waistband of her faded jeans and stretched the sleeves over her hands to warm them.

Her eyelids shut to the familiar *chug-chug-chug* of training aircraft engines starting up in the background. When a door slammed closed, Tris shot upright.

"Hey, Woody. Man, you scared the crap out of me."

"Gotcha!" Woody Westin laughed as Tris caught her breath. Woody wore his "uniform": a pair of baggy Dockers, an old t-shirt, and tennis shoes, with a sweat-stained Westin Charter Company baseball cap that covered his blond buzz cut.

He motioned Tris toward his office. On her way, she accidentally banged into the coat rack where she'd hung her captain's jacket last night; along with some old pilot shirts from her collection, and the custom-tailored pants from her former job at Tetrix, it completed her pilot uniform.

Tris loved wearing that jacket—a visual representation of all she'd worked so hard to achieve. The pants, however, embodied everything that was wrong at her last job. She couldn't see how Tetrix, a company whose management required her uniform slacks to be fitted perfectly down to the last stitch, and tough enough to survive a nuclear war, could be oblivious to the toxic work culture of their flight department.

Tris followed Woody into an office the size of a kitchen pantry and unfolded an armless metal chair he kept in a corner for visitors.

Woody read a phone message on his desk, then leaned back in his chair and cracked his knuckles. "So, thanks for coming in. I guess that trip was crazy yesterday—bad weather out east?" He didn't wait for an answer. "You see the new flight on our schedule? That trip from Exeter to some place out in who-the-hell-knows-where Canada and back? Can you make that happen?"

Tris nodded. "Phyll told me about it yesterday. We fly empty to Iqaluit on April 11th, and then back to Exeter the next day with our passenger. That's about two months away, so there's plenty of time to plan it. An angel flight. That's quite a coup."

Woody flashed a wide, gap-toothed smile. "It sure is. We need to pick up the wife of an executive and bring her back here for treatment at Exeter Medical Center. The company's own jets are all down for scheduled maintenance that week, which is the only time the specialists can see her. Anyway, I can't stress enough how important this trip could be to our business. I mean, if we can get spillover trips from Tetrix, who knows? Maybe some of the other local companies will follow suit."

Tris mentally swatted away the mention of Tetrix and ignored the familiar tightening in her throat. "What's the passenger's story?"

"I don't have all the info yet." Woody thumbed through some notes on his desk. "I guess the guy's wife has Lou Gehrig's disease.

They're Americans, but the company relocated them out there for some reason. You know the area, right?" He squinted at Tris, his expression inviting her to fill in the blanks.

"I could locate it on a map, but I never got to Iqaluit while I was flying for, uh, them. I heard some of the guys mention it, and it just sounded like a fuel stop in between Northern Europe and the US. The company has a small office there. The executives we flew—the high-level folks—never visited it."

Why did it have to be *them*?

Woody nodded. "You realize that as the pilot-in-command on this mission, you'll have to liaise with the Tetrix flight department on passenger details, timing, etc. You okay dealing directly with those folks?"

A cold bolt of anxiety sliced through her. Aviation was a small community, and companies based at the same airport tighter still. She'd known that taking another job at Exeter would put her right in the sights of her former coworkers. Logically, it was only a matter of time before she ran into them again. She heard Dr. C's voice in her head: *Every thought, every contact, has a tail.* Her disastrous experience at Tetrix had left her reeling, but time had passed, and the wounds had at least scabbed over.

"Of course. I'll get started on the flight planning. Anything else I should know?"

"Maybe." Woody paused and tapped his desk a few times with his pen. "Jimbo and I are looking at buying another 350—you know, expanding the business. There's one for sale out in Phoenix that could be right for us. We need to run the numbers. If we can make a deal for it, it'll happen fast." He looked around and finally grabbed a half-eaten roll of Tums that had migrated behind one of his desktop airplane models. He popped two of the chalky discs into his mouth.

"So, busy times coming. I'm gonna need a new Chief Pilot a lot faster than I thought. A second airplane means I won't have time for those duties anymore. I know we talked about it, you know, 'in time.' Well, time's *now*." Woody smiled and winked.

Tris tilted her head back, eyes fixed on a water stain in the corner of the ceiling. She wasn't expecting this promotion now. Woody'd always said *eventually*. It was a dream come true—to have complete authority over pilot hiring and training. The promotion also carried the astonishing consequence that she would fly a *Tetrix* executive's ailing wife to obtain medical treatment as the head of Westin Charter's entire flight operation.

A quicker timeline meant longer hours, and that equated to less time for her personal life. She'd promised Dr. C—promised *herself*— that she'd concentrate more on life outside of work.

But *Chief Pilot*! It was the right next move.

She wanted it.

"Tris? What's that smile about?" Woody asked.

Tris realized she hadn't responded to him. "I'm just happy. And . . . surprised. I wasn't expecting this so soon. Thank you."

"Good. I'll need the new Chief ready for that angel flight. I'll confirm with our friends at the FAA, but I think I can do all the training in-house and complete your qualification. Unless the FAA wants to fly with you." He rolled his eyes at the mention of the federal agency. "Can you put together a formal training plan?"

"Sure. I'll get started right away. You'll let me know if we need to involve the feds?"

"Will do."

"Great." Tris hesitated, then made a decision about something she'd been meaning to ask Woody for a while. The company was expanding. She'd be its Chief Pilot. There would never be a better time to ask.

"Woody, I'd like you to approve a captain upgrade for Bruce."

Woody's eyebrows rose but his expression stayed non-committal.

She pressed him. "Look, he's worked hard, done everything we've asked of him and more. And with another airplane, you're going to need a second captain."

Woody squinted, then shook his head. "I don't know. You sure about him, Tris? I mean, he's a good co-pilot and all . . ." He pushed the brim of his baseball cap up and rubbed his forehead. "You sure you're ready to tie your own success to this guy?'

"He's earned the chance, Woody. I trust him."

"And I trust you," he replied, tugging his cap back down. "All right. Let's get him upgraded."

The tiles were set, each domino perfectly placed. How they fell would be entirely up to her.

Three

THE PARKING LOT was full, forcing Tris to drive around several times before a space opened up. With each circuit, her grip on the steering wheel tightened and she slid further down in her seat. She couldn't be too careful.

The squat, three-story medical building where Dr. C had her therapy practice also housed the offices of a couple of Aviation Medical Examiners. Tris hadn't known about the AMEs and the steady stream of Exeter pilots in and out of the building when she'd chosen Dr. C. By the time she realized that she might be recognized, she'd already bonded with her therapist.

Dr. C had helped Tris immeasurably as she struggled with the emotional consequences of losing Bron and the year at Tetrix that followed. With her help, Tris wrestled with depression, re-learned how to exist in the world without constantly questioning other people's motives, and discovered how to trust people—a very few people—again. Seeing her was worth a calculated risk.

Tris parked her old Corolla in a spot vacated by a huge sedan.

A few feet away, a woman pushed an older man in a wheelchair. Nearby, a couple of high school girls carrying backpacks smoked cigarettes and drank Diet Pepsi. No one she knew.

Still, she pulled her ski hat down just above her eyebrows and zipped her parka all the way up. It was 35 degrees outside, so bundling up wouldn't attract any attention. With only five minutes left before her appointment, she crossed her fingers and walked as close to the building's outer wall as possible. Tris had an explanation prepared for why she was there—she always did—but it was better not to be put on the spot.

Safely in Dr. C's waiting room, Tris took off her outer layers and thumbed through the magazines for the latest issue of *People*. A bit lowbrow for someone with a Masters in English Literature, but she loved celebrity gossip. Another thing she was good at hiding.

The red light next to Dr. C's office door meant she was with a patient. Tris flipped the pages of the glossy magazine and leaned back to read an article about Tom Hanks. *The Green Mile* had just come out; she'd wait and see it until after she read the book.

A hinge squeaked as the entrance door to the waiting area opened. Tris instinctively bent her head and shifted her body toward a corner of the room. She imagined Woody, or one of the local mechanics—anyone who knew she was a pilot—sitting down next to her, looking confused, asking, "Hey Tris, what are *you* doing here?" She'd have to make up something, anything but the truth. A hasty lie formed in her mind.

Thankfully, it was only the mailman. He left some letters by the closed door to Dr. C's office and went about his business. Her skittishness was not a put-on. It had been over a year, and she still hadn't told anyone—not even Danny or Diana, her two best friends—that she was seeing Dr. C.

Her pulse was still racing when the red light clicked off, the door opened, and Dr. C appeared. Petite, with white-blond hair, she wore a twinset, skirt, and her usual sly smile. Oh, the things she must hear in that room. Naturally competitive, Tris wondered whether she was the most troubled person Dr. C had ever treated.

"Are you all right?" The doctor asked, noting her uneasiness.

Tris jumped up. "Sorry. The mailman spooked me." She rushed past Dr. C to the office. "I know, I know. After all this time, it's just silly. But still . . ." Tris's words trailed off as she balanced on the edge of an armchair. She rubbed her hands up and down her thighs.

Dr. C closed the door and sat on her office chair. "Not silly at all. I completely understand your career concerns."

Tris had explained how the FAA dangled a sword of Damocles over pilots who sought counseling. Therapy was considered a danger sign, regardless of the reason. Even a whiff that a pilot was in treatment resulted in swift and devastating action. Her medical certificate could be suspended; without it, she couldn't fly. She knew a couple of male pilots who'd openly sought marriage counseling, but so far, they were the only ones to get a pass from the FAA.

Tris remained at the edge of her chair, her forearms on her thighs, hands clasped.

Dr. C extended her hands, palms down. "Relax. I know you had a fright, but it's over. Or is there something else going on?"

Finally, Tris leaned back against the chair's soft cushion. "Woody may have found another airplane to buy. He's stepping up the timeline on my promotion to Chief Pilot."

Dr. C nodded. "I see. When we last talked, you said you wanted the promotion. Now that Woody wants to move more quickly, is that still true? How do you feel about it?"

Tris bit back a *fine*, deliberately fighting her learned response to always say something positive. Here, in this room, she didn't have to be the good soldier. Her answer could be stripped to the bone, honest.

"Well, I guess I *should* be happy about it."

"You should? Who told you that?"

"No, I mean—of course I want it. And I'd never say no to Woody. No, that's not exactly right. I don't *want* to say no to him. After what he did for me? After Tetrix? If it weren't for him, well, I'm not sure where I'd be." She shook her head, still unable to believe her good fortune.

Dr. C sat poised with her pen hovering over the notebook in her lap. Her look softened, conveying real concern.

"Please, go on, Tris," she said.

Tris stared at a framed print of a large empty field with a small airplane flying in the background. She couldn't recall seeing it there before. "I really like my job as it is, flying the Royal, just a regular captain doing trips. The promotion will mean way more work, more responsibility." She paused. "But what if . . ."

Dr. C scribbled on her pad, then looked up. "What if what?"

Tris didn't answer right away. The two women considered each other in silence, and then Dr. C broke the stare by jotting down another note.

Tris noticed a new throw pillow resting against the divan's plump cushions. She preferred to sit upright rather than recline on the couch. These meetings were too important. If not for Dr. C, she'd still be riding the constant swells of depression and loss.

"What if I can't? I mean, what if I can't do it?"

The old insecurities bubbled up, born of early career challenges and the trying year at Tetrix, where her every move was questioned. Her many successes still couldn't quiet the doubt. What if they never could?

Dr. C shrugged. "Woody offered you the promotion. He wouldn't have done that if he wasn't sure, would he?"

"No."

The older woman fingered her string of pearls and cocked her head slightly to the side. "If he's sure, why aren't you? You've come a long way, Tris. Is there anything—anything *real*—in your training or experience since you've worked for Woody that supports your concerns?"

"No."

"Then what is this really about, Tris?" As if she could read her mind, Dr. C asked, "Will this promotion give you what you need? Or just more responsibility at work, without any new challenges outside of it? Will that satisfy you?"

"Will it *satisfy* me? I still don't know what my career is supposed to look like. I *have* to move forward, move up, and I have. Woody pulled me out of his flight school and made me his very first charter captain at Westin. Wasn't that moving up?"

"Of course it was, Tris. But I wonder . . . do you think it's finally time to do more in your personal life?"

Was it? She was still alone. Bron was gone. She'd held Danny at arm's length long enough for him to move on and marry Em. There was no one else on the horizon. Work, home, her cat. Was it enough?

"I want to be satisfied with what I have. I'm sitting here, my heart is in my throat, and I want to tell you I'm satisfied. But I'm somehow . . . unfinished. Like there's something I'm missing."

"What's missing, Tris?"

"I don't know."

Those internal toxins, guilt and shame, coated Tris's throat like bile. She still hadn't mentioned the angel flight, the contact with Tetrix she would be sure to have over the following weeks, or her recent visit with Bron.

Dr. C smiled what Tris thought of as her "little" smile, the one she used as a segue between topics, as opposed to the "big" smile she used when Tris made her laugh.

"Time to figure out what that is, eh? What's missing."

Now it was Tris's turn to smile. "I guess so."

"So, anything new to share about your life outside of work?" Dr. C leaned forward, pen lying on her pad. The movement was meant to gently prod Tris into a conversation she might not be ready for.

"I went to the cemetery."

The space between them buzzed with faint, low-level static. She'd done the one thing she'd told Dr. C, promised *herself*, she wouldn't.

"And how do you feel about that?"

Tris raised her hands in the air and exhaled in surrender. "Sitting here, right now, I feel stupid. And *weak*."

Dr. C's brows cinched. "And while you were there?"

"At peace. Comforted. Like there was no place I'd rather be."

Four

DANNY TERRY'S MOBILE phone rang as he cleared the sliding glass entrance door to the Denver Airport Inn. "The Wife" popped up on his caller ID. Emily.

"Hey baby."

His roller bag bumped along the uneven hallway floor and snagged on raised areas of carpeting rife with amoeba-shaped blotches in all colors and sizes. If he got bored later, he could wander the halls and count the stains. The rug-freshener-and-mold scent of intermittent cleaning matched the scuffed trim and faded wallpaper.

Danny stopped in a vestibule, loosened his tie one-handed and listened to Em tell him about the dishwasher repair she scheduled for the next day as he checked the rest of his missed calls. One missed call earlier from Em. Nothing from crew scheduling. *Damn.*

The ink on their marriage certificate had still been wet when he got the call to interview for his dream job, flying for Legacy Airlines. It was all coming together—the plum job, the wedding, the life—like it had for so many of his friends.

Danny had been almost forty when he got married. It was time. He and Em had a big wedding in the same banquet hall as her parents had. She'd worn her mother's dress, and her dad had cried when he walked her down the aisle.

The planning had been a bitch. Danny was relieved to be flying during most of it and dreaded the end-of-day calls with Em about flowers, bridesmaids, and bands. Her parents were paying for it, sure, but he could never wrap his head around the fuss. How silly to spend so much effort and money on a party that would only last six hours.

When the day finally arrived, the wedding was amazing. Watching as the details that had once annoyed him came together in a beautifully arranged pageant, Danny gained a newfound respect for Em's planning and organizational skills. Still, he couldn't shake the feeling that he'd been a prop in that big show. His job was to reflect Em's glow, answer her vows, slide on her ring, feed her cake, and balance out the photos.

Maybe all grooms felt that way.

Em loved him. He was sure of it. And now they were taking the next step and trying to have a baby. But not tonight.

"Hey. You in the hotel?" She'd turned the conversation back to him. She wasn't really one for small talk. It was one of his favorite things about her. Em got to the point. Just like Tris.

"Yup. Spent the whole day on call in the crew room. And this hotel sucks. I'm almost afraid to lie on the comforter even in my uniform. I shouldn't be here long, though. I'm sure I'll get a trip. Especially with all the weather in Exeter. A crew's gotta be held up somewhere."

"Right. So, hon, there's no chance you're going to be extended this time, is there?" Em was referring to the last reserve stint he did. Legacy Airlines crew scheduling kept him on duty an extra day, which they could do under the pilot contract.

"Why? What's up?" Had to be a family thing. There was always something going on with her people.

28

"Did you forget it's Bruce and Heather's anniversary party this weekend? How could you forget?" Em zoomed from asking a simple question to accusing him of something. It was one of Em's personal habits that he didn't care for. He let it pass.

He remembered the party all right. Em had practically taken Bruce's head off when she learned that he'd invited Tris, and she'd accepted.

"Right. Yeah, I'll be there. They can only extend me for a day, which would mean I'd be home on Friday night at the latest." And tired. And not in the mood to do anything but sleep over the weekend. Em knew it, too.

"I'll pick up a bottle of champagne and sparkling grape juice for Heather," she replied cheerfully, the tension of a few seconds before gone. "I mean, it's an anniversary party, after all. Can't wait to see you, baby." And he knew she meant it.

"Me, too. Love you, Boo." He was pretty sure he meant it.

The lock to his hotel room clicked open. What the hallway had previewed was spot on. The room had barely enough space for its full-size bed, three-drawer chest and shelf that doubled as ersatz desk. The uneven particleboard surfaces looked bloated and water soaked. He flipped the light on in the bathroom. Clean enough.

His first trip to Denver, ever, had been to interview for the Legacy job. He'd taken an interview prep course "guaranteed to land the job," the ads promised. The company's consultant, a tiny woman with a slight lisp, had actually told him how long to count in his head between hearing a question and answering it, what questions he should joke with the interviewers about, when he should smile. It was surreal.

And it worked.

Now that he was on the seniority list of this mammoth airline, every passing day would bring him closer to a better schedule, nicer overnights, and more money. His current ride, the Boeing 737, was the smallest plane in Legacy's fleet. Since airline pilots were paid by the number of passengers they carried (how many people they could kill at any one time, as the gruesome inside joke went) when he had enough seniority to fly the big iron, the 777 with almost 300 passengers, his lifestyle would look a lot different.

Maybe then—with more money, more time off—Em would relax into their marriage, forget about his history with Tris.

Maybe they both would.

Five

LEMASTER REGIONAL AIRPORT sat in the middle of a corn-field fifty miles west of Exeter. Typically hosting small single engine props whose owners lived to poke holes in the sky, its one runway was so narrow no jet could land there, so the airport rarely got commercial traffic.

Tris and Bruce brought in an executive to visit a nearby corn-processing plant. After landing, Tris expertly negotiated the tricky taxiway, a cracked concrete strip that dead-ended outside of a Mobile Mini trailer.

The corrugated steel container sported an "Executive Terminal" sign. Adjacent to its western wall was a larger structure used as a hangar and mechanic's shop. Its interior was warmed by a small space heater. Coffee cost twenty cents and was dispensed into paper cups by an old vending machine.

Tris and Bruce expected a long sit at the remote location waiting for their passenger. Then Phyll paged and said their itinerary had changed, they needed to return to Exeter, asap. Woody had hired mechanics to do an oil change on the Royal when their passenger's trip added an overnight stay.

Bruce looked up from the small card table where they were studying their dispatch release and surveyed the room.

"What's up?" Tris asked.

"Where's the lav?" Bruce stood and looked around again, as if he had missed something in the 300-square-foot box. Other than a teenaged girl sitting behind a folding table with a phone on it, they were the only people in the room.

Tris grinned. "Methinks this transaction will be 'au natural,'" code for behind a bush outside somewhere. It wouldn't be the first time either pilot pursued that option. Bruce grimaced and headed for the door.

As he reached for the doorknob, a loud *whoosh* of air pierced the silent ramp. Then something exploded. The building's thin walls shook.

"Fire!" someone screamed. The cry sounded like it came from the ramp.

"Bomb!" another voice bellowed.

Tris pushed past Bruce, who was frozen in place, and yanked the door open to the sight of a large fire burning on the ramp right outside the hangar. Plumes of thick smoke obscured her view of the fully fueled Royal, mere feet from the blaze. She looked around for a fire extinguisher. Her mouth was open, but no words came out.

"Run!" Bruce yelled over the sudden sound of a screeching alarm.

Both pilots squeezed onto the ramp and then hustled away from the building. They joined airport employees, rampers, mechanics, and small-aircraft pilots jostling for position on the street side of the building. Tris's captain's hat got knocked off her head. The hair tucked up inside fell below her shoulders as her hat bounced off of people fleeing the blaze, hit the ground, and was stomped on.

In a grassy area well clear of the tiny building, Tris gasped for breath, the acrid smell of sulfur still in her nose. A dozen others were already sucking in fresh air as they watched the activity from a safe distance. She couldn't spot Bruce anywhere.

Fire engines and an ambulance arrived, sirens blaring, lights turning in a blue and red wave. Firefighters carried their heavy equipment with speed and purpose.

Tris worked her way through the groups of people, looking for Bruce. He stood over by the opposite end of the hangar structure. At six-foot-six, he was visible even over the heads of rescue workers in full gear. His hand was clasped around his mobile phone, but he wasn't speaking. Tris hoped he would find a quieter place to call his wife.

Satisfied that Bruce wasn't hurt, Tris turned back toward their airplane. For security reasons, views of the ramp were obscured from where she stood, so she grabbed someone with an airport badge.

"I'm the captain of Four-Five-Quebec, the Royal 350 on the ramp," she said, hooking a thumb toward where her airplane sat. "Can you help me? How close is it to the fire?"

The man's eyes widened. "Ma'am, I can't let anyone back inside. It's too dangerous."

They were silenced by an announcement blared through a megaphone.

"Folks, this is Chief Timmons, Lemaster Fire Department. I need you to step further away from the building. Please *back away*."

"Excuse me, ma'am," the airport employee muttered as he rushed off.

Unable to see the airplane, Tris joined Bruce and braced herself, waiting for a huge boom, a signal that something full of fuel had blown up. Standing silent side by side, they exchanged glances and sighs.

Bruce held his mobile phone against his chest with both hands like a talisman. "What if we'd been on the ramp, Tris? Or on the plane? And couldn't get out? If I'd been hurt. What about Heather? What about my *son*?" He croaked out the last few words.

"But that didn't happen, Bruce. You are not in any danger. You're okay."

The crowd stood in small groups, watching, drawn together by the emergency. Bruce looked straight ahead. His expression—bereft and helpless—made Tris tear up involuntarily. Not for herself, but for him, for his family.

She heard, "I'm okay. Yes, I'm fine," over and over, spoken in urgent tones into mobile phones amid the frightened assembly. People gave each other reassuring pats on the shoulder, some held hands, and others hugged.

Their connection, forged by fire, at once touched and saddened her. It was one thing to be responsible for others' lives when she flew an airplane. Life and death were always in the back of every pilot's mind. But passengers were strangers, and her dedication to them a professional commitment.

It was something else entirely to be responsible to people who valued *your* life. How long had it been, how much had transpired, since someone had loved her so much, depended on her so implicitly, that *she'd* be terrified *they'd* lose her?

She understood Bruce's fear perfectly.

When the gunpowder exploded, she'd been afraid, sure. She worried about Bruce, the plane, the workers.

If she'd been hurt, whose life would change?

Six

THE FLAMES HAD scorched part of the Lemaster ramp but never reached the Royal or destroyed any equipment. The scene had looked and sounded way worse than it was, and, slowly, people went back to their jobs, their planes, and their lives.

A grey cloud hung in the air, giving the ramp an eerie, early-morning look. Yellow police tape stretched around the temporary building, past the hangar and along at least half of the asphalt ramp. A uniformed officer slowly removed the barrier.

"The danger is past. Crisis averted," Chief Timmons brayed through his megaphone. "You can all go back to what you were doing." He paused, looked down at a piece of paper. "Will the crew of a Royal 350, Five-Four-Five-Quebec, please come see me?"

Tris and Bruce walked toward the fire chief as everyone else moved away.

"Sir, I'm Tris Miles, the captain of the Royal."

Timmons removed his thick yellow and black uniform glove and shook hands with Tris.

He consulted his notes as he spoke. "A box which held a canister of gunpowder was accidentally crushed, breaching its protective metal casing. Someone must have thrown a match near it, and it ignited the black powder," he said, eyes fixed on the crew.

"Thanks for the information. But what does that have to do with us?" Tris asked.

Timmons looked back down at his notes. "That box was part of a load of freight that was supposed to go on your airplane. But it had no label on it. It was HAZMAT, but whoever packed it didn't put the required label designating it as EXPLOSIVE. Did you know that ma'am? That you were carrying hazardous materials?"

Tris took a step back and raised her hands. Bruce's face lost all color. "No way. I had no idea. Our company ops specs prohibit us from carrying any type of combustible material," Tris said, rattling off this regulatory fact a bit too quickly to emphasize that she and Bruce had no way of knowing what was in the box. As pilots, all they did was review the bill of lading, and check weight estimates to make sure they were reasonable and within the limitations of the aircraft.

Timmons pulled off his helmet with his non-gloved hand, placed it under his arm and scratched his head. "All right ma'am. I understand. But you're gonna have to tell that to the local police."

"Police," she heard Bruce whisper. He'd stepped behind her and was crouched down on the grass. "HAZMAT," he spoke again, incredulity framing his voice.

Tris put her hand on his shoulder. "Bruce, we're both going to have to talk to the cops. They're still in the hangar. Come on."

Slowly, he got up, and followed his captain back inside.

After Tris reiterated to the Lemaster police that the crew had no inkling what was in the unlabeled box, it was Bruce's turn. She went back outside for some air and stayed until she spotted the officers leaving.

She found Bruce, doubled over in an old metal chair in the middle of the hangar. He stared at the ground, tears staining his face. His chest extended fully with each deep breath.

She gasped at the sight of this man, bent over, crying—still shaking like a frightened child. This wasn't Bruce, her stalwart co-pilot.

"So." She sat down next to him and knocked his knee with hers. "Just another fun-filled day at the airport, eh?" Her attempt at levity fell flat.

"Tris, there was no HAZMAT sticker on it. Nothing. And it was our freight. I *touched* it. I actually picked it up, put it down, and kicked it aside. I *kicked* it."

Bruce didn't say what she was sure both pilots were thinking— that he could have been the one who damaged the box, or the container inside. Tris tightened her left fist, nails biting into skin.

It could have ignited in flight.

Bruce stared straight ahead. She put her hand on his back. It was 30 degrees outside, maybe 45 in the hangar, yet he'd sweated through his shirt.

"It's all right, Bruce. It's all right," she repeated softly.

Just then, the ambulance parked on the ramp spun its lights and pulled away. "How many got hurt?" Bruce whispered as he watched it leave.

"I don't think anyone. It's empty."

Bruce grabbed his head with both hands, tightened his fists and rocked back and forth. "I feel sick, Tris. Really sick," he said.

"It's okay. You're fine," Tris said, and patted his arm.

Bruce leapt from his chair and rushed toward a garbage can. He bent over it and vomited.

Tris moved out of earshot and pressed #2 on her phone's speed dial. Woody answered on the first ring. "Tris? What's up? How are you? I was just about to call you for a status report. I'm listening to updates on the radio. Sounds like the fire is out. When can you take off? I need the Royal back here for an oil change. The mechanic's been sitting here for hours."

"We're *fine*, by the way, as in not hurt. But Bruce—I don't think he can fly." She looked over at her co-pilot, still bent over, retching.

"Why not? You guys have to get the plane home. Can't you handle it, Tris? I mean you want to be the Chief Pilot here right? Fix it."

She closed her eyes. "Woody, we were a few feet away from a fire that could have burned down the hangar and caused our airplane to explode. That's unnerving, to say the least. But it was due to a mislabeled box of gunpowder that was supposed to go on *our* aircraft. Someone tried to transport gunpowder on our aircraft. Good God, what if . . ." She let her voice trail off, then spoke with authority. "Anyway, I can fly. Bruce can't."

Bruce might come around and be his old reliable self. Or he might not. Tris avoided her own internal inventory. She had to get that plane home.

"Lemme see what I can do. I'll try to find someone." He hung up.

Tris draped a passenger blanket over Bruce's shoulders when he finally sat down next to her. "Hey Bruce. You want me to call someone? Maybe Heather?"

"*No*. She was freaked out enough when I told her what happened."

They sat for another hour or so, and finally Bruce was well enough to walk over and bring back some fresh coffee from the Starbucks a couple of blocks away. He handed Tris her venti French roast and walked back outside.

Tris sipped in silence when the metal door they had escaped through swung open. Backlit by the now-setting sun and lingering smoke from the fire was a man in a bomber jacket. As her vision adjusted, Tris noticed broad shoulders, a full head of bright red hair, and matching russet beard with strips of gray.

When he saw Tris, his eyes moved to her epaulets.

"Are you Captain Miles?"

"I am."

"Mike Marshall." She grasped his outstretched hand firmly. "Woody called me. I'm current and qualified on the airplane. I can help you get it home." He nodded toward the turboprop that sat motionless on the ramp.

His words emerged through a filter, as though they'd been underwater. The eyes that met hers were blue, but not like the sky. Deep blue like tinted glass, a window to the soul.

Tris took a step back and folded her arms across her chest, anything to increase the personal space between them.

He kept smiling and moved closer to her. His arm reached out. Tris backed up further.

"Uh, I thought you'd want to see my license and medical," he said, offering them to her.

"Of course," she mumbled and looked down at the two small documents that made pilots legal to fly.

The sound of a mobile phone shattered her mounting attraction. It was Woody, calling to tell her what she already knew— he'd found a pilot to help her ferry the airplane home.

She ended the call and turned to Mike. "Can you do a thorough pre-flight and get fresh weather while I let my co-pilot know what's going on? He's not feeling well. I'll brief him."

"Will do." Mike strode off, seeming to know his way around the hangar.

He was already in the right seat when she boarded the airplane with Bruce and their updated flight plan. A quick scan of the cockpit revealed that he'd performed all required checks.

"Ready to go home, Captain?" Mike's eyes crinkled at the corners, above a wide smile.

"I sure am. Engine-start checklist please."

CHRISTINE

*I'm already walking like a drunken sailor.
Soon, I'll be stuck in a wheelchair. And as
more time passes, I'll lose the ability to
perform the most basic daily functions. I'll
waste away until I'm just bones in that chair.
Or a bed. Or in a bed in a hospital. Or
hospice. Just today, I couldn't reach the top
shelf in the kitchen without using a stool,
which seemed so heavy but, in fact, weighs
only two pounds. I checked.*

*And it's happening so fast. Too fast. So fast
even the doctors are stumped. "Christine, you're
a special case." They made it sound like I
should be proud that less than a year after my
diagnosis, I struggle to walk to the mailbox.*

*We had just put the past behind us, now this.
It makes me want to punch something. But
there's no one to blame. And there is no cure.*

*Yesterday, after we made love, all you could
talk about was the treatment, the trip to
Exeter, the future. I just wanted to scream,
to beg you, "Please, for the love of God,
shoot me in the head. If you love me don't
make me do this."*

You see, I want to end my life now, before I can no longer kiss you, my love, or hold you, or use the bathroom by myself—among the many things I'll be asked to let go as this disease claims my body, little by little, day after day.

If my work, my experience, has taught me anything, it's that I can say goodbye—to you, to all of it. I can give it all up, but only on my own terms.

Seven

WHEN TRIS CALLED Bruce at home the next day to check on him, he sounded like his old self.

"You sure you're ok?" she asked.

"Positive. But you can bet I'll be quadruple checking our freight from now on. So, what about Pinedale?" he asked. The trip was scheduled to leave later that day.

"Actually, the passengers called to delay it a few days. Which works out great for us. Seriously, Bruce, are you all right?" As Bruce's friend, she hoped he was truly over what happened. As his captain, Tris had to be sure he was fit to fly.

Bruce didn't hesitate to respond in a tone that convinced her. "I'm fine. I'm ready for Pinedale. Heather's been following me around like a mother hen. I love that she's concerned for *me* with that huge beach ball she's carrying."

Tris chuckled. "You still calling him that? He's got a name, right?"

"Oh yeah. But Heather has sworn me to secrecy. Given her

hormones, no way I'm pissing her off," Bruce said, his light tone more reassuring than his words.

"Okay, Bruce. See you on Thursday for Pinedale."

Yet when the day arrived, the trip was beset with problems. Right at takeoff time, there was a line of thunderstorms passing through Exeter. The two pilots stood at Westin's old HP desktop looking at the live Doppler radar.

"Are you sure we can do this?" Bruce asked for the third time as the latest forecast spit out of the company's dot matrix printer.

Tris fought the urge to snap at him. She'd already explained how they could dart between cells without too many heading changes, and easily clear the storms to the west which, conveniently, was their direction of flight.

"I am, Bruce. But my question is, are you?"

Bruce straightened his back, raised his eyebrows and peered down at Tris. Finally, he shrugged and said, "Let's go."

Tris deftly flew the airplane around the storms, and the rest of the flight was uneventful, until they pulled onto the ramp at the remote airport in Wyoming with a flat tire. Tris spent thirty minutes lying on her back next to the strut relaying damage info to Woody. Four hours passed before a mechanic Woody dug up met them at the airport and changed the tire.

The exhausted crew ended up on an unscheduled overnight, which catapulted Bruce into a bad mood, since Heather was expecting him home that night.

Dinner brightened his frame of mind considerably. Tris and Bruce chose a saloon-themed restaurant with actual batwing doors. The floors were covered in sawdust. Exhausted and slap-happy, they called each other "Podner" and split a pitcher of beer.

The next day, on the way home, Tris found herself impatient and restless. She could usually ignore Bruce's constant pen clicking, doodling on the flight release and incessant knuckle cracking, but his tics all screeched like nails on a blackboard.

After a mercifully uneventful flight back to Exeter, she was anxious to be by herself. When Bruce shoved his hand in his pocket and began clicking coins together, Tris almost lost her composure.

"You can head home, Bruce. I'll finish up the post-flight items. Go ahead. Go."

But instead of thanking her and leaving, Bruce stood by the airplane with his hands on his hips.

"*You* want to take the garbage out? Cross the belts for the cleaning crew? Isn't that *my* job?"

Tris had to let a few seconds pass rather than risk saying something she'd later regret. "Bruce, if I tell you I'll do it, I'll do it. Go home."

He clucked his tongue and made a show of hoisting his backpack over his shoulder. It was rare for the two of them to even disagree much less squabble. Always so eager to please, Bruce's behavior often bordered on worship.

And, just like that, as if snapped out of a trance, Bruce returned to his old self. "Okay, *Podner*," he said with an exaggerated drawl, "guess I'll see you this weekend at the party, right?"

Tris grinned. "Wouldn't miss it, *Podner*." She was looking forward to seeing Heather. And Danny.

Tris was searching for one of the mechanics to see whether there was any residual damage to the airplane's rim when Woody called her name.

"My office, now," he said, and sped away.

"Hey Woody. What?" she said, opening his office door moments later, her hand and head curled around the doorframe.

"Come in. Sit down a second, would you?"

There was no room in his office for her flight bag, so she

dropped it in the entranceway, a not-so-subtle signal that she was done for the day.

If Woody got the message, he promptly ignored it.

"Trip go okay? Except for the flat tire?"

He didn't look like he wanted a long answer.

"Yes."

"You know how big a financial hit I took on Lemaster? Having to hire a rent-a-pilot? And the mechanic I paid who sat around all day waiting to fix an airplane that wasn't there? Crap on a cracker!" Woody had both elbows on the desk and his hands clasped together.

She nodded in her most sympathetic fashion. "I know. But at least we completed it. No one could have predicted . . ."

He interrupted her. "Where's the syllabus?"

"Which one? Mine for Chief Pilot or Bruce's? You have Bruce's." She pointed in the general direction of the large pile of papers on his desk.

"Chief Pilot. I need to run it by the feds to make sure my new guy meets the specs."

It was an odd choice of words. Tris was his "new guy." She shrugged it off. "I've been here at the airport, or on a trip for the last few days. Give me a little time." Irritation crept into her voice and she couldn't cover it.

"How about Friday? That'll give you three days. Then you're due back for a trip."

She was still nodding as the phone at Phyll's desk began to ring. Woody got up and walked to the door so quickly Tris barely got her feet out of the way. Something was on his mind.

Tris followed him out. She had enough to worry about. He'd tell her eventually.

Eight

THE EMPTY WAITING area at Westin Charter was rarely so quiet. Phyll was gone for the day; Woody had answered the ringing phone at the reception desk and listened intently as he scrawled notes. Tris wasn't sure if he was done with her, so she dropped into one of the empty chairs.

Her mind went straight to Bruce. No getting around it, he was—off. He never snapped, never copped an attitude, never, *ever* talked back to her, no matter how difficult the day. Even at Lemaster, he hadn't acted out. She let it go. Bruce had earned his share of mulligans, and Tris would gladly credit him with the one he'd used up today.

Woody finished his conversation and called to her. "Tris, listen, I have something to tell—well, to ask you." He hesitated, scratched the back of his neck and pursed his lips as she walked over. "We just got a call from Tetrix. They have some info on our angel flight passenger. A whole dossier, so I'm told."

No surprise there. Tetrix always overdid it on paperwork. "And?"

Woody nodded. "Phyll's out tomorrow. I'd like to see what they have, and I'm sure you're curious. Can you swing by Tetrix and pick it up? Now?" He exhaled.

Tris hadn't been back to the Tetrix hangar since she resigned from her co-pilot position almost two years ago. Every now and then, she'd hear the voices of the pilots she used to fly with on the radio. Deter, Zorn, Basson. Even Dicky Lord. She recognized them all, and each word they spoke brought a quick pang of fear mixed with regret. The reaction passed more quickly now, thanks to the work she'd done with Dr. C.

Her recovery was about to be tested again.

"Fine. Who do I see about it?"

Woody looked down at a pink phone slip. "Brian Zorn."

"My old boss," she said evenly.

At her initial job interview, she'd told Woody everything. How proud Zorn had been about adding a female pilot to the Tetrix flight department; how he dumped her training on Ed Deter, a retired military pilot who hated female aviators and consistently undermined her. Tetrix captain Larry Ross befriended her, but his own internal demons overpowered any interest he had in helping Tris succeed, and eventually ended in catastrophe.

"I know what you think of them," Woody said quietly, both his expression and voice compassionate. "But, hey, it's business. I told Zorn that you were leading the charge on this flight, that you were my guy."

Tris had to smile. *My guy.* "No problem."

He clapped her on the shoulder with a wink.

She was warmed by the memory of Woody's words the day she was hired: *Tetrix didn't know what they had. I do.*

Nine

SHE'D HAVE BEEN more comfortable if she drove, but Tris chose to walk to the Tetrix hangar in the biting cold. She zipped up her parka and borrowed a warm ski cap from Woody. A captain's hat was more ornamental than functional, and it was twenty degrees out. Still, she carried the hat to wear when she was inside. No way she was going back to Tetrix in anything other than full captain's regalia.

With each step, she imagined how she'd take off her coat, straighten her uniform jacket and slide the middle button into its hole. She rehearsed what she'd say when she stood opposite Zorn. "Yes, I'm pilot-in-command on this angel flight," and "Yes, Westin is doing very well. We're expanding. In fact, Brian, I'll be flying the angel flight as Chief Pilot." Maybe even, "I'm fully in charge of this important assignment."

Her eyes teared in the cold and she wiped them furiously, lest anyone at Tetrix think she'd cried on her way over. At the keypad to the parking lot gate, instead of pressing the red button for assistance, she entered the code she remembered from her time as a Tetrix employee. 5-0-2-6. The gate slid open.

The wind picked up suddenly. Cold air twisted around her, attacking every inch of exposed skin and snaking up her sleeves. She ducked her face down behind the collar of her parka, but it didn't help.

Tris looked around the parking lot to see who she might run into. None of the cars looked familiar, but that didn't mean she'd avoid seeing one of the pilots she used to fly with. Those guys got new cars every year, it seemed.

A woman whose voice she didn't recognize buzzed her in. The first thing Tris noticed was that the entrance lights were off. When she opened the door, it was nearly dark inside. Tris could see her breath.

Tris greeted the woman at reception, who was also wearing a parka, along with a scarf and a knitted hat with earflaps and a pom pom.

"Hi. Are you from Westin?"

"Yes. Tris Miles." Tris held out her hand. A large red mitten grabbed it.

"Okay. Here it is." The red mitten gestured to a folder on the desk with a post-it note that read "Westin Charter."

Tris looked around. The entire area was dark. "Where's Brian?"

"He's gone. Everyone's gone. Our heating system went out. It's ice cold in here."

Tris chuckled. "Thanks. Tell him I said hi."

"I don't understand this medical brief at all." Woody pushed his chair away from his desk. It banged into the credenza behind him, causing the three airplane models arrayed on it to wobble.

"Me, either," Tris replied. "But I'm not sure we need to. Our passenger has ALS. And she's what—oh, man. Forty-two years old." She stopped to catch her breath. "Says here that she's 'ambulatory,' so I guess she can walk. She doesn't need oxygen or special services. Unless any of that changes, basically she's just another passenger."

The thick file that Brian Zorn had left for her was comprehensive. It included pages of medical information, copies of newspaper clippings, and some photographs.

Woody tapped the manila file folder. "Zorn said the guy—a high-ranking exec for them—was crying when he brought this paperwork to the hangar. His wife only has this one chance for treatment. There's no cure. How fucking sad is that?" He gestured to the photo on his desk of his wife Giselle. "You know, if it weren't for her, I'd be lost."

Woody said this so often, Tris was ready with her standard reply. "And wearing plaid pants every day."

Woody grabbed his briefcase. "Okay. You've got this, Tris. I'm outta here."

Tris followed him back out to the waiting area. She watched him bundle up and head out, as she flipped through the file.

She read a fact sheet about the town they were landing in. Iqaluit was the capital of the Nunavut territory of Canada. The word itself meant "many fish." Major local industries included hunting and fishing, and the inhabitants' primary method of transportation in the winter was snowmobile.

Tris found a flyer from the local airport where the Royal would originate the angel flight. The list of services included fuel, weather reporting, and catering, "With Appropriate Advanced Notice." She'd better have Phyll call them well ahead of the trip.

The physician's report for patient "Edgemon, Dr. Christine Marie" was stapled to the left inside cover. It included basic facts about their passenger's diagnosis, written with a plethora of medical jargon that could not disguise the grim trajectory of the disease. It would be fatal, but before it was, it would rob Christine of all physical abilities. Walking. Speaking. *Swallowing?*

Tris scanned a few of the other documents. Christine had been a practicing psychologist in Exeter. She and her husband Erik had moved to Iqaluit for his career as Regional Director of Project Management with Tetrix, and lived in a town called Happy Valley, according to a clipping from the *Nunatsiaq News*. Dr. Edgemon had put out her shingle as a grief counselor and volunteered with the local Inuit who had little if any access to mental health professionals.

Thumbing through the photos, Tris saw what had to be their wedding picture. The groom wore a white tux and tails. Christine wore a wine-colored midi-length dress that looked like it was silk or satin. Probably a second marriage.

Her husband beamed at her through kernels of rice caught in mid-air. Christine had her head turned, an oddly alarmed expression on her face. She seemed to be looking for something—or someone— she'd hoped wasn't there.

In one of the newspaper articles, an interviewer asked her how she felt about leaving Exeter, the big city, for the desolate landscape of Nunavut. "It was a unique opportunity to make a new start for ourselves. We'd just gotten married, and wanted to shed the past, to leave our previous lives behind for something that we could build from the ground up. Together," Christine had answered.

And that remote location at the tip of North America was what they chose? What did they need to break away from that required so much distance?

Another photo portrayed Christine and her husband Erik at a ribbon-cutting ceremony in Iqaluit. The two stood on a dirt patch surrounded by snow and ice. Tris couldn't make out any roads or buildings. Several people in the background were hunched over, grabbing the sides of their hats. Her husband embraced her with both arms, his head resting on her shoulder. The camera caught Christine's blond hair in flight around her head, which was turned. She looked off, wide-eyed and anxious.

What's she so afraid of?

Tris rubbed her eyes. No sense creating melodramas from wedding pictures and grainy newspaper photographs. She straightened the papers inside, closed the folder and put it in her angel flight pile.

Time for the day to be over.

Ten

THE SHOPPING LIST made no sense. As Heather's pregnancy advanced, her handwriting got worse. Bruce felt around in the glove compartment of the Bronco for his reading glasses. He'd only started wearing them recently, when he couldn't fake it anymore.

Vanity and ego kept him from carrying them in the airplane, even though he couldn't always read the notes on his navigation charts without squinting. When Tris wasn't looking, he'd pull his mini-magnifying glass out of his shirt pocket to make sure he wasn't missing anything important.

At his most recent aviation physical, he'd put drops in his eyes and made sure to pull the corners back with his fingertips. Someone had told him that it would help his vision test at the required 20/20. So far, so good.

He scanned the list and saw "wakers." What were wakers? Bruce turned the list to the side slightly. Oh, *crackers!*

Heather couldn't do the anniversary party shopping, so it was up to him. The list included finger foods, hors d'oeuvres, pigs-in-blankets: things that were easy to assemble or that Heather could heat in the oven and serve. Too bad. He was hoping she'd make one of her famous from-scratch quiches. Lately, she could barely stand up long enough to take a shower without having to rest, so he guessed that cooking for the party was out of the question.

Inside the store, Bruce walked diligently from aisle to aisle, filling his arms. He hugged two blocks of Cracker Barrel sharp cheddar, a large box of Ritz crackers, and a dozen eggs as he reached the frozen foods aisle.

Bruce spied the brand of mini quesadillas he liked and scooted toward the freezer to grab them. In front of the glass door, he stopped to secure his selections, and managed to free one hand without dropping any items.

A chubby young store employee wearing an apron with the name Roy embroidered on it approached him. "Excuse me, sir? Do you need a cart for those items?"

Bruce was confused. "What? Why?"

"Well," the store employee continued, "it looks like you're about to drop those items, sir. Perhaps a cart would make things easier for you." Roy turned toward a row of empty shopping carts a few feet away.

Bruce's cheeks flushed. He wanted to slap the pushy kid across the face. But then he'd drop his groceries.

"If I wanted a cart, don't you think I could, you know, walk five feet over there and get one? I don't need a cart. Now beat it," he said.

Just as Roy's mouth dropped open, he was joined by another male store employee, much older.

"Hello, sir. Is there something wrong? Something I can help you with?" the second man asked. His shirt had the word "Manager" stitched on it, but no name tag. Other shoppers had slowed their march through the aisles and were milling about. A woman stared at

Bruce; her bag of broccoli florets suspended in mid-air.

Bruce wasn't sure what was wrong. The kid had asked if he needed a cart. "I don't need a cart. I *don't* need a cart! *I* don't *need* a cart!" he insisted. With that, Bruce dropped his items on the floor where he stood, zipped up his coat and walked out of the store.

The temperature was below freezing, and a light snow swirled around him. Next to the grocery store was a Baskin-Robbins. Bruce hated ice cream, even as a child, but he had to get out of the cold. The door had a bell that rang when he opened it, and another ostensibly helpful store employee—this one female, also young, with terrible acne and a severe ponytail—asked him if he'd like to sample their new chocolate raspberry flavor.

Bruce didn't understand. Why would he want ice cream? "No, no thank you," he said. "I . . . I'm looking for . . . an ice cream cake. Yes. I need a cake for a party tomorrow."

The young clerk frowned. "Well, sir, if you need a custom cake, you know, with, like, a special name on it, you have to order it a week in advance. We may have something, you know, that is pre-made that you'll like. If you can come to, like, the end of the counter, I can show you." She wore a full-on smile now, complete with braces.

Bruce looked at the cakes sitting side-by-side in the display. "Happy Birthday Jim," with a vanilla ice cream golf ball on top, was right next to "Good Luck Mandy," which looked like chocolate with a red ice cream rose.

Birthdays in his house were celebrated with whatever cake his mother could get on special from the store at the last minute.

That will never happen to my son.

A son. *His* son. "Another boy," his mother lamented. Every time she mentioned her first grandchild, that's what he heard. "I can't win for losing, another boy. Well, it'll save on clothes anyway. Lots of hand-me-downs." And didn't Bruce know it. Some of the things he'd worn as a child had belonged to his brother Ben, who was ten years older than he was. He'd be damned if any of those threadbare offerings would ever touch his child.

Every possession Bruce had growing up was ripped, scraped, scratched or broken. He'd had his heart set on a new toy for his seventh birthday, just one.

When the day came, Bruce ripped the shiny wrapping paper off his gift to find one of his brother Jack's old fire engines.

When it was time for cake, his mother proudly served an unclaimed special order she'd picked up on sale from the grocery store. "It's a Boy!" was spelled out in a blue icing flourish across the top.

Another boy.

"Why can't I have my own cake for once?" he'd cried. He never got the answer.

When his parents weren't working, they were huddled together in their bedroom doing something they didn't want their sons to see. Sometimes they came out arguing, and Jack would herd his two younger brothers quickly into the garage, where they'd hide until the screaming stopped.

When they neglected to feed their sons, Jack would slap American cheese between two slices of Wonder bread slathered with mayo and ketchup for Bruce and his brother.

No. No hand-me downs for his son. No cheese sandwiches. His kid was getting everything new, even if Bruce had to steal it. *His* son would be served the best baby food money could buy, and he'd eat it in a highchair surrounded by his parents. And he'd never be afraid, never have to hide in his own home.

Bruce stuck his hands in his pockets, then patted down his coat, searching for his gloves. He must have dropped them in the grocery store. *I can't go back in there.*

He finally responded to the clerk, still waiting patiently for his order. "It's my wedding anniversary this weekend. Have anything for that?" How would he carry an ice-cream cake to the car without his gloves?

"Here's one that's chocolate and vanilla. Would you prefer strawberry? Or maybe, like, one of these combination brownie and ice-cream cakes?" Her hand floated over the display like Vanna White highlighting a solved puzzle.

But he didn't want an ice cream cake. "Sorry. No. My mistake. I'm sorry. Thank you," he said, as he bustled out the door back into the snow.

The Bronco was now cold inside. It would be at least five minutes before the heater started working on the old truck. The shopping list lay crumpled at his feet. He bent to pick it up. There was another grocery store on his way home. He'd try again.

Eleven

FINALLY HOME, TRIS found Orion sleeping in one of his many beds in the living room, this one near the patio door. Light filtered through the vertical blinds, making him look like a small furry Zebra. He yawned and rolled over, inviting a belly rub. Her touch immediately activated his purr, like a small motorcycle that needed a new muffler.

White Oleander lay partially open on her couch. She'd finished it before she left for Pinedale. *The Green Mile*, the first Stephen King novel she'd ever bought, had been pulled off of her bookshelf and was in the "ready" position on the coffee table.

Tris kicked off her shoes, changed into sweats and went to the kitchen. The refrigerator door resisted her pull and when she yanked it open, it caught her leg. She yelped and hopped up and down in front of the open fridge. She grabbed for a Diet Coke, and a whole row of the red and white cans rolled onto the kitchen floor. One clipped her big toe before coming to rest against the trashcan.

Tris swore, put the escaped cans back inside the fridge, and grabbed one she hoped wouldn't blow up in her face. She popped the top slowly, tipped it over and watched the dark liquid fizz and pop as it slid into a glass of ice. Tris placed the beverage on a coaster and curled up with the book in her big leather recliner. Tiny holes and scratches dotted what was once a pristine brown. That was Orion's doing. Still rubbing her toe, she smiled down at the longhaired Tuxedo, who was now snoring.

What was she so stressed about? At that very moment, safe in her own home with her cat snoozing a few feet away, there was nothing to protect, nothing to win or lose. Yet earlier that day, leaving Pinedale, she'd found herself entranced by the bill of lading for the freight on her aircraft, looking for—what? A sign that something wasn't right?

It's the captain who sets the tone of every flight. Was Bruce more twitchy than usual today because she'd hummed off-key? Did he pick up on her discomfort?

She cracked open *The Green Mile*. Reading usually calmed her, but after fifteen minutes, she dropped the book, reached for her now-sweating glass and tapped her fingernail against it. Would Dr. C answer the phone if she called? A glance over at the answering machine revealed a steady light. No new messages. She paced to the kitchen and back.

Dr. C had once suggested that Tris take anti-anxiety medication. She'd laughed out loud. That would ground her for sure. She couldn't even claim their pricey therapy sessions on her insurance for fear of leaving a paper trail, much less take any prescribed meds. The last time she had gotten her First Class Medical renewed, Tris had broached the subject of therapy with the AME, a harried man who certified pilots as safe to fly as a side business to his thriving occupational injury practice.

"Well, if you said you were in therapy, the regulations tell us we'd have to investigate further, and possibly defer your medical." He didn't face Tris, and sounded almost like he was talking to himself. "Yeah, that starts a whole big process. We have to get records, maybe talk to the therapist. Don't want a poorly-adjusted pilot up front with lives at stake, do we?"

Tris wanted to ask whether a troubled pilot wouldn't be better served by a few hours with a shrink than putting on a brave face and toughing it out in the cockpit. But she wisely kept her mouth shut.

Pilots didn't go to doctors for any ailment short of broken bones or chest pains. Once reported, there was a record. Records led to questions. And questions sometimes ended careers.

She had once asked if Dr. C believed she was a danger in the cockpit. To hell with the FAA, if she couldn't fly, she wouldn't fly. That was Dr. C's opportunity to laugh. Then she shifted back into therapist mode and asked, "Do you think you are?"

She didn't then. She didn't now.

What am I so anxious about?

Breathe deeply. Relax. Pet the cat.

After doing all three, Tris returned to planning. First thing, organize her own training. Make sure she could qualify as Chief Pilot before the angel flight. Then, check in with Bruce. His training was going well. Today's annoyances were all inconsequential. And, even after his upgrade, when they flew together, she'd still be pilot-in-command. She'd manage the work environment for both of them, hopefully doing a better job of it than she'd done the last couple of trips.

Bruce's knowledge, flying and adherence to company procedures were impressive. It was time to step up his training by letting him fly from the left seat. It was the only way to truly give him the full experience of command. He was ready.

Her mobile phone buzzed. The caller ID came up "Unknown."

"Hello?"

"Tris?"

"Diana? Hey, thanks for calling me back." Diana had taught Tris how to fly back in the day, became her mentor, and remained one of her best friends. A training captain for a freight carrier in Brussels, Belgium, she and Tris could talk about their careers in a way neither could with their male peers. As Tris transitioned out of Tetrix, Diana had done her best to be available, despite the time difference and the demanding flight schedule that took her into some of the most difficult to navigate overseas airports.

"Hey. How's it going?"

"It's going," Tris replied. "I wanted to tell you the good news. Looks like Woody wants to move me up to Chief Pilot. And fast."

"That's great." Diana sounded distracted. "Look, I'm calling in between legs here. You're excited about this right? You sound a little tentative."

"I am, and I can't put my finger on why," Tris said. "Woody has really put the hammer down and told me he wants it done asap. Before the angel flight in April."

Someone spoke to Diana in the background, and she answered, "merci." Tris always gave Diana leeway if she couldn't talk, but she really wanted her friend's advice.

Tris continued, "What if I can't, Di? What if I can't . . ."

Diana jumped on her comment. "That's ridiculous, Tris. It's been years since your bad training experience at Clear Sky. Forget it. This promotion is perfect for you. You've earned it, and you *deserve* it. And the timing—I mean, wouldn't you love to do that medical flight for those assholes at Tetrix as Chief Pilot?"

"Oh, it's crossed my mind," Tris chuckled. "The more I think about it, the more I want it. And not just to shove it at Tetrix. You're right. I've earned it."

Another voice said something to Diana, and she replied, "Okay. Be right there. So, Tris, I'm coming to Exeter on Tuesday. I was hoping to stay with you for a day or two."

"Sure. The airplane's down for maintenance next week, so no problem. You taking vacation?"

"Uh, no. I'm on leave, actually. Look, I'll explain when I see you. I'll call you when I figure out what flight I'll be jump seating on."

There were several seconds of dead air, which Tris attributed to the international connection. Diana was probably using a calling card from a pay phone in who-knows-where.

"Di? You still there?"

"I'm here. Look, Tris, I gotta go. We'll pick this up in person—Tuesday, okay?"

"Great. Bye."

"Ciao."

Back when Diana was training her, they would talk for hours about their careers, their personal lives. Diana always had the right words. Tris sank into the leather chair, which now seemed built specially to fit her, and smiled for the first time all day.

CHRISTINE

*Erik, I know what you're thinking. That I
agreed to go, to get the treatment.*

*But on that phone conversation with the
doctor, you talked, I nodded.*

The hope in your voice broke my heart.

*If we participate in this clinical trial, I'd
just be a guinea pig for some new drug that
may or may not slow the progression of the
disease. And for the privilege of being a test
subject, they'd set me up with one of those
computers the patients in the US are using.
So, when I can no longer speak, raise my arms,
or even type, I can select letters with my
eyes. The words I'd create would then be
"mechanically generated," which is code for
"spoken in the voice of a cyborg."*

And the treatment is in Exeter, of all places.

*I felt as though my life ended in Exeter once
before. I can't bear the thought of returning
to have it happen again, for real.*

*Who knows whether the treatment would have any
effect at all? "No guarantees," they say all
the time. And I might not even get the*

*medication—only a placebo. And then I'd have
to watch this disease continue its unabated
destruction in Exeter.*

No Erik. I simply cannot die there.

Twelve

DANNY WASN'T AT Heather and Bruce's party when Tris arrived. Since Danny's wife Em was Heather's sister, she'd assumed they'd be there early. After she hugged Bruce and gave Heather a kiss, the couple went off, hand in hand, to greet other guests.

Tris didn't recognize anyone else, so she grabbed a beer and moseyed around the place, smiling at the other guests. A large "Happy Anniversary" banner was draped over the kitchen island, its lowest point almost touching the top of a three-tiered server filled with mini quiches.

When the front door finally opened for Danny and Em, both looked agitated, but they quickly smiled and greeted Heather and Bruce. After they dropped their coats off, Danny and Em migrated to the kitchen. Danny sat on a bar stool at the island. Em stood next to him, but each looked in a different direction.

"Damn these shoes," Danny said under his breath, "I can barely walk in them. I can't believe you made me wear them." He lifted one foot and his face twisted in pain.

Tris had been leaning in a doorway behind them but was close enough to hear. As she headed towards the couple, the air thickened with the familiar mix of jealousy and loss that always seemed to surround them.

"Hey, guys."

Em's hand grasped Danny's as if remotely activated. "Oh, hi," she said. Tris could almost hear the air leaking out of Em's deflating smile and caught Em's eye roll. It made her a little sad. She'd always hoped they'd be friends.

Danny wasn't her destiny. Many times, Tris wished he were—prayed to wake up one morning and realize he was "the one." He'd tried so hard, and for so long.

Unfortunately for Danny, he would always be the person who had called her that horrible night, who told her Bron had died in an accident while driving to his crash pad. He related the horrific details, unaware that Tris had put Bron at that deadly intersection.

Loyal, loving Danny supported Tris when the burden of her guilt and grief seemed too much to bear. He'd stood by her during the nightmare year at Tetrix, when every trip, every workday was a minefield of harassment, verbal abuse, and disdain. And when he approached her finally, respectfully, for love and companionship, she pushed him away.

Tris had hurt him, badly. But their friendship survived. She loved Danny, just not like Em did. He deserved way better than Tris could give.

"Hey, Tris." Danny finally looked up from his Blackberry.

"Hey, stranger. How's life on reserve at Legacy?"

"Can't complain. Well, of course I can. But I won't. It sucks. But it's not forever. As soon as I can hold a line and get off reserve it will be easier."

"Livin' the dream, eh?" Every pilot's private joke.

"That I am, Flygirl."

Tris blanched at the use of Bron's old nickname for her. She'd asked Danny to stop calling her that.

Danny quickly caught himself. "Sorry, Tris. I didn't think."

She waved it off and he asked about the fire at Lemaster. Everyone wanted to hear details from someone who'd been there.

Em had been talking to a woman Tris didn't know. She turned her attention back to her husband, playfully grabbed his arm and pulled him toward her. Em marked her man with a kiss and whispered in his ear before turning to Tris.

"Well, I'm going to scope out the desserts. Good to see you," she said, her cold tone leaving no doubt that it was anything but. Danny flipped his eyebrows up quickly, in an "I'm so sorry" way.

"I know. Don't worry about it." Tris accepted Danny's unspoken apology for his wife's abrupt exit.

Despite everything she'd done to him, Danny was still her best friend, as he had been Bron's. They'd grieved Bron's loss together. Their connection had tightened after his death, and despite their private jokes and the bond she and Danny had forged by the many hours flying together at Clear Sky, there was a persistent sadness between them. Danny was the last living connection to her days with Bron, the only person still in her life who had borne witness to their relationship.

Tris needed Danny. But she had absolutely no right to.

They continued their conversation in the living room when a rush of cold air flew in from the open front door. A bearded, red-haired man wearing jeans and a green and black flannel shirt approached the two pilots. His blue eyes fixed on Tris like a spotlight.

Mike Marshall.

Thirteen

"HEY MAN." MIKE spoke to Danny, but his eyes never left Tris. "How are my friends over at the old shop?"

Danny grasped Mike's extended hand and smiled warmly. "Good. They miss you. Still talk about the one that got away."

Mike looked at his feet. "Yeah."

Tris surreptitiously tugged her loose sweatshirt down. Her new V-neck sweater, the one that hugged her curves, lay at home on her bed. It was just Danny, Em, Bruce and Heather, she'd reasoned as she slid the oversized top on over baggy jeans. There was nothing she could do about it now, so she released her hair from behind her ears and tried to fluff it.

"Mike Marshall, meet Tris Miles. Tris used to be at Clear Sky, you know. Now she's over at Westin."

Mike's eyebrows rose. "Oh, we've met. How are you?"

Danny's gaze bounced back and forth between them.

"The 'Disaster at Lemaster'," Tris said, as she met Mike's eye. "Mike was the pilot Woody sent to help us fly home. Mike, how do you know this crowd?"

"I'm Heather's cousin. Bruce didn't tell you? Ah, you know, that day was so crazy I'm not surprised he didn't think to mention it. So, Clear Sky, eh? When were you there?"

"Me? '95 to '97. I was this guy's new-hire training partner when he did his captain upgrade training." She motioned to Danny, who was now intently watching Em. She'd migrated to the dessert table and was popping individual cheesecake bites into her mouth like beer nuts.

"Sorry, guys. Gonna go check on the wife." Danny left the two of them alone.

"So, you like working for Woody? I've known him for years. Used to instruct for him," Mike said, his expression thoughtful.

"Yeah, me too. And then I started the charter company with him."

"And you're his Royal captain." Tris was pleased that he looked her in the eye instead of zeroing in on her breasts like most men did.

"Captain for now. Woody's been delegating his Chief Pilot responsibilities to me. We'll make it official within the next month or so. He wants to expand the company, get another airplane, make Bruce a captain. Progress." She looked around for Bruce but didn't see him.

"So, you're growing? That's great."

"We'll see. What's the old saying about new airplanes? 'I'll believe it when I see it on the ramp.'" Both pilots laughed and shared a knowing gaze.

"How about you? Are you just flying contract trips, or do you have a full-time gig?" When Mike and Danny were talking, it sounded like Mike had been at Legacy. But that didn't make sense. If Mike had gotten a job at Legacy, he'd still be working there, not freelancing.

Mike glanced at some photos of Bruce and Heather hanging on

the wall and didn't answer right away. Then he stepped closer to Tris. "I'm in between gigs right now. Looking for something new, and local."

The tingling sensation that ran through her body was so strong, she was afraid she'd cry out if he touched her. Sexual energy surrounded them, thwarting her internal censor's usual point-counterpoint and inspiring her to put voice to thought. "We'll need a new co-pilot on the Royal once I get Bruce upgraded. You interested?" After all, she'd gotten to know Bron when they flew together.

He pursed his lips together in a slight smile and thrust his thumbs in his pockets. And then she realized her mistake. "Oh wait, sorry. That's not going to be the right fit for you, with all of your experience." Embarrassed, Tris looked down at her salt-stained work boots. Why hadn't she worn her new Uggs?

If Mike was affronted by her suggestion that he fly as a co-pilot, he didn't show it. He smiled and responded without a hint of arrogance, "Yeah, I've got a few thousand hours in that Royal you fly. I'm hoping to hire on as a captain somewhere."

Tris nodded. "Of course. Good luck. And thanks again for helping us get out of Lemaster that day. What a cluster."

"Hey, can I get you another drink?" Mike lightly touched her shoulder and gestured toward the kitchen. He'd barely made contact, but the generated heat zinged through her down to her toes.

"Another beer would be great. I'll snag us some seats."

She soon found a spot at one end of the crowded couch.

Mike squeezed in next to Tris and handed her an MGD. Their thighs touched, and Tris relaxed into the contact. The couch was made for maybe five people to sit comfortably, and now there were six of them scrunched together. The guy at the end had his butt hanging off the cushions.

A sharp peal of laughter rose over the din in the room as their small talk hit a lull. It crackled past like a flash of lightning, leaving her a bit breathless. Mike took a sip of his beer and smiled at her.

A man pulled a chair up next to Mike and began talking. Mike briefly introduced Tris, and then turned back to converse. Suddenly unsure of herself, Tris leaned back against the rear couch cushions and sank almost a foot behind Mike. All she could see in front of her was a row of shoulders, and she didn't have enough leverage to push herself through them.

"Hey? What are you doing back there? I thought you were ignoring me." Mike found Tris buried in the squishy cushions.

She struggled for purchase, frustrated by her helplessness. "I can't seem to get out of here."

"Here, let me." Mike gallantly extended his hand.

Tris grabbed his forearm and let him pull her forward. Mike then crowded in next to her and made a comment, but all she heard was what sounded like running water inside her skull. Tris looked down at her knees while she blushed, lest she give something away.

Airplanes were a safe topic. "So, Mike, where else have you flown? Do you know Danny from Clear Sky?"

His leg muscles tightened against her thigh. "After Clear Sky, I went to Legacy. I know him from both."

Tris couldn't hide her surprise. "Legacy? And you're not still flying for them?" She scratched a spot on her arm that didn't itch, then ran her thumb around the mouth of her beer bottle.

"Nope." Mike raised his beer, took a long draw, swallowed and belched softly. "Excuse me," he said, his eyes trained on the floor in front of him. "Well, Legacy isn't for everyone. I was still on probation . . . and, well . . . I ended up quitting."

Tris had no idea what to say next. To have an opportunity like that and quit during the first year? Didn't make sense. Something had to have happened, but this wasn't the place or time to probe.

Mike playfully bumped her shoulder, and his lips spread into a mischievous smile. "Hey, looks like they're going to pop the champagne. Let's go get some."

Tris smiled back, and let Mike take her elbow and guide her toward the festivities. She leaned into his side, his flannel shirt soft against her cheek. Her heartbeat bumped like an African drum solo. She straightened up, slightly, enough to put a few inches between them, but not far enough away to make him think she wasn't interested.

Mike was in the bathroom, Danny was talking to a woman who Tris thought might be his mother-in-law, and Em and Heather were huddled at the dessert table. Em gestured with both arms, each movement an exclamation point at the end of whatever she'd said. Her torso was rigid, and her voice low enough so Tris couldn't hear it.

Tris needed a break, a minute to steady herself, by herself. She'd been to Bruce's house before, and while it was small, the master bedroom was far enough away from the action in the living room to provide solitude. She walked quietly down the corridor in that general direction and saw the bedroom door ajar.

At first, he was hard to see. The bed was covered with jackets, purses, bags, and other accouterments of party guests. But there was Bruce, sitting on the edge of the bed, bent over, his chest on his knees.

She stood in front of him. "Hey, Bruce?"

He blinked rapidly, as though he didn't recognize her. But then he grabbed her wrist. "Hey Cap. How are you?" he said and tightened his grip.

Tris gently removed her arm from his grasp, sat down next to him, and put her hand on his back. Should she call for Heather? No, she'd have to shout and that would bring unwanted attention.

She donned the most convincing smile she could muster while his eyes darted around the bedroom in a loop between the windows, the closet, and the door.

"So. Tired of the party already?" She tried to joke him out of his trance.

"Party? Yeah. I guess."

"Buddy, are you okay? Did something happen?"

Bruce looked around the room, his brow furrowed, as if he were trying to find something he'd misplaced. Then his expression cleared and the look of the smart, purposeful co-pilot she knew returned. He leaned in close to her.

"So, the Pinedale trip. I keep thinking about it. Like, sometimes I think what if we didn't get around those thunderstorms? And in my dreams, I see us in the plane, getting tossed around, except it's not you and me in the cockpit. It's Heather and the baby."

"Bruce, are you nervous about the baby?" Tris spoke softly, after glancing over at the open door to make sure no one was lurking in the hall.

"No. Well, yes. No. I don't know. I think it's the usual first-time dad stuff, you know. But there's something else, since Lemaster . . ." His voice trailed into a whisper.

"I know. It freaked me out, too."

Bruce didn't respond. He shook his head and covered his face with his hands.

Tris proceeded carefully. "There are options, you know. Maybe you should see someone. Just once or twice. To talk about it."

He suddenly came alive. "A therapist?"

She nodded.

He sat up sharply. "Are you kidding? That would totally fuck up my career."

Tris wanted to tell him that there were ways. If he was careful, he could get help. She'd done it and was better for it in and out of the cockpit. The risk was manageable. She'd teach him how.

"Anyway," he took a deep breath and exhaled slowly, "it's not the baby, or even Lemaster. Not entirely. It's Legacy."

"Legacy? What about it?"

"They granted me another interview. My third. And last, if I don't make it. They want me to schedule it within the next ninety days."

Bruce needed to make more money. He was at the age and experience level where most of his peers were moving on to bigger companies, with more opportunity. Bruce was clearly desperate to go to Legacy—she knew it and suspected that Woody did as well. It was the next appropriate step. But he'd blown the two interviews he'd already had, and Legacy only gave applicants three chances.

Tris quickly did the math. "Then schedule it as far out as you can. After the angel flight you'll be a captain. You can impress them with that experience. You'll get the job this time." *She* could make him a captain in time for his interview. She'd do it for Bruce. Woody was right. As Chief Pilot, her success and Bruce's would be intertwined. How proud she'd be to help him get the job at Legacy.

They sat in companionable silence for a while. Then Bruce laughed, and turned the conversation to their Pinedale passengers, the only bright spot of the trip: a married couple who had renewed their wedding vows in the dusty town where they'd met twenty-five years before.

"Those two were really into each other, eh? I mean, I thought the guy was gonna carry his wife over the threshold of the ramp."

Tris chuckled. "It was nice. Kind of cute. Hard to imagine that in my future. I'm not as lucky as you and Heather." More silence. "Bruce? Hey, let's get back to the party. Before people start to worry about you."

He smiled at her appreciatively. "Like you did, Cap?"

"Roger that."

Fourteen

TRIS LATCHED THE aircraft's lavatory door and did an awkward pirouette to turn around in the tight space. Despite filling it with all the Ozium she had onboard, the lav stank. She'd order a cleaning after today's long leg.

Exeter to Jackson Hole, Wyoming, was a lot of work, but a great payday. And the best part was the crew got to stay overnight.

She stopped on her way back to the cockpit and spoke briefly to her passengers, a family of five who had an estate in Jackson. He was the Chairman of a huge Exeter drug company whose corporate jet was down for maintenance. The crew had bought a chew toy for the family's dog, an even-tempered Golden Retriever. The dog was snoring on a club chair, one of its paws resting on the plush gift.

As a charter captain, it was Tris's job to be both a strong pilot and a good host. After all, people paid what most would consider an insane amount of money to be in her professional space, to have a more comfortable and personal travel experience than the cattle-car environment of Exeter's discount airlines. It was incumbent upon the crew to pamper them both in the air and on the ground.

This group was tidy. They had stacked their sandwich trays neatly, along with their used paper plates and plastic utensils, near the trash bin. This would save her and Bruce time when they landed since there was no hired cleaning crew on the road.

The Royal was a big step down from the standard of luxury this family was used to. Tris wished she could commiserate with them, since she came from flying a larger, more spacious airplane with opulent fixtures and frills.

Memories of piloting the Tetrix Astral into the exquisite valley of Jackson Hole brought a wave of nostalgia. The moment Tris crossed the Tetons for the very first time was one she'd never forget—flying over snow-covered tips so close they looked like they'd scrape the bottom of the fuselage.

Tris slipped back into the left seat and nodded to Bruce that she had the radios. Bruce would fly the challenging approach into Jackson Hole, one that tested every pilot's skills even in the beautiful weather they had today. First, they'd glide over the Teton Range, then dive almost straight down into a steep valley surrounded by mountains. Not for the faint of heart. And tomorrow's departure would be even more harrowing.

Assuming Bruce did well today, she'd put him in the command seat tomorrow for the trip home. He needed that experience, and Tris was determined his training be thorough.

She'd judged and critiqued Bruce's performance ever since they began flying together. The two debriefed every flight, going over what went right, and what went wrong. Bruce listened and processed her suggestions, tips, and critique. She was pleased and proud when he incorporated them all into his flying.

But this was different. Pilot training was the mission-critical skill of a Chief Pilot. It wouldn't matter if she could expound on the details of the airplane's systems or know charter regulations and FAA procedures cold. If she couldn't successfully train Bruce as a captain, get him upgraded—well, then she wasn't qualified for the job.

The syllabi she'd drafted for herself and Bruce were still on Woody's desk. He'd rushed her to get them done but hadn't approved them yet. She cut Woody some slack. Booking charter trips was the highest company priority and Woody was a one-man sales department.

Bruce interrupted her reverie. "Excited about the overnight?"

"Oh yeah. We're lucky that Phyll could get us such a great rate. This place, Bruce." She took a deep breath and exhaled slowly. The hotel they were booked into was right on the Snake River in Teton Village, and had unimpeded views of the entire Teton Range. Tris had stayed there with Tetrix years ago.

Tris dreamed of the day she could retire in Jackson Hole, or someplace like it. Every time she visited, she was entranced by the tranquil beauty of the setting. But how could she ever afford it? She lived month to month, with little left over for savings.

Chief Pilot pay would make things a little less tight. Maybe she could start putting money away for retirement so that someday she could walk outside her home, turn in any direction and see magnificence. Step One: Finish her Chief Pilot training. Step Two: get Bruce in the left seat.

Grand Teton rose before them, its high peaks teasing the wide cerulean sky. When the entire Teton Range came into view with Yellowstone in the distance, the landscape shone in its full majesty.

Bruce was monitoring the instruments, as he was supposed to. When he looked up at the stunning natural beauty all around them, his mouth opened wide. "Wow," he said softly, as they started their descent into the valley. They'd been cleared for a visual approach, and he scanned the area as they flew across the field and turned parallel to Runway One-Nine.

"This is amazing," he said after calling for flaps, and then after the gear was down, "Oh my God." It *was* breathtaking. There was no other way to describe it.

Bruce clicked the autopilot off, and Tris instinctively guarded the rudder pedals. Her right hand hovered near the power levers, and her left shadowed the yoke. Nothing was wrong. She was simply doing her job.

Bruce had called for and completed all required checklists as he turned the Royal perpendicular to the field on a perfect base leg. The airplane's descent rate was right on. They had a direct crosswind, so Bruce carried a little extra speed on final approach. Exactly what she'd have done.

Less than a minute from landing, the wind picked up. To stay on track, the nose of the south-flying airplane pointed to the west. Tris moved up slightly in her seat. Bruce's features were taut, his eyes trained outside.

When the Royal started to buffet, Tris turned to check on the passengers. Predictably, they'd all stopped whatever they'd been doing, and stared at the pilots. They were looking for a sign of strength, some indication that whatever was tossing their airplane around was no big deal. The cockpit was their confirmation, their comfort. If the pilots were calm, they'd try and stay calm, too.

Bruce's right hand was firm on the yoke, tighter than normal but short of the dreaded "death grip." After all, it was just a little wind shear. Still pointed almost forty-five degrees off the runway centerline, fifty feet above the ground, Bruce pressed the rudder and kicked the nose of the airplane forward.

The left main gear touched softly on Runway One-Nine, followed almost immediately by the right, and then the nose wheel. After his perfect crosswind landing, Bruce let the plane roll to the end of the runway before turning off. He'd given the passengers the best possible ride and a soft touchdown. The extra runway used was a small price to pay.

Tris nodded appreciatively. "You'd have landed a little sooner normally, right?"

Bruce was used to Tris grilling him on procedure. "If the runway was contaminated with, say, ice or snow, to avoid a go-around back into bad weather, sure. And thank you."

She nodded. "Yes, nicely done. I'm going to have you fly us home tomorrow from the left seat. You ready for that?"

Bruce tensed for a split second, then nodded. "You bet, Cap."

"Let's shut down, get these folks unloaded and get to our overnight."

An older man with a long gray beard wearing reflective gear marshaled them into a parking spot. Tris didn't recognize him. She prided herself on remembering the ground crews at airports she'd visited. Experience had taught her that a friendly relationship, a handshake, and a decent tip for going above and beyond—carrying passenger bags, cleaning the lav and toting out the catering—went a long way in the aviation game. She'd say hello before they left.

Bruce would "kiss them goodbye," code for chaperoning the passengers to their transportation and making sure they were safely on their way. The passengers' limo was waiting, and, incredibly, each of them asked for their own luggage so they could help roll it to the car. Their older child even popped his own bag in the trunk, while his father, the Chairman, left his for the driver to handle and hopped in the long black luxury vehicle. The Chairman said something to Bruce, and Bruce responded. They shook hands, the limo pulled away, and Bruce headed back to the airplane to help Tris finish cleaning.

"Cap," he began tentatively.

"Uh-huh?"

"Hey, look, about the party the other day. You know, when I was … weird?"

Tris had been organizing her charts but stopped to pay closer attention.

"Yes? What about it?"

"You know. I was a bit, maybe, overwhelmed. And nervous. Heather. The baby. Legacy."

Tris looked down. Her strongest memory of the party was seeing Mike again. She'd almost forgotten about those odd moments with Bruce.

"No problem, Bruce. We're good."

He gave a quick nod and redirected himself to the business at hand. "We putting it in the hangar overnight?"

"Well, what would you do, Bruce?" She loved to turn his questions back on him. He'd be the one deciding soon enough.

Bruce grimaced. "Let me check the overnight weather. Be right back." He jumped down the air stairs and sprinted into the executive terminal.

She busied herself brushing crumbs off of the seats and collecting trash. She crossed the seatbelts, made sure all the seats were forward and tray tables stowed. The rug needed a quick vacuum. Tris grabbed the full bag of trash and went to request a shop vac. She ran into the bearded ramper she hadn't recognized before.

She smiled and held out her hand. "Hey. We haven't met. Tris Miles."

"I remember you." He touched her hand quickly and turned away.

"Wait. What? You do? Have we met?"

"Yup. You came in here a couple of times in an Astral." He laughed and jabbed his thumb toward the Royal. "That little prop your ride now?"

Ah. She was used to being looked down upon by other pilots who flew bigger, more sophisticated aircraft. But a *ramper?*

As he turned away again, she called after him. "I need a vacuum. And a lav service." He kept walking.

"*Now.*"

He smirked. "You sure that's what the captain wants?"

Despite the cold, Tris hadn't yet put on her parka, so she rotated the sleeve on her uniform jacket so he could see her epaulets. "I am sure," she said evenly.

He looked at the four stripes and shook his head.

"Yes, *Captain,*" he said as he walked off to comply with her request.

Tris didn't know whether deep-seated disrespect for her authority drove his rude behavior, or if he was just a jerk. Thanks to what she'd learned from Dr. C, all Tris needed to shake off the encounter was to breathe deep and look around.

From the top of the Royal's air stairs, Tris could make out busy ski runs, lifts going up and down the mountains, skiers in bright colored clothes and hats shifting their weight back and forth as they flew down the slopes. No way that guy was going to disrupt her enjoyment of this wintry paradise.

She must have still had an odd expression on her face when Bruce came back out.

"What happened?" he asked and blew into his ungloved hands. The wind had picked up again, and the sun was going down.

There was no point focusing on the encounter. She was over it. "Nothing. So?"

Bruce smiled. "We don't have to pay for a hangar. No precip expected tonight."

The rude ramper walked by, glaring at the two pilots.

Bruce cocked his head. "What's up with him?"

"Got me," Tris said. Now in her parka, scarf hanging loosely from her neck, she pulled her shoulders back and grabbed the handle of her overnight bag. Bruce walked in stride behind her as the two pilots passed the ramper, who struggled to attach a drain tube to the lavatory cap on the aircraft's fuselage.

Just moments before, she and Bruce had flown over a mountain range the sight of which nearly made her heart stop. Now they were headed toward an all-expense-paid night off at a five-star resort.

Mr. Rampie was about to scrub their fetid lav.

Tris waved, smiled, and told him to have a great day.

Fifteen

A BURLY TAXIDERMIED bear stood at the entrance to the Snake River Lodge. Reared up on its hind legs, teeth bared, it looked poised to devour anyone who walked past. Tris was not a fan of the wall-mounted moose heads in the lobby, or animal trophies generally, but she loved this bear. Something about his ferocious expression, paws raised and ready to shred an attacker, made her feel somehow shielded from the harsh winter environment. While she waited for Bruce, she reached up and petted its head.

It was cold. Tris eventually shoved both hands in their thin leather gloves deep into the pockets of her parka. Impatient to get going, she rocked back and forth on the heels of the red and black cowboy boots she had dusted off for this trip.

Tris was taking Bruce on the nickel tour of downtown Jackson before dinner. First, they'd hit the square and walk under the famous Antler Arch. They'd have a beer at the Million Dollar Cowboy Bar. Yes, she told him, they really had saddles instead of bar stools.

Her mobile phone rang. She didn't recognize the number on

the caller ID, but it might be their passengers with a flight update. While she was technically off-duty, she was on the road, and Woody paid for the phone, so she had to answer it.

"Hello. Tris Miles."

"Tris? Hey, Tris. This is Mike. You know, from Heather and Bruce's party? And, well, Lemaster, but I hate to lead with that."

His voice had a sexy scratchy tone, like he'd just woken up. For a second, he sounded like Bron.

She held the phone closer to her ear. "Oh, hey. How are you? *Where* are you?"

"Actually, I'm on an overnight in Medford, Oregon. In a Royal." First the location, then the equipment. Typical greeting among pilots.

She laughed. "Ah. Nice. But I think I can do you one better."

"Oh yeah? How's that? You in Miami or something?"

"Miami? I'll never figure out people's love affair with that place. No. Much, much better. Jackson Hole."

A slight whistle accompanied his long exhale. "Wow. Where are you staying?"

"Snake River Lodge."

"The one with the big bear?"

"Yep. I'm standing right next to him." Tris leaned against her stiff furry friend and grabbed one of his extended paws.

"Tell him hello for me, would you?" The proverbial ice broken, Mike paused. At first Tris thought it was the connection.

"Mike?"

"Yeah, I'm here. So, uh, Tris? Uh, are you around this weekend? Like, to possibly go out? With me? To do something?"

Tris squeezed the stuffed paw. "Love to. When?"

Moments later, after they'd set a date, Tris twirled around the arms of her static furry partner in an improvised Texas Two-Step. Bruce tapped her on the shoulder from behind.

"What's up here?" he asked, interrupting the impromptu dance. That warm feeling she'd developed a few moments ago still lit her from inside.

Bruce clinked the keys to the rental car. Curtly, he asked, "Wanna get going?"

"Let's go," she said, and caught the keys Bruce tossed over to her.

The town of Jackson sat on the east side of the Snake River. As they drove away from the lights of Teton Village, the stars were in bright relief against the ink-blue winter sky. Those thousands of individual flickering lamps were bright enough to light the road and looked close enough to touch. Her favorite constellation, her own personal North Star, was right where it should be: shoulders cocked, belt at an angle, and sword pointed toward her, so near it seemed she could prick her finger on it. Orion.

Usually Bruce commented on everything he saw, a mostly endearing quality.

Tonight, he was quiet, uncharacteristically withdrawn. Tris was in too good a mood to probe, buoyed by her upcoming date with Mike. She was off-duty and didn't want to concern herself with Bruce's problems. He might still be on edge because of the flight into Jackson Hole. The focus, the effort involved, and the intense concentration—it stayed with pilots long after they left the airport.

But when they parked along the square and Bruce passed on getting his picture taken under the arch, she could no longer ignore his behavior. He often rallied out of a bad mood when they were ready to investigate a town he'd never been to before. Tonight, he just wanted to get to the bar.

"It's over there." Tris motioned to the Million Dollar Cowboy Bar. Bruce walked toward it without another word.

The two of them hopped up on their mounts and leaned

forward. Once he had taken a few pulls on his MGD, Bruce put the bottle down and checked his pager. He huffed, and then tossed the rectangular leash on the bar.

"Heather paged me twice. *After* I talked to her for twenty minutes at the hotel. I don't know—"

"How's she feeling?" Tris asked.

He drained his beer. "Depends on the day, which I guess is pretty typical when it gets this close. Nah, it's not the baby."

Bruce signaled to the bartender for another beer, then put two fingers toward his mouth in a V-shape and shot Tris a familiar look. If Bruce was smoking, he was agitated. But she nodded. She wanted one, too.

He pulled an open pack out of his back pocket. It was depressed in some places, crushed in others, so he must have had it for a while. Bruce fished around inside it and pulled out two Marlboro Lights. He passed her one and lit them both.

"Heather and I had a fight last night," he said softly, between puffs. That was unusual. Of all the couples she'd known over the years, Bruce and Heather were one of the strongest. A few minutes in their company left no doubt that they were a perfect match and truly devoted to one another. It was especially clear when they were around Danny and Em, whose connection wasn't as solid.

"Really? Why?"

"So, yeah, got that Legacy interview coming up," he continued, "And, sure, I'm psyched about it and all. You know I can use the money—the money I'd eventually make. Danny said he's barely clearing what he made as a captain at Clear Sky so far. Heather's focused on me making it to Legacy this time. So, it really matters that I make captain."

"You're on track. What's the issue?"

"So, we were thinking... well, *Heather* was thinking what if

Woody buys another airplane before that angel flight? Like, soon? He's gonna need things to happen fast, right? You know, get my internal upgrade done and take the new plane through proving runs and get the FAA to sign off on it for charter ops. He'd need a pilot who could do that. Immediately, right?"

Tris stiffened at the implication that she might not be that pilot. She checked her breathing and took a sip of her beer and a long drag on her cigarette. The practiced non-reaction reaction of the professional pilot.

"*I'll* be the Chief Pilot, Bruce. *I'll* do it. Who else would do it? And why would you and Heather fight about it? You guys never fight."

"Rarely. But, yeah. That's what I-I-I told Heather. That you'd do it. She s-s-said . . ." Bruce only stuttered under extreme stress. He hadn't stuttered at Lemaster. Something important was up.

"Bruce, what did Heather say? I won't be upset," Tris coaxed him.

He spoke while looking straight ahead, not at her. "She wanted to make sure you were up to it, I guess. That you were the best person to do it. She really likes you, but, Tris, this is so important to us."

She turned to face him. "Bruce, look. I've got your back. You know that."

"Yeah." He nodded and drank deep.

They smoked in silence for a little while.

Tris looked out the window at the sparkling night lights. Then she remembered something from her last overnight in Jackson.

"Hey, you wanna get out of here?" She motioned toward the door.

He brightened. "Yeah. Whaddaya got in mind?"

Tris sported a devilish smile. "You by any chance got swim trunks or some extra clothes in your bag?"

"I've got a pair of sweatpants. Why?" Bruce faced her now,

intrigued. Finally, the Bruce who loved adventure had arrived.

"As I recall," she said, "not far from here, toward Yellowstone, there's a natural hot spring right off the road. No sign, but a big clearing, and a pool of bubbling hot water. Want to see if we can find it?"

"Aw, *hell yeah*." Bruce drained his beer, picked up his lighter, and reached for his credit card to pay the bill. "Let's go."

He hopped off his saddle, his mood considerably brighter. The real overnight was about to begin.

Sixteen

BRUCE CLOSED HIS eyes and willed himself to remember the geothermal phenomenon they'd found last night, right where Tris expected it to be; steam rose off the bubbling hot water into a night ignited by so many stars he could not stop looking up at them, trying to gauge how far away the faintest flickers were. He and Tris had sipped beers pulled from the six-pack they'd bought at a convenience store along the way and blasted classic rock from their rental car's radio.

With a blink, the soothing vision disappeared. Bruce sat in the left seat of the Royal, waiting for Tris to seat the passengers and close the door. Outside the cockpit grandiose mountain peaks rose to almost thirteen-thousand feet. They'd amazed him yesterday. Now, they terrified him.

"You want to be a captain? Be one," she'd said earlier, as she gestured to the left seat. The captain's seat.

He'd practically memorized the airport's safe departure instructions and repeated them again in his head: *right turn out, climb to fifteen thousand.*

I can do this.

A tug zoomed by the airplane, dragging its tow bar along the ramp, the thick metal cylinder screeching and throwing up sparks. Its noisy travels ended when it banged into the side of the hangar. The building's metal door rattled on its hinges.

So did Bruce.

Please God, do not make me fly today.

Only a miracle could delay takeoff now. His stomach was almost empty after a breakfast of black coffee and a hard-boiled egg. Yet he was nauseated, as though he'd scarfed down a Grand Slam breakfast at Denny's.

"Hey. Bruce. You want the Before Start checklist?" Tris asked for the second time. Hadn't he answered her?

"Yup. Please."

Keep it short. Got it, got it, got it. I'm fine. It's fine. Time to start up the engines and get outta Dodge.

"Fuel quantity? Bruce?"

"Uh. Yes. Checked." He pointed at the gauges. Plenty of fuel if they had to come back in an emergency. But how would he turn around? With those mountains right in front of him, to the side, behind him?

And then it hit him. He couldn't. He had to clear the rock in front of him. Period.

No. No. No.

No problem.

"Okay. Ready to start number one? Propellers clear?"

Bruce switched on his internal autopilot and plowed through the checklist until both engines were turning. His neck muscles tightened, and he longed for last night's hot tub to release the tension.

Instead, he had to taxi to the runway.

"Ground control for taxi, please?" he suggested.

Idiot. Don't ask. Command!

His body rigid, Bruce forced his head to turn from side to side to make sure the airplane didn't hit anything as they crawled forward. All eyes were on him. Sure, Jackson Hole was a tough airport. But in broad daylight, with clear skies and no wind, he couldn't fuck up. No excuses.

Just short of the runway they were cleared for takeoff. Bruce carefully lined the Royal up on the white runway centerline. On his right, the direction he needed to turn, there was an active ski run. That visual reference would make departure a snap. He'd follow the run straight out of danger. And climb, climb climb.

Behind him, their passengers were seated, reading. He pushed the power levers forward, slowly gaining speed. He took a deep breath. *Too slow.*

"Westin Charter One, cleared for *immediate* takeoff." The voice was cold.

"Roger, Westin Charter One is rolling," Tris replied to ATC. "Bruce, *go!*"

The airplane broke ground seconds before a Falcon 900 touched down behind them. He could sense Tris's eyes on him.

"Bruce, where are you headed? You need a right turn." Tris pointed at the copy of the departure procedure that was on the clipboard in front of him.

"Correcting." His brain told his hands to move the yoke, his feet to tap the rudders. How easy it would be to follow that run off his right side. It was crowded, a line of skiers in colorful clothing marking the pathway.

Just relax. It's fine. You're fine. Nothing can hurt you.

"You're not correcting fast enough. You gotta clear that mountain ahead. Turn now! Bruce!"

As she spoke, ATC called them. "Westin Charter One, I need an immediate right turn on course. Confirm."

As if from nowhere, a wide peak rose in front of them.

"TERRAIN. TERRAIN, PULL UP!" screamed the airplane's anti-collision system.

Bruce yanked the yoke up and to the right, causing the red stall warning light to flash. Thankfully the horn, which sounded like a truck backing up, didn't activate. Tris's hands crept as close to the power levers as they could without making contact, warm behind his own sweaty ones; guarding the power, ready to take control.

The abrupt turn out of Jackson's airspace removed them from harm's way. Once they were level at cruise altitude, checklists complete, Bruce tried to catch his breath.

Relax. Relax. You cleared the obstacle. Nobody died.

Why didn't you turn sooner? Why?

Bruce focused on the flight instruments, trying desperately to avoid conversation with Tris, who sat less than two feet away.

Was she angry? She looked it. And surprised. And confused.

"Bruce, you were two hundred feet low crossing the mountain-top. You understand that, right?" she finally said.

"I'd never have hit it, I swear." Sweat made the back of his neck itch. He reached to scratch it, and his hairline and collar were soaking wet. All because of a little climb out of an airport in visual conditions. The easiest of maneuvers.

Got it, got it, got it.

He had to gain control of himself, to move, to dissipate some of his nervous energy.

"Hey, I'm going to hit the head," he said. Tris nodded and pulled out her oxygen mask. It was procedure to have it ready when only one pilot was up front. "I'll check on the folks while I'm back there."

"I have the airplane," she said.

"You have the airplane."

The catering tray and drink cooler were right behind the pilot seats. He could bend over and make it seem like he was inspecting them while he caught his breath. Everything was fine. This wasn't a check ride, nothing was at stake. It was just another flight with Tris, like he'd flown a hundred times before.

But it wasn't. She was assessing him, judging him. Grading him. Which meant she could fail him.

"So, how's it going?" He hurled the question in the general direction of the passengers.

Everyone nodded and mumbled, "Fine, fine."

"How's the weather in Exeter?" the Chairman asked.

"Oh, great, great. Should be a smooth flight."

He made his way to the lav and splashed cold water on his face. Back in the cockpit and belted in, he took control of the Royal from Tris. Nothing but blue sky ahead, no delays into Exeter. All was well.

"So, how are they doing back there?" Tris asked.

"Why? Did they say something?" The words were out of his mouth before he could stop them.

Tris folded up the chart she was consulting and put it aside.

"Look, Bruce. That departure. You've done that same sort of thing a dozen times. If there's something going on I don't know about, if you're uncomfortable with command responsibility, now's the time to tell me. I can fly us home, no problem."

"No, no, everything's fine." He laughed it off. "I guess I was so overwhelmed by the sights on the takeoff. So beautiful." *Ugh. She'll smell that bullshit a mile away.*

Tris pressed harder. "You aren't always going to be doing that departure in visual conditions. What if it were snowing? Or nighttime? So you couldn't see? You've gotta hit that crossing restriction at the right altitude every time."

"Of course. I will." He couldn't imagine being in command, having ultimate responsibility for a flight into or out of that airport.

What if an engine failed? What if Tris wasn't there to help him? What if no one was?

Wait, wait. No.

He could do it. Today was a one-off. Heather, the baby, the upgrade, the *interview*. So much was riding on him.

Did I really do that? How could I have blown that departure? I knew it by heart.

Something familiar, from long ago, bubbled up inside. Not fear—he wasn't afraid. This was worse, much worse, but he couldn't quite remember. He heard the echo of his mother screaming, something about a dirty plate, or an unclean room, or bad grades, or one of the long list of ways he never measured up to his brothers.

Shame.

Tris cleared her throat. "So, when's Heather's shower? If I can't make it, I want to send a gift." She smiled over at him.

Such a nice person. I don't deserve her.

"I think next week? All I know is that she told me I needed to be out of the house. And, really, I'm not super interested in it anyway. All those women, and the girlie stuff and all."

"Yeah, I'll bet. Like breast pumps and diapers and baby monitors. But especially breast pumps."

He hated talking about those things, and she knew it. He laughed, and the tension in the cockpit finally dissipated.

Both relaxed now, they talked easily while the miles flew by.

"How's Mike?" he asked, when they were nearing home. He shot Tris a goofy smile and a little bit of a sideways leer. "You two looked like you hit it off at the party."

"Yep. I talked to him yesterday, in fact."

"You two going out?"

"This weekend."

"Cool. Hey, you know he's looking for a full-time flying gig,

THANK YOU

FOR READING
ANGEL FLIGHT

BY R. D. KARDON

PLEASE POST A REVIEW ON

AMAZON.COM

GOODREADS.COM

BOOKBUB.COM

right? Maybe you could point him in the right direction. If you know of something?"

ATC interrupted. "Westin Charter One, we need you to start your descent. Descend and maintain one-seven, seventeen thousand. Exeter altimeter Two-Niner-Niner-Seven."

Tris clicked the mike. "Out of flight level three-one-zero for one-seven thousand. Two-nine-nine-seven, Westin Charter One."

Bruce had the autopilot put the aircraft in a descent. The weather was good, though a bit windy. He'd have his hands full putting the plane down on the runway, but he'd done a more difficult crosswind landing the day before.

"Before landing checklist complete," Tris called when they were fully configured and cleared to land.

"Five hundred," the robotic voice of the airplane's altitude alerter droned.

"Airspeed," Tris alerted him. He was a bit slow.

Bruce put his hands on the power levers and could have sworn he pushed them forward.

"Airspeed." Now Tris's hands crept up behind and lightly touched his. He jolted, gave the airplane too much power, and the nose shot up, further decreasing speed.

"Steady Bruce. You got this. Level it off, and land," Tris said, as calmly as if she were discussing where to have lunch. He goosed the power, and the extra speed caused them to land further down the runway than usual, but he'd regained control.

"Okay, Bruce, we'll talk about it later. You've got the tiller. Can you get us to the ramp?"

Why would she even ask? How insulting.

"Of course, Tris. I've got it."

"All right." She keyed the mike. "Exeter Ground, Westin Charter One taxi to the ramp."

"Hey Westin Charter One, Exeter Ground. Welcome home. Cleared to the ramp. You know the way."

Tris asked Bruce to stay after he finished his post-flight duties. There was no one else around, so each of them grabbed one of the leather chairs in the waiting area. The scent of burning coffee from a carafe nestled on their ancient Bunn-O-Matic coffeemaker filled the room. Bruce got up without a word and switched it off.

He couldn't look at Tris.

"Okay. What happened?" she asked.

"When?"

"First, there was the departure from Jackson, when you didn't follow the departure procedure and had us heading straight for solid rock. And then the aircraft destabilized on the approach into Exeter, one you've flown, I don't know, hundreds of times. So. What happened?"

Bruce wanted to tell her everything. Explain why he lost his concentration, why he didn't seem to be able to perform the most routine task. But he didn't know.

The nausea returned. "I wasn't myself. I'm sorry." He scratched at his stomach absent-mindedly. It was like someone else was at the controls of the airplane, another pilot, not him at all.

Tris raised her eyebrows and held up her open palms. "Bruce. The passengers and the plane were at risk during both phases of flight. At real, physical risk."

"I'm sorry," he whispered.

"Sorry's not enough. You were dangerous, Bruce."

When he mustered the courage to look at her, he read doubt all over her face. "You gonna tell Woody?" he asked.

It was quiet for a long time. Maybe she hadn't heard the question.

"Okay, time to go home." Tris got up. She patted his shoulder and rolled her bag out the door.

She never said she wouldn't tell.

CHRISTINE

I know you will be mad at me at first—you'll have to be angry to move on, that's part of grief—but you must understand. I beg of you, please, Erik, for me, please understand.

We both chose to live in this land that held no memories, where we could rebuild our lives from the ground up. Our life in Iqaluit was my second chance. You'd been struggling so much at Tetrix, and I was constantly looking over my shoulder, expecting Warren to appear wherever we were, despite the restraining order. It was fate—the day my divorce was final, you got the offer for the job here.

There it was. A chance for both of us to get out from under the thumbs that were crushing us.

Remember the day we got here? Man, it was cold. Just us, in that house with no heat. But the sub-zero temperatures we endured those first days was nothing compared to the chill of being in the same town as Warren. How long was it, how many weeks, months, before I stopped being afraid he'd followed us here?

Erik, you took me, reeling, miserable, on the

brink of a breakdown and walked me back. We
made it through, made it home, and home is
here.

I love our life, exactly the way it is today.
At first, I loved Iqaluit for the desolation
it offered. But what seemed so stark at first
was revealed to be a place we both regard as
rich, beautiful.

My work here has given me comfort, since it
has taught me that, in time, the way we lived
is what you'll remember, not the way I died.
Not the ugly parts you'll be dealing with
while you listen to this. Time will pass,
you'll heal, and the sight of the diner will
remind you of when we lost power and sat at
the counter drinking cider all night. Or the
snowmobile ride to Amka and Tuk's wedding in
parkas and ski pants—and that crazy cummerbund
with the polar bears on it that you insisted
on wearing. I laughed so hard I almost fell
off, which made me laugh even harder, since if
I had fallen, I don't think you'd have found
me until spring.

I will be at peace, beyond pain and beyond
help long before that airplane touches down in
Exeter.

Wait—

PART II:
THE AMENDED FLIGHT PLAN

March 2000

Exeter, Illinois

Seventeen

WHITE, BLACK, AND NAVY BLUE. Nothing seemed appropriate. Her clothes closet was a sad homage to what *not* to wear on a date. Tris vowed to do some shopping, someday, at someplace other than Target or a pilot uniform supply store.

Mike's plan for the evening was loose: have dinner at a local Italian place, and then either head to O'Slattery's for a drink and live music, or maybe see a movie. So like a pilot—decisive and crisp in the cockpit, hesitant outside of it.

So like her.

Tris settled on a relatively new pair of jeans and a long-sleeved black t-shirt with a satiny trim. She smiled at her profile in the full-length mirror. The tight fit around her chest would normally make her self-conscious, but tonight, it was the perfect look.

Mike wasn't picking her up for another hour. Her least favorite part of dressing up was putting on makeup, so she'd delay it until the last minute.

Today's study material covered her couch. Orion's head rested on the federal charter regulations manual. His body sprawled out over the three page-training plan Tris had prepared for Bruce's upgrade, crushing and wrinkling it into valleys and ridges.

Jackson Hole had scared her. But more important, it challenged her confidence in Bruce. She'd trained enough pilots to know that each reacted differently when they were being judged—check rides were designed to make sure pilots could handle themselves under stress, with plenty of distractions. Bruce had failed—obviously and repeatedly—on the flight out of Jackson, then botched a simple approach into Exeter. How could she trust him to command an airplane on his own in bad weather, in an emergency, or with passengers aboard?

As long as she sat next to him, their passengers were not at risk. But Jackson had shaken her. He'd practically flown the Royal into solid rock.

Tris hadn't made a final decision or discussed her impressions with Woody. Not yet. She and Bruce had an easy trip in a few days. They'd fly empty to Saginaw, Michigan, pick up two people, bring them to Parker Field, an airport about seventy-five miles from Exeter, and then fly back empty. She'd have him do all the paperwork, fly every leg and talk to the passengers. If it turned out that he needed more training, more experience, Woody would have to know right away. But she had to be sure. Ending Bruce's upgrade training had consequences for everyone involved, including her. This was her call, and she had to make the right one.

Tris sighed. It was time to be purposeful about makeup. In the bathroom, she flipped through a drawer of disorganized tubes and tubs of chemical compounds designed to make women look better. Tris never wore more than mascara and Chap Stick when she flew, and put face paint on so rarely, she had to psyche herself into it.

She pressed a plastic tube and flesh-colored liquid plopped onto a tiny sponge. It felt greasy as she rubbed it on her face. The drawer held only one color of blush, which she dusted on her cheeks. Silver eye shadow went on next, to go with the grey-brown tint of her eyes. The whole idea of cosmetics seemed silly. After all, she hadn't been wearing any of this when she met Mike, and he'd asked her out.

Her first date jitters intensified when she realized she'd gotten out the curling iron but forgotten to plug it in. Her hair fell straight down her back toward her bra strap. She pulled the brown locks forward, where they came to rest alongside her breasts, making them look even bigger.

All dressed and ready to go, she checked her watch again. Mike's arrival time was now minutes away. Other than a few one-night stands—she fondly remembered that guy on an overnight in Minneapolis, the one who'd bought her a drink after Bruce had gone to his hotel room—she'd been off the market.

The intercom buzzed right at 6:30 p.m. Her heartbeat reached a crescendo as she pressed the button.

"Hello?" She tried to sound as if she had no idea who was at the door.

Was that crazy?

"Hey, Tris. It's Mike."

"Come on in. You can meet my cat."

Ugh. You can meet my cat. So lame.

Despite the long build-up, she was startled by Mike's knock at the door. There he stood, one hand in his pocket, and a bouquet of fresh flowers in the other. Tris blushed so deeply, she was sure the color of her cheeks matched the red roses.

"Hey, Tris," he said, handing her the flowers, "Great to see you."

"You too. These are lovely, Mike. Let me put them in water.

Come in." She considered the front pocket black t-shirt he'd tucked into his straight-leg Wranglers. His reddish beard had been trimmed since she last saw him, and he'd gotten a haircut.

Mike walked straight over to the sliding glass patio door, like he already knew the layout of the apartment. She gestured toward Orion, who took up the only empty spot on the couch next to the pile of books and papers.

"Studying up, I see."

She laughed. "Well, avoiding studying mostly. But, yeah."

"For your promotion or Bruce's?"

She was in the kitchen looking for a vase. "Bruce's? Have you talked to him about it?" she asked cautiously. Discussing Bruce's recent performance with Mike would be unprofessional, although she realized she'd love his opinion.

"Well, we were all together at a family thing yesterday. He mentioned it. Seemed excited."

"Is he? Well, he needs training. Everyone does. To upgrade," she said coolly while she touched the petals of a perfect red rose.

Mike had already turned his attention to her purring feline.

"What's his name?"

"Orion." When he gave her a quizzical look, she continued, "After the only constellation I can consistently recognize in the sky."

Mike laughed and softly stroked the cat's head. "Well, it's a beautiful night tonight." He walked over to her vertical blinds again, parted them slightly and peered outside. "Let's see if we can't improve on your star-identification skills after dinner, eh? I know a great place to park and look at the sky."

She grabbed her coat, and they walked out to an evening of glittering possibilities.

"Birmingham was kind of a big small town," Mike said about his hometown in Alabama as he twisted the top off of a bottle of Dos Equis.

"But you have no accent. None," Tris protested.

Mike grinned and called up a grossly exaggerated southern drawl. "Why ma'am, Ah can't buh-leeve you'd say that. Bless yo' heart."

Mike and Tris sat in the front of his Honda Accord with the seats all the way back and the sunroof open despite the cold night air. Above them, airplanes on final approach into Exeter Airport seemed to float by. Tris closed her eyes as she listened to Mike talk easily about his childhood, his stories hinting at a broader education than the classic Aviation Management degree.

After dinner, they'd picked up a six-pack, and Mike had driven them to this place, an out-of-the way turnout near Exeter Airport. He seemed to know the spot well—she was probably not the first woman he'd brought there.

She shed that thought as quickly as she had it and relaxed into the moment. There was no place to rush to, no schedule to keep and no need of company other than the man sitting next to her. The two pilots made themselves part of the night.

Tris talked about Pittston, where she grew up. "Check out the definition of 'small town' in the dictionary, and you'll see a picture of one of our two traffic lights. There was absolutely *nothing* to do. For fun, my friends and I would ride our bikes to the Parker's gas station and convenience store, Pittston's social hub. We'd sit for hours, as kids came and went, maybe grab a can of soda from the vending machine, sometimes buy a donut from Mrs. Parker. We kids called her 'Old Midge,' because, well, no one's mom or dad could remember a time she wasn't there, behind the counter, selling donuts."

Then Mike broke the unspoken first date compact and mentioned an ex-girlfriend. "You're not my first Patricia, by the way," he said playfully after the two had quietly sipped beers for a bit, referring to Tris's full first name.

"I beg your pardon?" She used a haughty tone in jest.

"My very first girlfriend was named Patricia. No kidding."

Tris decided to go with it. "Oh really? And how long ago was this?" She was legitimately curious but covered it with mock disdain.

He took a long swig of his beer. "When I was three, I think. My mom's best friend had a daughter named Patty who apparently I would chase around, yelling 'Atty, Atty.' Personally, I think it's family legend."

The tension making its slow march toward her shoulders disappeared. "Ha. Well, saving the best for last, eh?" *Oh my God, did I say that?* She quickly brought the topic back to airplanes. "So, you're flying contract right now or—?"

"Contract. So, ready to learn some new constellations?"

"Ready," Tris said, and sat up in her seat.

"You know Orion . . . and he's right . . . there," Mike poked his arm through the sunroof. "See him?"

"Yep."

"Okay, then. Look up and to the right. Looks like a funky rectangle, or maybe a trapezoid? You got it?"

She wasn't sure. "The thing that looks like it has a crooked handle at the bottom? Is that it?"

He nodded. "Yup. That's Taurus."

Tris beamed. "Seriously. Wow, now that I know it, it seems so obvious. Thanks, Mike."

He cupped her shoulder and gave it a squeeze. "Ready for another fun fact?"

"Sure."

"Orion's shoulders? You see how one looks lower than the other?"

"Right."

"The higher one is called Betelgeuse. That's the star that the movie "Beetlejuice" was named after. Theory has it that the star, Betelgeuse, was the doorway to the infinite blackness of outer space. In the movie, Michael Keaton's character was the doorman to the underworld."

"Bullshit." She playfully pushed him away. "Really?"

"Really. Look it up." Mike pressed a button and the sunroof started to close. "Ready to move on?" He twisted the key in the car's ignition

"Sure. Where to?"

"Well, I have a few thoughts. All this constellation talk makes me want to get a better look at that cat."

Eighteen

"DID YOU HEAR? Mike and Tris are out on a date tonight." Em's words wafted out of the kitchen, where she stood at the stove stirring tomato sauce. She sounded almost giddy about it. Danny let a twinge of jealousy pass and stifled a sigh. Em didn't bring up Tris unless it was to remind him that he'd pursued her for nothing. He'd hoped she'd be over it by now; she had a ring on her finger, after all.

"Nope. Hadn't heard." He pretended to be engrossed in the issue of *Aviation Week* cradled in his lap. A college basketball game was on TV, the sound barely audible.

They'd had a quiet, low-key day. Danny ran some errands in the morning while Em did laundry. He was on his second of four days off and had finally started to relax. But when Em talked about Tris, it usually led to an argument.

"Yeah, Heather told me. You know how the information pipeline works."

Danny had to laugh. In Em's family, gossip traveled faster than any airplane he'd ever flown. "Well, good for them."

He caught a whiff of Em's meatballs and inhaled deeply. She was preparing his favorite meal. How lucky he was to be married to someone who could cook. Em and Heather had an Italian grandmother, who, family history had it, cooked for wealthy locals in the small town she grew up in on the Amalfi coast. When she immigrated to the US, her favorite pastime had been to teach her two granddaughters how to cook.

Danny got up to join his wife in the kitchen. Em already had a bowl of shredded Parmesan cheese and a cruet of olive oil ready for the crusty bread she'd picked up.

A cat-of-the-month calendar hung from a pushpin on the wall. In addition to the family parties, his flying days, and other miscellaneous appointments, it now had baby stickers on a series of days during the month when Em was most likely to conceive. Their fertility calendar.

Having a baby was never something Danny expected he'd have to work at. But now, having sex with his wife had become a mandatory part of the schedule. Em was in her early thirties, and her doctor said there was no reason to think she couldn't conceive. She'd gone off the pill only three months ago.

But Heather was younger than her sister, and her pregnancy had pushed Em into baby overdrive. He looked at the calendar again. This month, the days she was most likely to get pregnant conflicted with his flying schedule. Just then, Em pushed past him to grab something from the fridge.

"I know. Not this month, I guess." Her disappointment was palpable.

Danny didn't necessarily agree. So many of his friends had "oops" babies. Surely, he and Em didn't have to consult a calendar to become parents.

"Oh, I don't see why not." He smiled and moved up behind his wife, put his arms around her and rocked her back and forth. Like a scene from a movie, she turned slightly, and he pictured her dragging him to the bedroom.

Instead, she pointed a sauce-filled spoon toward his lips.

"It's hot. Be careful."

Danny slurped the steaming concoction, then grabbed for the glass of water Em had sitting by the stove. He put out the small fire the piping hot sauce had started on his tongue. "It's delicious."

"Thanks baby." Em stirred the sauce thoughtfully, and Danny wandered back to the couch. He noticed a pile of clean clothes in a basket that needed folding. He ignored it and turned up the sound of the game.

"So, anyway," Em said, "about Mike. I guess Bruce was able to give him a line on a new job where he works."

Danny was focused on the UConn game. "Who?"

"*Bruce.* Bruce told Mike about a job at the place he works."

"Great. Good."

"Yeah, it would be awesome if they worked together."

"Sure. Okay." Danny only half heard and wasn't particularly interested.

The oven door swung open. A wave of heat and the smell of fresh garlic bread floated into the living room. Em pulled out the fragrant tray with the His and Hers potholders they had gotten as a wedding present.

"I wonder how much she knows," Em continued.

"Huh? Who?"

"Tris."

Danny couldn't hide his annoyance. "Knows about *what*?"

"Mike's ex-wife."

"What's there to know?" His interest was piqued.

"Did you set the table yet, hon? It's time for dinner."

"On my way."

Nineteen

DIANA'S FLIGHT FROM Newark was late. Snowstorms had raged up and down the east coast all week causing havoc in the congested Northeast airspace. Tris sat in her now-cold car, the engine off, and willed her mobile phone to ring.

Thank goodness she had a few days off before the Saginaw trip. The last person Tris wanted to see right now was Bruce, although she'd have to face him eventually.

Tris squirmed against her shoulder harness and glanced out the window.

Mike had asked her out again, and she'd enthusiastically said yes. All she wanted was to hang out with Mike and talk about him to Diana.

Her mobile phone chirped.

"Di?"

"Hey. I'm here at arrivals. Can you get me?"

"I'm already in the Hampton Inn parking lot. Can you grab the van?"

"No problem. On my way." Exeter was crowded, so pilots made ample use of local hotel parking lots. They would grab the free van at the terminal and tip the drivers handsomely.

Ten minutes later, when Diana got out of the van and grabbed her bags, she stopped to light a cigarette. Tris could tell right away that something wasn't right.

Even from a distance, Diana looked stooped and tired. Tris drove closer to the hotel entrance to pick her up, and almost stomped on the brakes when she saw Diana's face.

Her skin sagged noticeably. Although she'd always tended toward plump, Diana's clothes hung on her. She looked more like a scarecrow in a pilot costume than the former Air Force captain she was.

"Hey girl!" Tris said brightly through the open passenger door window, overcompensating to hide her shock. Tris was stunned to see Diana without makeup. Usually, she put a full face on, from moisturizer to powder.

"Hi Tris. Trunk open?"

Tris nodded and lifted the release handle again to make sure. Diana dropped her bag in and slammed the trunk shut. She opened the passenger door, plopped down and shot a side-eyed smile at Tris. She didn't reach over for a hug. Maybe she was just tired.

Tris couldn't wait. "Hey, Di," she said as she pulled away from the hotel, "So great to see you. I have so much news. I met a guy."

Diana's expression was deadpan. "Can I smoke?"

"Sure, with the window open. But, come on. What's wrong?"

"You still smoke occasionally don't you, Tris?"

For as long as it took to finish the cigarette, Diana looked out the window. All Tris heard was inhaling and exhaling.

When they got to her apartment, Tris finally got a good look at her friend. Her appearance was worse than it initially seemed.

Diana was wan. Deep dark smudges rimmed her eyes, and her skin was blotchy. It looked like she hadn't even washed her face.

"Di, you look terrible. What happened?" They never pulled any punches. After all, Diana had taught Tris how to fly, and a pilot can't dance around critical issues in the cockpit, or in life. Honesty and safety came first—before friendship, before loyalty, before love.

Diana looked around the room, as if she'd find the perfect response scratched on the walls. "I don't know where to start, Tris. I'm being 'reviewed.' Reconsidered as a captain."

Tris didn't understand. "Reviewed? Reviewed as in decide whether to keep you in the left seat?"

"Yes."

"What? That's crazy. Why?"

Diana moved the index and middle fingers of her right hand to her lips, as if she were still smoking. Then she started to cry. "I lost my concentration in *actual instrument conditions*—started a right turn that should have been a left. I caught it, but still. And then, after landing," she took a deep breath, "I turned the wrong way onto the ramp, off of a runway I'd landed on a thousand times." She wiped her face with the back of her hand and sniffed deeply, then blew her nose with a Kleenex Tris handed her.

"I was flying with a guy I've known for years. I helped train him when he first started at the company. And you know the first thing he did when we pulled onto the ramp? Told our boss. Now I'm on review. After *five years* and a spotless record."

Tris sat expressionless on the couch next to Diana, frightened by her mentor's loss of composure. She forced her brain into problem-solving mode, grasping for what logically came next. But all she could think about was Bruce.

"What was their justification for putting you on review? You can't be the first pilot that ever made a wrong turn. I've done it.

Everyone's done it." Her heart beat like it would come out of her chest. Tris fought to sound neutral.

"I didn't want to question them about it. You know how it is. I can't push back. They control my pilot records. The last thing I want on my record is 'unsafe.'" She paused. "That's what my first officer said. That I was *unsafe*." She buried her face in her hands and then looked up, tears pooled in her eyes. "What would make this guy do that to me? What does he gain?" She turned away, sobbing.

Tris was afraid to speak, even to breathe. Wasn't this exactly what she was about to do to Bruce? Did *he* deserve it?

Diana composed herself and dabbed at her eyes. "So," she sniffed, "the plan is for me to be on leave for a while. With pay, thankfully. At least they did that. They want me to see their in-house medical guy, who's here in Exeter. And then I'm headed home—well, to my mother's house. *My* home is in Brussels. In base."

Diana got up and walked back and forth, first wringing her hands, then shaking them. Tris desperately wanted to calm her friend. But she had nothing.

"What are you going to do?"

Diana shook her head. She held up two fingers in a V and motioned to the patio. Tris got up and unlocked the door.

"I'm gonna have a smoke," Diana said, and stepped out into the freezing night.

Twenty

TRIS SAT IN Dr. C's waiting room organizing her thoughts. This was her first appointment in a while—since before Jackson Hole, Diana, Mike.

And Bruce.

Bruce. The Saginaw trip they flew the day before should have been a breeze but ended up a cluster-fuck. The passengers were late. Then one of their kids, a four-year-old girl, had a meltdown on the ramp. The mom used one hand to try to calm the child, and rhythmically flipped her own bottle-blond hair with the other. The father boarded their two older children, and then stood on the ramp checking his watch every two seconds between hard looks at his daughter, as if she could be stared into submission.

Finally, Tris got them all tucked in. Then, on takeoff, Bruce was two hundred feet low on departure. Tris alerted him, twice. They were in visual conditions and fortunately air traffic control wasn't too pissed off; they weren't asked to "call the tower" on landing, a sure sign that a pilot is going to be reported to the FAA for busting a required altitude. And at least this time there weren't mountains in front of them.

Tension in the cockpit was high the whole way home. Neither pilot said much, other than to call for or respond to checklists. Tris couldn't get her visit with Diana out of her mind, and Bruce was barely responsive to her attempts to converse.

The two pilots pasted smiles on their faces to get their customers unloaded and on their way after landing. Bruce quickly finished his post-flight duties and rushed out of the hangar without saying goodbye. He knew something bad was coming.

Here, in her therapist's office, she recalled how he couldn't look her in the eye.

"How are you, Tris? What's been going on?" Dr. C's usual opening lines.

Tris tried to organize her thoughts enough to answer, but her words galloped out. "So much. So much has happened. I'm so confused. And disappointed. But excited. Just, so much . . ."

"Where do you want to start?"

Tris didn't want to talk about Lemaster. But it was where the current string of events began.

"So, first. Remember the guy Woody called to fly the plane home after the fire at Lemaster? Mike? Well, we went out on a date."

Dr. C had been tapping her pen against her thigh. Her eyes widened uncharacteristically. "Really? And how did that go?"

Surging adrenaline caused her words to sound jumbled, disorganized. "Fine, but that came later. It's Bruce. I really screwed up. I could have killed him. And me." Tris popped up from the chair and paced the room, arms loose at her sides.

Dr. C nodded slightly, put down her pad and pen, and stood. She reached out and gently placed her hand on Tris's shoulder.

"Tris. Calm down. Why don't you sit and tell me how you

could possibly have done something like that?"

Tris sat, gulped a few breaths, and closed her eyes, shaking her head back and forth. She leaned forward, arms on her thighs, hands clasped together, and whispered, "I made a series of bad decisions. You know, the error chain?"

The flying public always looked for pilot error—the one thing a pilot did wrong—after an in-flight disaster. But those tragedies were generally the result of multiple faulty judgments, tiny cracks in a flight's foundation which, on their own, caused no damage; yet, when sequenced one after the other, resulted in catastrophe. Like JFK Junior's crash—so many bad choices. *Like Diana. Someone who has ten times the experience I have.*

"So, tell me about your decisions. And how they created a disaster."

Dr. C still didn't get it.

"No. I mean, one more. If I'd made one more bad decision. If there had been . . ." Tris rubbed her hands together. Their calloused skin scratched like sandpaper. She looked around the room for some hand cream.

"I let Bruce sit in the left seat—the *pilot-in-command's seat*— on a takeoff out of an airport surrounded by mountains. And he almost flew us into one." Her body spasmed as if shaking off a chill. "Directly into a mountain. A mountain he could see. Right in front of us."

Dr. C gasped. "That's horrible. What about your passengers?"

Tris closed her eyes and leaned back. "They didn't notice. Thank goodness."

"Tris, I understand why you're upset about this, but he was flying poorly, not you. Sounds like no one was hurt. Isn't that correct?"

How could Dr. C not understand? "I put him in the situation.

I trusted him to be better than he was. I should have known that he couldn't do it—it was too much for him. I'm supposed to have the judgment of a Chief Pilot—how could I miss that he wasn't ready?"

"You mis-calculated. You know better now."

Tris could only muster a slight nod.

"Why are you being so hard on yourself? Everything's fine now, isn't it?"

Tris forced a contrite smile. "We're all alive, if that's what you mean. I decided in the exercise of my best judgment that Bruce could handle the departure out of Jackson Hole. Except he couldn't. When I was at the party..." Memories of her own watershed moments—her busted check rides, her struggles to complete initial training at Clear Sky, how Danny had rescued her—swirled through her mind.

So long ago. Danny had stood by her, made sure she got another chance—and then another—until things finally clicked. Didn't she owe that to Bruce? But her problem was mechanical. She didn't *know* what to do. Physical skills could be taught, honed, improved. And she had learned them.

No. It's not the same.

Bruce had failed in an airplane in flight—not a simulator—where living, breathing people could have died. His errors were of judgment, and, in trusting him, so were hers. There was no way around it—she'd have to do the same thing to Bruce that Diana's co-pilot had done to her.

It made her sick.

Dr. C bent toward her. "What were you saying about a party? Did something happen at a party?"

"Well, Bruce kind of confided in me that he was ... well, not feeling a hundred percent. That he was nervous. And then on the trip itself—I should have *seen it.* Why the *hell* did I let him fly?" She nearly shouted the last words.

"Tris, please. Tell me how you're feeling."

Tris spat out a laugh. "How am I feeling? Horrible. Like I'm turning on Bruce. And now I have to tell Woody that I was wrong, Bruce isn't ready like I said he was. Like I *argued* he was, to convince Woody to upgrade him."

"So? Surely Woody's misjudged a pilot's skills before himself, don't you think?"

Tris nodded. "Probably. But that's not the worst of it."

Dr. C's brows cinched. "No? Why not?"

Tris covered her face with her dry, scratchy hands. Pulling Bruce's upgrade could affect the angel flight, Woody's expansion plans, her own advancement. Yet there was a worse consequence, by far. Something that would destroy their trust.

"I'm the one who has to tell Bruce."

CHRISTINE

*Sorry, baby. I had to run to the bathroom.
That's happening more and more now, and
sometimes I almost don't make it. I'm
losing . . . function. Oh God.*

*You can't understand what it's like to
lose control of your body. You can't feel
that, or see the changes in the mirror like
I can, when I dare to look. My failing
body with my tired, scared face on top of
it.*

*I may look the same to you, but my body itself
is a lie. And let's not have lies between us,
Erik, no unexpressed resentments, no fake
happiness. That was my only rule for this
marriage.*

*My body is creeping toward destruction. No
other way to say it. Sometimes at night I
actually think I hear it. Like the crunch
crunch crunch of the termites gnawing through
the wood frame of our house in Exeter.
Remember? A little bit more every day.*

And that's the truth.

But here's another truth, Erik. This sad, sick

body will soon be gone, but I will always be with you.

Please keep listening, don't stop this tape because you don't want to hear it. I know you don't want to, that you just want to throw this thing against the wall, but Erik, please don't stop listening.

I became a grief counselor because when my dad died, nothing made sense anymore. People who always acted normally were compelled to plant syrupy sweet platitudes in my ear. My patients tell me that's the worst thing about losing a loved one—that people have no idea what to say, but think they have to say something, anything.

When my father killed himself, everyone thought they had the answer. "He's in a better place." "His pain is gone." "You'll move on." What a bunch of crap. If anyone says those things to you after I'm gone, walk away.

You've heard me say it so many times in speeches, interviews. And now I'll say it to you.

Death is a project to be managed. It sounds cold, right? But it's true. And project management, well, that's what you do, baby. Erik, if I didn't think you could handle this— after what we went through with Warren, the

125

move here, my diagnosis—I wouldn't even consider it. But you can. And it's what I want.

You know, it's not the first time. I thought about this once before. Right after I first met you, right when Warren and I split. I was always afraid. Afraid that every door I'd open, he'd be there. Every time I'd turn around, he'd be there. And I remember thinking on one particularly dark day, "What the hell. If this is my life, it's no life at all."

But the very next day that blackout curtain Warren pulled over my heart just parted. Because the very next day, Erik, you said you loved me.

Twenty-One

THE BEDROOM SMELLED different. The morning aroma of sleep and warm feline now included a new, musky scent. Tris rolled onto her back, and there was Mike. Her Wedgewood blue comforter flowed in time with his easy, rhythmic breathing. How long had it been since she hadn't woken up alone?

Mike stirred, and in those soft moments between asleep and awake, he reached for her. His eyes stayed closed and his hand fluttered in the air until she grasped it. They both lay there, hands clasped between them. He squeezed a gentle acknowledgement, confirming that the promise of the previous night was, indeed, for real.

They'd ordered pizza, watched *The Thomas Crown Affair* and talked. Conversation was steady, but not forced. The rights, wrongs, rigors, successes, and disappointments of their lives, their careers, would be fodder for future evenings together.

The two were as comfortable together as long-time partners, not like relative strangers on a second date. Touch came easily, and rather than shy away, they moved into each other, as longing filled the spaces between them. They took their kisses and caresses to her bed, murmuring together late into the night.

When conversation slowed, they simply went to sleep. Tris slept better than she had in months.

Having Mike sleep over was a natural end to the evening. There were no clunky transitions from date to overnight marked by oblique suggestions or implied want. They didn't have sex, and that felt right.

Tris smiled at Orion, lying on his back at the foot of the bed, four legs in the air, waiting for someone to scratch his belly; the ultimate sign of his approval.

What looked and felt right in the dark sometimes warped in the light of day. A slip of sunshine peeked through the curtains. Mike was in her bed. The familiar alarm in her chest—anxiety stoked by the unknown and unwanted—was not.

Tris sat up and swung her legs over her side of the bed. She yawned and stretched, wearing only an oversized t-shirt and a smile born of nascent intimacy.

Then her shoulders dropped, and her torso sank on top of her knees. In a few hours, she'd have to tell Bruce she wasn't going to continue his upgrade training. First, she'd explain to Woody that Bruce wasn't quite ready to be a captain. Woody had his doubts anyway, so she wasn't concerned about what he'd say.

She hated to give bad news, to say no, to disappoint anyone, let alone Woody and Bruce, both of whom she liked and respected. Bruce's hopes, his confidence, would be crushed. How do you tell someone they've botched a huge career opportunity, yet leave them feeling valued?

Distracted, Tris squealed in surprise when Mike's strong arms grabbed her and pulled her back down on the bed. Without a word, he kissed her cheek, and held her. Her body's warning signal never came.

"Okay, buddy," she said, wriggling out of his grasp. "I need coffee. Want some?"

"Mmm," he mumbled as he moved back to his side of the bed. "Yes. I do." Tris grabbed her robe from a hook and slid into it, then donned her moose-head slippers. She flexed the stuffed nose and big ears that protruded from the front of the threadbare footwear. They hardly kept her feet warm anymore, but she loved those slippers.

"But then I've got to go. I'm talking to someone about a job this morning."

"Yeah, you mentioned that last night. So, what airport? What equipment?" she asked, but he'd already stepped into the bathroom and turned on the light and fan. Tris went to the kitchen and pressed the start button on her old Mr. Coffee.

"What are you up to today?" Mike called to her a few minutes later. She waited, mug in hand, for the full pot to brew. Someday, she'd remember to buy a new coffee maker that had a pause function.

"Errands this morning. Later on, I'm headed to the airport to sit down with Woody, then Bruce." Mike didn't say anything, so she wasn't sure he'd heard the last part. It was just as well.

She poured coffee into two mugs. Maybe Bruce had discussed his recent flying difficulties with Mike, given their family connection. No, probably not—pilots didn't discuss their shortcomings with other pilots.

Mike entered the kitchen, his hair wet and combed back, dressed in the jeans, button-down chambray shirt, and lace-up boots he'd worn last night.

"Well, I'm going to take my coffee to go if you don't mind." He grabbed the mug she'd set out for him. "So, I guess we'll have to find a time for me to give this cup back to you, eh?" He hugged her and kissed the top of her head. She caught the faint scent of black cherries. "Tonight, perhaps?"

"Sure. Stay in or go out?"

"Oh, I think stay in." He gave her a squeeze. "I'll pick up Chinese. Up for it?"

"Perfect."

Mike was out the door in seconds, her question about his interview unanswered.

I'll ask him later. Lifting her steaming mug of coffee with both hands, Tris inhaled the aroma of French roast mixed with Mike's black cherry scent. Man and mug both smelled like peace.

The gravel patch that bordered the Westin Charter hangar was muddy from last night's rain. None of the regular crew of homeless people that usually lined the hangar walls was around, although their bags and shopping carts stood in a disorganized array. The stink of wet garbage coming from the dumpster was so potent that Tris pinched her nose and breathed through her mouth.

She'd parked next to Woody's car. Luckily, Bruce hadn't arrived. This wasn't the first time she'd have to have a tough conversation with a pilot about training. And as Chief Pilot, it would surely not be the last.

Inside the hangar, one of the mechanics was checking the Royal's engines. He waved at her as she walked by, taking care not to trip on electrical cables or various tools and airplane parts that were strewn in a semi-circle around a large multi-drawer toolbox.

When Tris entered the office area, she found Phyllida pouring herself a "cuppa" from the Bunn, the Westin Charter schedule pressed securely under her arm.

"Hallo Tris," she said, "stopping by for a wee chat?"

Tris thumbed toward Woody's windowless office.

"Yep. With the gaffer." Tris jumped at any chance to use the British slang Phyll taught her.

Phyll's brow furrowed. "Well, take care then. He's in a bit of a snit."

"Why?"

Before Phyll could answer, Woody poked his head out. "Hey Tris. C'mon in." When she stepped inside the tiny office, Woody shut the door behind them.

"Go ahead," he said, sitting at his desk. "It's your meeting."

She unfolded the metal guest chair and sat. "Woody, we need to talk about Bruce..."

"Oh, yeah," he interrupted. "That training outline you did is very good. I meant to tell you. How's he doing?"

"Well, thanks. About that. I don't think he's ready for upgrade."

Woody tapped a paper clip on the desk. "No?"

"No. Honestly, I think he's a bit overwhelmed with everything that's been going on with him. First, you know, the baby's coming. Then Lemaster. What a horror show that was. He took it hard. As part of his training I've given him the left seat, had him make some judgment calls." She paused, internally questioning her well-rehearsed speech. "And he's fine on the ground—*great* on the ground. His planning and preparation get four stars. But, on the last few flights, his airmanship... he has simply not been himself." Her voice trailed off. She wriggled in her chair and looked away from Woody before continuing. "He will not be ready to upgrade in time for the angel flight. He's not ready to be a captain."

Woody unbent the paper clip, pulling it open. "And more training won't help?"

It was a fair question. "I don't think his physical skills are the problem. I can't trust his judgment. He's become... unpredictable."

"Really? Have you talked to him about it?"

There was no way to talk a pilot out of freezing in the cockpit. Tris shivered as she recalled the departure out of Jackson Hole. "I've debriefed him after every flight, of course. But I haven't told him that I'm recommending his upgrade training be suspended. Just for a little while. Maybe until after Heather delivers. I wanted to tell you first."

Woody nodded. "So, you're withdrawing your recommendation that Bruce upgrade, eh? We're close to a deal on that second airplane. You know this'll leave me with only one captain now. Who's gonna fly the trips I want to book to pay for it?"

"I know. And I'm sorry. As your Chief Pilot, I can interview new captain candidates right away."

Woody spun the twisted piece of metal between the thumb and forefingers of both hands, eyes fixed on the dexterous operation. "Okay. So, let me see if I've got this. In your best professional judgment, a few weeks ago, Bruce was ready. And now, you tell me, in your best professional judgment, he's not. Have I got that right?"

The blow struck right at her pilot-in-command authority. She hoped it was just his frustration, that Woody wasn't intentionally trying to be mean.

"That's what I'm saying. I'm so sorry."

Woody lifted a piece of paper from his desk. "This kind of screws me a bit, Tris. You have to know that. I mean, we're almost ready to pull the trigger on that second Royal. And now I've got a crew problem. Is Bruce good to fly as co-pilot, or do I have to go out and get another one of those too?"

Tris willed herself to stillness, calling on the many times at Tetrix she'd forced herself not to react; to stay calm for the good of the airplane, her passengers, herself.

She kept her response brief and monotone. "As long as he's flying in a supporting role, he's been fine."

Woody lifted a piece of paper from his desk. It looked like a resume, but she couldn't be sure. "That's it, then. When do you tell Bruce?"

Tris looked up at the clock on the wall behind him.

"In about ten minutes."

Twenty-Two

IN A LITTLE-USED anteroom in the Westin hangar, Bruce listened to his dream of flying for Legacy dissolve.

Bent over in his seat, forearms on his legs, hands dangling between them, head bowed, he forced himself not to cry.

Tris hesitated, breathed in and out slowly. "Based on what I've seen on the last couple of trips, if I continue to push you toward upgrade right now, it'll be too much. You won't make it."

"Tris, look. I know I've been distracted lately. I'll do better. I know I can do better. I have to have this. I—" His voice broke, and he closed his eyes.

When they opened, Tris was rubbing her forehead. Bruce could see this was killing her. She offered a whiff of hope. "We've got the trip to Manchester coming up in a couple of days. It's not Bangor, but the route will be close to the one we're doing on the angel flight next month. I'll have you plan and fly both legs. We'll see how it goes. But Bruce . . . no promises."

He couldn't look at her. His shoulders trembled as he fought back tears.

"Bruce, you're going to be a captain someday. And you're going to move on to whatever next step in your career you choose. It's all going to happen. Maybe not at the speed, or in the order that you think it should, but it will happen. You're so smart, and such a great pilot. But you're carrying too much right now. You've got to offload some stuff, buddy." She tried to give him a friendly pat on the leg, but he rose abruptly and backed away.

"Okay, Tris. I get it." He hesitated, and his entire body went limp. He dropped back into the chair opposite her again. "You talked to Woody?"

"Yes. I had to."

"What did he say?"

"That you'd stay in the right seat until you were ready to upgrade. No one is forcing you out, Bruce."

Bruce nodded his head. "Thanks, Cap." He tried to smile. "And your Chief Pilot training? How's *that* going?" Sarcasm crept into his voice. He couldn't help it.

Tris twisted in her chair and looked up at the ceiling. "Well, so far I haven't heard back from Woody about my training proposal. He still has to approve it. And, the plan is still to have it done before the angel flight. Hopefully, by then, Woody will know something more about . . ."

"Okay. I get it. Thanks, Tris. Hope things work out for you." Bruce pulled his keys out of his pocket and headed for the exit.

Outside, he stood by the driver's door, and let his fingers locate the familiar boxy house key. He pinched it while the remaining keys dangled on the chain. His own key ring felt unusual in his hand, like it belonged to someone else. The car key, the heaviest and largest one he had, sat between the one that opened the storage shed at his apartment complex and the grocery store hangtags Heather had put on there.

Heather. He had to come up with a story that made this whole disaster seem like a big mistake. He looked over at Tris's car. Tris.

That girl has not a care in the world. No real responsibility. Nothing like the ones I have waiting for me at home. She has the Chief Pilot job to look forward to, and a new boyfriend. At least for now.

What did he really know about her? She had been Woody's Chief Flight Instructor before he started the charter company. Before that, she'd flown a jet for Tetrix. How in the hell did a pilot go from that to this? Early on, he'd heard some rumors floating around that she'd been fired for failing a check ride, or that some guy there tried to sleep with her, and she bitched about it. He'd never had the nerve to ask her what really happened. When she'd plucked him out of the scrum for the prized position of co-pilot on the Royal at shiny new Westin Charter, he was so grateful he forgot about it. What did he care?

He had needed this co-pilot job; it was a big step up for him. Boy, that seemed so long ago, but it was only, what, a year? He had been about to marry Heather. The timing made sense.

Heather had never liked that he was a pilot—not at all. His parents lived next to a pilot and his family; he flew out of Exeter, was the pilot on some corporate jet. Every time the guy went on a trip, the wife went over to his mother's house and bitched.

Heather didn't care for Bruce's mother either. He didn't blame his wife for that; no matter how neutral his mother's conversation started out, it always degenerated into frustration at how hard her life was, how badly it'd worked out. Bruce had warned Heather about his mom before they were married, warned her about his dad, too. Both his parents had a way of sucking people into their bitter, disappointing point of view.

Heather had said she didn't care. But once the glow of being a newlywed wore off, Heather avoided her in-laws.

Bruce had assured Heather that the two of them would never become like those neighbors, or his mother and father. Westin Charter was the perfect compromise. He took the job at Westin, got a week's vacation to get married, and four months later had a bun in the oven.

Bruce never told Heather about his first interview at Legacy, which came a week after their honeymoon in Oahu. She was so happy, opening boxes of wedding gifts and decorating their freshly painted two-bedroom rental home. He'd hoped to surprise her with news of the new job, the career position that would set them up for life. So, luckily, he was spared that awkward conversation.

The wind picked up and cut through his flimsy Westin Charter windbreaker. *Idiot. It's twenty-five degrees out with the wind chill. Why'd you leave your parka at home?*

Despite the refuge the inside of the Bronco promised, Bruce couldn't seem to stick the key in the lock, turn it and open the door. Every time he tried, his right hand flopped down on his thigh. What if the engine exploded or caught on fire? There was no checklist for this, for a car. What would he do if it burst into flames?

No, no that won't happen. That's insane.

Thinking how he must look, standing there, Bruce opened the Bronco's cargo bin and huddled over his golf clubs. He slowly removed them from his golf bag one at a time, as if to make sure they were okay. They were made of the finest tungsten steel. His Big Bertha had its pom pom cover on it. Nothing had changed.

Bruce pulled the bag out of the trunk. A pilot who pulls their clubs out of the trunk is reorganizing. Lake-effect snow began to swirl around him as the wind speed increased. He clasped his hands together and blew into them.

If he got a job at Legacy, he'd need a bigger car, because he'd need a larger overnight bag. He had to get the job at Legacy. Once he did, he could buy a bigger car. There'd be room in his trunk for everything he needed. He hefted the bag back in.

They'd hired Danny. Christ, if they hired that guy, Bruce should have no problem. But Danny had all that command time from his captain days at Clear Sky. Bruce's smile dropped into a scowl. His chance to get that same experience was in serious jeopardy.

Tris had given up on him. Maybe she didn't have the chops to train him.

He looked over at her car, parked just a few spots away. For a moment, he imagined swinging Big Bertha against its front windshield, glass flying. She wouldn't be hurt, just inconvenienced, the way she had inconvenienced him.

That's ridiculous. What are you thinking?

There were still options. The Chief Pilot job wasn't filled yet. Hadn't Mike met with Woody again today? It was a flicker of hope. After all, Mike had so much experience in the Royal. Surely, he'd catch something she couldn't, teach Bruce some tricks, give him the right push. Maybe Heather had been right about Tris after all.

Glad I suggested Mike talk to Woody about a job.

It's not over.

Another strong gust of wind blew through his windbreaker. Finally, he could unlock the Bronco, stick his key in the ignition, and start it up.

Twenty-Three

TRIS NUDGED MIKE'S foot out of her way and plopped down next to him. "Hey. Don't be such a couch hog," she joked.

This was only her second time at his place, though it turned out he lived less than two blocks from her. She could see her patio from his bedroom window.

His tattered couch wasn't much of an improvement over the old brown sofa at her place, the one she'd bought second-hand from Bron. She assessed his other furnishings—an old coffee table whose glass top had a long diagonal crack, a bookcase that wobbled when she'd brushed past it. There wasn't much. In fact, most of the small one-bedroom apartment was taken up by boxes.

"How long have you lived here?" she asked.

"Not long. Actually, I moved in right around when I met you."

Mike had no photos on the wall, or in frames around the living room. It wasn't long ago that Tris had finally taken the photos of her and Bron off the walls and collected the ones that were sprinkled on surfaces throughout her apartment. At first, she had to force herself not to open the drawers she'd hastily shoved them into, not to give in and try to re-experience the moments they captured.

They were still there, but she thought of them less and less. And it had been weeks since she'd had the urge to go to the cemetery. She still loved Bron. But he was no longer her life.

"Penny for your thoughts?"

She must have seemed very far away, luxuriating in how comfortable they were together, how they'd managed to establish a close, easy intimacy even though they hadn't had sex.

"Not worth that much, I'm afraid."

He took her hand in his. "I'll be the judge of that, ma'am." Mike said in an exaggerated southern accent.

She nestled against his chest and picked up *Hearts in Atlantis.* It was due back at the Exeter Public Library the following week. The hardcover book teetered in her lap while she lay next to Mike, so she straightened up and flopped to the other end of the couch. There, that was better.

Mike was reading Katharine Graham's autobiography, *Personal History,* which he'd borrowed from Tris's collection. He slumped down, positioned himself in the opposite corner of the couch, cracked the spine of the paperback and dug in.

What a bonus that he shared her love of books. He'd minored in English and told Tris how jealous he was that she had a master's in English Lit.

There's nothing sexier than a man who reads.

Mike was in the kitchen making dinner when Tris woke up. His book was open, face down, on the coffee table. Hers rested companionably on her chest. She had no idea how long she'd been out.

Something sizzled, and Tris remembered that they had bought flank steak and vegetables. Mike was making fajitas. She couldn't believe her good fortune. It had been a long time since a man had cooked her a meal. In fact, she wasn't sure anyone ever had. Bron had been a take-out guy, and she'd been more than willing to go along.

Mike talked a lot about the importance of diet. Pilots were frequently forced to eat whatever they could find on the road. Exeter in particular had only a few healthy offerings in the terminal. The closest place to eat near Westin Charter was a Pizza Hut that made those greasy individual pies in bulk and left them to congeal in semi-heated servers. The guys all called them "death discs." Tris avoided them at all costs and only grabbed one when her blood sugar tanked and she was desperate.

Tris walked up behind Mike, who was playing air guitar with a spatula. She pinched his butt while he strummed.

"How did you learn to cook?" she asked playfully, reaching for the spatula, which he now held above his head, out of reach.

"My ex-wife taught me." Matter-of-fact.

Tris stepped back. "Your ex-*wife*? You were *married*?"

Mike moved the food around in the pan. "I was. Hey, can you get me the red pepper flakes, please?"

Tris slowly moved across the kitchen to the pantry. "Yeah? What was your favorite dish she used to cook?"

He smiled and pointed toward the cast iron skillet full of sizzling sliced steak and vegetables. "This one."

Mike seemed at home in the kitchen, his red and black flannel shirt untucked over his pants, feet bare, spatula in hand. He hummed as he stirred.

And he'd opened the door.

"You never mentioned an ex-wife."

"She cheated on me. We got divorced. Then she died." He said unemotionally, as if he'd tasted a piece of skirt steak and declared that it "needs salt."

"Oh, no. What happened?"

He lay the spatula down on a spoon rest and ignored her question. "Dinner is ready in five. You're hungry, I presume?"

The man tells her that he'd been married to and cheated on by an ex-wife who since died, and then smiles like Wolfgang Puck. He moved closer to her, but she wrenched away, awkwardly pretending to grab something from a cupboard she had to turn her back to open.

"I am. For dinner. And for information. Mike, every time I ask about your past, about things you've brought up yourself, you blow me off." She couldn't let it drop.

"Not now. This isn't the time. Let's eat." He grabbed the plates he'd already stacked and topped with napkins and silverware and headed to the living room where he proceeded to "set" the coffee table. All the while, he softly sang a U2 song. She couldn't remember the name.

Twenty-Four

WHILE A LATE winter snowstorm raged outside, Tris and two of the Westin mechanics were in the hangar telling pilot jokes.

"Hey Tris, what's the difference between a pilot and a jet engine?"

Tris could not count the number of times she'd heard this joke. "I have no idea."

"The jet engine stops whining when it gets to the gate." All three of them laughed before getting back to discussing the minor mechanical problem that arose during flight. The familiar smell of dust and machine oil rose from a dirty rag tucked in one of the guys' back pockets.

Tris was giddy, almost manic, to have landed safely in Exeter before the storm hit. She and Bruce didn't think they'd make it. Des Moines was their alternate if they couldn't get in, but neither pilot wanted to end up there. They got lucky.

Phyll popped her head through the door to the main office and motioned her inside. She cornered Tris in the vestibule, blocking her entrance to the waiting area and Woody's office. The dark space was illuminated by Phyll's paisley leggings, neon green turtleneck, and pink feather boa.

In contrast to her clothes, Phyll's voice was soft and her expression grave. "I think you might want to wait a bit before you go in."

"Why? What's up?"

Phyll hesitated. "Woody just got back from lunch and is quite keen to speak to you. About staffing. Pilot staffing, right?"

Tris had to be careful here. Had Woody mentioned something to Phyll about Bruce? *Please don't let him fire Bruce.*

An exterior door slammed, and Tris looked instinctively toward the noise. First, she heard Woody's voice, then another man's, oddly familiar. His partner Jimbo? She thanked Phyll and continued inside.

"Hey Tris. Finishing up the trip?" Woody had his golf bag slung over his shoulder. Mike stood beside him.

"Tris. You know Mike Marshall. Mike, I believe you've flown with Tris Miles."

Tris grabbed Mike's extended hand. Mike faced her with smiling blue eyes that last met hers when he kissed her goodbye at his apartment door.

"Hi Tris." He shook her hand in a business-like manner.

"Thanks. Nice to see you again." Still in uniform, she straightened up and twisted her shoulders slightly to emphasize her epaulets. Someone had to be the alpha in this encounter. It might as well be her. "So, uh, Mike, what are you doing here?"

Woody laughed. "Tris, Mike's an old friend. That's why he was available on short notice that day Bruce couldn't fly. We hit some golf balls over lunch at the indoor place."

Both men chuckled at some subtext that lingered between them.

"Oh. Nice," she said. It was anything but. Mike had failed to mention that he was playing golf with her boss.

"Tris, follow me. Mike, wait here a minute." Woody opened his office door.

Tris bumped Mike's arm as she walked past him. He smiled in her direction. Her muscles relaxed, and she closed the door to Woody's office behind her, sat back in her chair and crossed her legs.

"Aw, crap on a—okay, sorry." Woody was thumbing through some phone messages and then pulled a piece of paper out of the pile on his desk. She recognized the training outline she'd prepared for Bruce.

"Yeah. So, Tris. About our plans here . . ."

"Look, Woody, if this is about Bruce's upgrade, please listen. I know you're disappointed, and I know I was the one who suggested it. Our last conversation was pretty short, and I can give you some additional details about why I changed my mind."

Woody cut her off. "No, this isn't about Bruce. Well, maybe. Listen, Tris, about Mike Marshall." He motioned toward the door. "We're getting close on that second airplane. And who knows, maybe a third. Business is good, we're growing. Mike's qualified on the Royal. He was a training captain on it before he went to the airlines."

Tris reached for the arms of her chair to brace herself, then realized the chair had none, so she grabbed the seat instead. She almost mouthed Woody's words along with him.

"I'm hiring Mike, Tris."

"Here? As what?" She forced her voice not to crack.

"A captain, of course."

"Instead of Bruce then? For the second airplane?"

Woody considered his desk. He didn't like conflict. Rummaging around, he pulled out the Chief Pilot training outline she'd prepared.

"This is great, by the way," he said.

Tris clung to the edges of the flimsy metal chair. "Woody, what's Mike's title?" She could barely contain her anger. Promises had been made. And earned.

"Okay, look. He's qualified to be Chief Pilot. He's done the job before, at another charter company, and with a Royal. I don't need two Chief Pilots aboard. I said I'd give you a chance. If you still want it, of course I'll consider you."

"You'll *consider* me. After promising me the job." Woody raised his hand in protest, but Tris cut him off. "And if I don't get it?"

Now it was Woody's turn to assert his authority. "Tris, I'll choose the best pilot for the job. And if I don't choose you, you'll still be a senior captain."

She fired back. "Senior, except for the Chief Pilot. If you choose Mike, that is." Tris thumbed toward the door. Anxiety coaxed her to say something sarcastic, maybe even hurtful, to Woody. Her years of training checked her tongue.

"Yes. That's right. If you want to look at it that way, yes, I'd be bringing in Mike ahead of you." Woody paused. "Mike thinks he can get Bruce upgraded. Look, Tris, I have to say, I'm not sure I agree with you about Bruce. Mike shared some ideas he had . . ." Woody cupped at the air in front of him, as if he were trying to grab words that accidentally escaped.

Tris gasped. When did all of this happen? "Woody, has Mike even flown with Bruce? Ever? Because Bruce has sat beside me in the Royal for a solid *year*. And I'm telling you that I'm *sure* he's not ready. Let me tell you more about the flights . . ."

Woody dismissed her with a wave of a hand. "Yeah, let's get him upgraded," he said, shuffling papers on his desk. "He knows our procedures, he's reliable, and we can use him as captain when neither of you is available or hire him out to other charter companies and charge a fee for his time. Otherwise, he'll fly as first officer, exactly as he's doing now. And if we get a third airplane, we'll need him."

Tris squirmed in her seat. "Woody, really, please listen—"

Woody shook his head. "No." His extended hands, palms flexed, pushed away her comments. "Tris, you are a critical piece of what we're building here. You know I plucked you out of that flight school over every other instructor who was drooling for this job, and I've never regretted it. Hiring Mike, considering him for the Chief Pilot job, those were my decisions to make as well. And I've made them."

"Thanks Woody," she muttered.

She opened the door to face her competition—the man she'd shared her bed with two nights before.

Twenty-Five

"HEY, TRIS, COME on. *Come on,"* Mike called, his voice an octave higher than usual. She walked as fast as she could to her car without breaking into a trot, to make sure it didn't seem like she was running from him. But she couldn't speak to him, not right now.

"Please stop," he called. She didn't.

Her fingers frantically combed the depths of her purse for her car keys as Mike came up behind her. He didn't touch her, but his sheer size blocked any escape. If she turned to face him, he'd see her shame. She'd failed to earn Woody's undivided loyalty. She'd slept beside this man who had betrayed her either all on his own, or along with Bruce, someone else she'd trusted.

"Why?" she snapped. "What for? Workday's done, co-worker. I'm headed home." She shuddered, and not just from the cold.

He touched her shoulder from behind. She wriggled toward the car. This was ridiculous.

"What do you want, Mike?"

"Look, Tris, give me a second."

"Why? To figure out how you're going to sell this to me as something other than what it is? That you went behind my back and talked Woody into hiring you, and now you're competing with me for the Chief Pilot position?"

Instead of defending himself, Mike nodded. "Yup. That's pretty much what happened."

"That night at my house? You know, the first time you slept over? You said you had a job interview. Was this it?" She gestured behind her to the Westin hangar.

"Yes. It was."

"Why didn't you tell me? Did you think I wouldn't find out?"

Mike looked away. "I didn't want to interrupt . . . to change the mood. Hell, I didn't want to upset you. We're just getting started."

She huffed. "Right. So. When I told you at the party I was being promoted to Chief Pilot at Westin, is that how you got the idea? Or from Bruce? Or both?"

The snow had stopped, but the blustery wind pummeled them.

"Hey, look, can we get in the car and talk about this? Can we please do that?" He walked around to the passenger side of her well-traveled Corolla.

Wordlessly she unlocked the car doors and got in. As soon as he heard the click, he sat in the passenger seat. Tris started the engine and turned on the heat. Ice-cold air rushed from the vents.

Tris stared out at the dumpster on the side of the hangar. She took silent inventory of the cadre of homeless men who lived there. Billy-Bob, Big Sal, and Shlomo were huddled near the wall. Where was Ike?

Tris tried to summon the tools Dr. C had taught her. Tried to be true to herself, be vulnerable, honor her feelings. The words all sounded so good in Dr. C's office, in the closed, guarded capsule where the two women discussed Tris's secrets. Out here, in the open, with no protective shield, her emotional muscle-memory yanked her toward a tried and true response—silence.

Mike looked out the windshield and took a deep breath. "Tris," he said, and then stopped. When he faced her, his eyes were soft, acquiescent. "Here's what happened. You know I'm related to Heather, Bruce's wife. After you and I met again at the party, well, I wanted to know more about you. So, I asked Bruce."

"When?"

"Before you get upset with Bruce, it started innocently enough. I was asking him, you know, what you were like, what it was like to fly with you. Look, I told you I was looking for a job. And, hey, it was *you* who said you'd be looking for a pilot."

"A co-pilot, Mike. I said we'd be looking for a *co*-pilot."

The temperature of the air spewing from the vents started to warm. Her internal ice wall cracked along its full breadth. Behind it, Tris found her power.

"I said *I* was going to be the Chief Pilot and that *we,* the company that is, would need to fill Bruce's seat when he upgraded." She smacked the steering wheel for emphasis, in contrast to her softly spoken reply.

Mike nodded. "Yes. That's true. But then Bruce came to me. He mentioned that you'd pulled his upgrade."

Her anger rose again, warming her cheeks. "He told you that? So he figured, what, if you were Chief Pilot, he'd have a better chance?"

Mike's head wagged back and forth. "It wasn't like that. Look, he asked for my help. My advice. What was I going to do? What would *you* have done?"

The weak plea left Tris undaunted. "It sounds like *my* pilot-in-command decision to delay the upgrade of *my* first officer was why *you* decided to compete with me for a job that you knew I fully expected to get. That I prepared the training outline for. That I *earned* working for Woody for the last two years. Sound right?"

"And you still might get it. Woody told me, and said he would tell you, that he hadn't decided. He really respects you. I respect you. Hell, *everyone* respects you." He smiled and bent in closer to her. "And some of us *more* than respect you."

She looked him in the eye. She wasn't buying it.

Mike slumped in the seat. The curves of his frown straightened into pursed lips. "Woody and I have known each other for years. Bruce mentioned me, told him I was looking."

A shrill, caustic laugh jumped from her throat. "And what? He called you? Just like that? And then he ends up hiring you. Fancy that."

The wind buffeted her old car. The snow had started to fall again, and if she didn't get going, she'd have to dig her way out of her parking spot. If she kept talking to Mike, she would surely cry—from frustration, from the inability to say what she really wanted to. That she'd been screwed. By Bruce and Woody, and by him.

Mike leaned toward her, as close as he could without touching her, close enough for her to smell those cherries.

"I'm sorry," he whispered.

"I've got to go." She put the car in reverse and waited.

"Tris," he said faintly, got out, and slammed the passenger door.

Twenty-Six

"IF ONLY HEATHER would stop complaining, then maybe I could get something done around the house. Everywhere I step, whatever I touch, she has a snide remark." Every few seconds, Danny would mumble, "Uh-huh," or "oh yeah," as Bruce's nit-picking soliloquy droned on.

The two men stood in line at the Greek place in the terminal at Exeter International Airport. Danny had a four-hour break between legs—airport appreciation time—and Bruce wanted to talk about his upcoming interview. But now he was on a roll that started with his crappy schedule, continued through his lousy trips, and finally settled on friction between him and Heather. He had yet to mention Legacy.

There were at least fifteen people in front of them in line. How Danny wished he could join the crowd of silent travelers behind them walking to and from their gates on this busy Thursday afternoon.

"I have my head under the bathroom sink, my body is curled around this pedestal and my feet are up against the tub. I got my

Maglite in my mouth, and I'm wrestling a PVC coupling." Bruce's words rushed on in a conversational stampede that threatened to trample Danny. When he stopped for a swig of water, Danny opened his mouth to speak.

Too late. "'Are you almost done, babe?' she asks, for what must have been the sixth time in five minutes. Danny, that girl is in the lav every ten seconds.'"

This dialogue was nothing short of bizarre. Bruce worshipped Heather. Danny had to tamp down any friction with Em when Bruce was around, he was such a devoted husband. Bruce and Heather's relationship was bullet-proof. Everyone knew it.

Danny's lips, desperate to curve into some reaction, finally chose a scowl. "She's pregnant. Pregnant ladies have to go a lot. Is this news to you? So, what'd you say?" *And do you always call your bathroom at home a lav?*

"'Workin' on it.' What else could I say? She wanted me to call Andy." Both men recoiled at the mention of their father-in-law.

Danny opted for diplomacy. "Yeah, Em is always asking her dad to come by and fix things. And, I know he's a jerk, sure, but I let him. It makes him happy, it makes Em happy, it'll make Heather happy and you can find something else to do while he's around."

Bruce shook his head. "No, man. I can't do it. I can't stand that he's friggin' talking all the time."

Danny laughed out loud. Like father-in-law, like son-in-law.

It was finally Bruce's turn to order, and Danny welcomed the conversational lull. They grabbed their respective lunches, packed in the see-through plastic containers airport vendors use to make sure travelers who don't speak English know what they got.

Bruce swiped some plastic utensils and napkins from a kiosk and headed to an out-of-the way table. They had to brush off a bunch of crumbs before they sat down.

"So, then she says, 'Let me know, please. I mean, I can go outside if I need to.' Like I'm gonna make my wife go outside to pee in March? With snow on the ground?"

"Hmm," was all Danny could think of to say.

Bruce flashed a mischievous grin. "Looks like Mike and Tris are going hot and heavy now."

"What does that mean?" Danny snapped. *Whoa, boy.*

If Bruce noticed Danny's overreaction, he didn't let on. "They've been dating pretty seriously, I think. And now they're competing for the Chief Pilot job. Man, can you imagine the pillow talk?" Bruce laughed at his own inane comment.

Danny wasn't sure what upset him more—that Tris had to compete for a promotion at Westin that she'd more than earned, or that she might be serious about someone. "You wanted to talk about Legacy," he said, putting down his plastic fork.

Bruce swallowed a mouthful of food. "Yup. So. What's the latest gouge? Anything new? I interviewed the last time a few months after you started, right?"

"I'm pretty sure nothing much has changed. But now you'll have that captain upgrade to show them, won't you?"

Bruce's shoulders rose imperceptibly, then dropped. "Yup. I'll have it. Almost wasn't going to get it. But it's s-s-still on track."

Danny caught the slight stutter. Sometimes when Bruce was under stress, or was lying, he would start to stutter, then catch himself. Bruce dropped his fork—more like threw it—into his plastic bowl and sat back in his chair. "Well, I think it's back on track now. My upgrade, that is. Went off the rails a little."

"Yeah? Some internal delay or something?"

Bruce bent over his food, picked up his fork again and began practically shoveling Greek salad into his mouth. He didn't take his eyes off of his plate when he spoke.

"Nah. Crossed wires, I think. A misunderstanding. Tris kind of fucked up a little."

Again, he had Danny's full attention. "Really? That's a surprise. What happened?" Danny added a chuckle, to bely his intense interest in the answer.

"Hey, you gonna eat that?" Bruce pointed to a wedge of pita bread on Danny's plate. Danny motioned that he could take it. Bruce grabbed it and used it to wipe up the juice at the bottom of his bowl.

"Well, look. I don't want to talk out of school, you know. But she really freaked out on a departure out of Jackson Hole. I guess she thought we were behind on the departure procedure or something. She got angry because we didn't make a crossing restriction." He paused, looked down at the table, and pushed away the empty bowl. "I kept telling her to calm down. But for some reason . . . I don't know. Yeah, ATC was pretty pissed. And so was Woody, I guess." He unwrapped a toothpick.

"Woody? Your boss? What did you tell him, Bruce?" Danny was emphatic, and immediately wished he hadn't been. Any hint of excessive interest in Tris would travel at hypersonic speed back to Em.

Bruce worked the toothpick between his back teeth. "I think Woody is having second thoughts about making her the Chief. Mike has been CP before on a Royal, you know." Bruce belched noisily into the air, attracting annoyed glances from nearby diners. "Woody says Tris is still in the running for it. But he'll probably get it."

Danny knew that Bruce had always supported Tris. And while everyone made mistakes, what he described didn't sound like her. In the thousand hours Danny flew with her at Clear Sky, she'd always been right on with procedures, especially in mountainous terrain, and never—ever—lost her composure. There had to be more to the story. For the first time all day, Danny wished Bruce would keep talking.

Instead, Bruce's pager buzzed. He checked it and asked to borrow Danny's mobile phone to call the Westin Charter office.

"Hey, it's Bruce," he said. Bruce listened for a minute, then his eyes widened. "Oh really? That's great. Thanks, Phyll." And he hung up.

"What's the trip?" Danny asked as Bruce handed him back his phone.

"Actually, it's a cancellation. For me, anyway. Tomorrow's trip to Burbank."

"What happened?" Danny asked nonchalantly.

Bruce's head bobbed up and down. "Mike and Tris are flying it, I guess. This will be Mike's first trip for Westin."

Twenty-Seven

THE HALLWAY WAS dark, the kind of dark that made Tris think she'd gone blind. She felt her way around the room—what room was it? It wasn't hers—and finally came to what might be a doorknob. It turned easily in her hand, no click or squeak of hinges as the door cracked open.

This time, just this time, let there be someone else behind it. Please don't make me see them again, sitting there playing cards.

She peeked in, and there they were. Bron and Mike. Sitting at a poker table, smoking cigars, piles of poker chips stacked beside them, a huge deli spread arrayed behind. The food was guarded by a man whose large biceps were dark with tattoos. His greased hair was tied in a man bun and he wore tight jeans and a Metallica t-shirt. She could only see his left ear, which had at least five studs curving up in a line from its lobe.

A holster bulged underneath the left side of his jacket, but she couldn't see if there was anything in it.

She opened the door wide.

"Read 'em and weep," someone said. *It sounded like Ed Deter. When did he arrive? Tris couldn't see him. Then, out of nowhere, Deter leaned over the table to scoop up all his chips, and the guy with the gun reached for his holster.*

Tris closed her eyes and ducked behind the door. Seconds later, the door disappeared. She was fully exposed.

"Hey, it's Kung Pao chicken," the man announced and handed *Bron and Mike a bag of Chinese food. Mike reached for it, a wedding band circling his ring finger.*

Bron held his cards.

"No!" she shouted at the shrill clack of her alarm. Only Orion was there to hear. It was four-thirty a.m.

Every night since Mike got hired, sleep competed with her demons. In the dream, Mike and Bron were always at a card table. Each time, Deter won the pot. And the burly man always reached into his holster and pulled out a different kind of takeout.

While Bron held the cards.

Tris made a mental note to tell Dr. C about it. When was her next appointment? Was it even scheduled?

The last place she wanted to be today was the airport. She'd ignored Mike's calls and answering machine messages, yet they were flying to Burbank today. That meant at least four hours together in the cockpit.

Woody was still negotiating the purchase of that second airplane, and Mike, before he could act as captain, had to fly a minimum number of hours under company procedures. Ironically, it fell to Tris to make sure he learned them.

At the hangar, the homeless were lined up, huddled as close to the wall as possible, some covered by newspaper, others by folded cardboard. She stepped quietly on the gravel path around them and carried her roller bag so she didn't wake them.

Woody had invited the disheveled group to sleep inside the hangar during winter. Each one had refused. They didn't want to be obliged or give up their independence.

Tris stripped off her gloves, loosened her scarf, and stored her roller bag in the airplane's baggage compartment.

"Hey Tris." she heard someone call when she came back down the air stairs.

Mike. She hadn't heard him come in behind her.

"Hey. Mike. So," she muttered, briefly flustered, "you want the first leg? Have you flown into this airport before?" She passed him the approach charts for Burbank airport in southern California.

"Yup. And didn't hit a gas station."

Tris couldn't help laughing. Mike was referring to the Southwest Airlines accident just days before where the crew landed way too long and rolled a 737 off the runway and right into a Chevron. Luckily, there were no fatalities.

"Great. Okay, then. You take it out, I'll fly us back tomorrow." She looked around for his overnight bag. "Where's your stuff?"

"Huh?" He looked sincerely confused.

"It's an overnight. Don't you bring toiletries?"

Mike looked off into the distance and rubbed his chin. She'd noticed this physical tic before. She'd ask him something, and Mike would rub his chin and consider it. Even asking him to pass the remote deserved due analysis.

"My 'go' bag's in the trunk. I'll grab it. Just wanted to check in with you first." He stood close by her, glancing over her shoulder to look at the trip paperwork she'd picked up. The captain's purview. She twisted slightly to highlight her epaulets. Petty, especially since Mike also wore four stripes on his shoulders.

"Want me to pre-flight?" he asked, recognizing that she was in charge.

"Yes, please, I already did a quick walk-around." Tris wanted to make sure to delegate all first officer duties to her co-pilot today.

When Mike rounded the tail of the aircraft to check out the number one engine, he called, "What about this?" He pointed to a pool of liquid on the ground. Tris hadn't seen it. Her face reddened.

She replied to the hangar door. "Not sure."

Mike made a noise of assent. "Yeah, me either. I'll grab a wrench and see what we can find out," he said, using aviation slang for mechanic. No attitude. Business as usual.

Thrown off by missing something, although her instincts told her it was probably water, Tris went to get some privacy in the cockpit. Surely once she powered up the gauges, she'd have noticed any low fluid volume. But she'd still missed it on the ground.

He's not judging you. YOU'RE the PIC.

"Nah. It's water," someone yelled.

"Great. Thanks," Mike responded.

Mike motioned to the entrance to the waiting area, and Tris nodded. He would bring out the passengers; they'd put the three executives aboard in the relative warmth of the hangar and then have the crew tug them outside.

Within minutes, they were airborne, pointed west. Other than required conversation, they'd been silent. Tension between them balled up like a twisted rope.

Tris broke the silence by broaching Mike's experience at the major airline he walked away from. "Bet you miss that 767 you used to fly for Legacy," she said, her chair pushed back, legs crossed. He couldn't walk away from her in the cockpit.

"I sure do. It was one of the lightest aircraft I ever flew." Mike looked wistful.

"Wow. Nice. Then what—"

ATC cut her off. "Westin Charter One, Kansas City Center."

"Westin Charter One, go ahead," Tris responded.

"Westin Charter One, light turbulence reported for the next ten miles. We can give you flight level three-eight-zero if you'd like."

Even though Mike flew from the left seat, Tris made the call. "No thanks. We're fine here. We're not experiencing any chop."

"Roger, Westin Charter One. Maintain flight level three-four-zero."

Tris confirmed, then picked up her "Coffee, Me, Skip the Tea" mug that Danny had bought her as a joke. It was her favorite. She supported it with both hands, guarding against jolts that could come at any time.

"Mike, I'm tired of dancing around the subject—why did you leave Legacy?"

At first, he seemed not to have heard, didn't acknowledge her or look over. But slowly, he put his charts away and pulled the privacy curtain behind them closed.

"Is that really what you want to know?" The words vibrated along with instrument needles and a loose metal panel that had thrown a screw. Turbulence had arrived.

Her anger boiled back up and her words came out quiet but deadly serious. "What I *really* want to know is how you happened to quit a job at Legacy Airlines, then came here to compete with me for the Chief Pilot position. Which you *knew* you were going to do while you shared a bed with me. That, Mike, is what I really, *really* want to know."

Recycled air hissed around them, mixed with dust and apprehension. Mike put his hands together and cracked his knuckles. Then he stretched his arms above his head and yawned. Tris was fascinated. He looked about to doze.

"Mmm-hmm," he hummed. His expression was open, eyes inviting. "Tris, I like you. I really like you. I want to be with you. I want to answer your questions about Legacy, because, let's face it, if roles were reversed, I'd have the same ones." He paused, and then looked away to run a quick scan of the instruments as the airplane bumped along.

"But," he continued, "don't ask me why I pursued the Chief Pilot position at Westin. Because you already know."

The words spilled out. "Don't patronize me, Mike." But was he? Tris opened her mouth to speak again, but this time Mike cut her off. The look in his eyes was sharp, intelligent but not at all unkind.

"I'm not. You know why. I was unemployed. And the perfect gig was right there, right in front of me, to fly for someone like Woody, a great boss, with people like you and Bruce, who I like and respect. Damn, Tris. This is not the watershed issue you think it is. In my position, you'd have done exactly the same thing."

Tris picked at a hangnail, and then bit it off.

"But here's the question *I* have," Mike continued. "If you think Legacy is such a great gig, that no one would ever leave, and certainly not to work for Westin, what are *you* still doing here?"

His words were caustic, but his tone wasn't; his eyes hadn't narrowed, his posture was open and relaxed. His expression was gentle and welcoming, like he might hug her.

Tris had to say something. But what? Her first instinct was to make notes, organize her thoughts in writing, but she fumbled her pen when she tried to grab it. It dropped between the right seat and the cockpit's side panel. Her arm slid down into that tight space; her body contorted, and her head rapped on the window.

The pen finally retrieved, Tris used a napkin to wipe off a smear of oil with a ball of dust stuck to it. There she sat, ready to write, to outline her eloquent thoughts.

She had nothing. No argument, no comeback, no suitable response.

Because she didn't know the answer. Sometimes when she

arrived for work, she caught Woody looking at her quizzically, like he couldn't quite figure out why she was still working there. He'd shake his head, mutter, "overqualified," and follow it immediately with, "I'm a lucky bastard!"

Tris had the skills, the judgment, the background to be at Legacy. If she wanted it. If.

After a sip of her own brand of liquid courage—coffee produced by the mighty Bunn—Tris punted. "Let's have dinner tonight in Burbank, okay? And we can talk about the choices we've each made in our careers. But, Mike, no bullshit." Fear bubbled into her consciousness. She stifled it. "If we're going to do *this*," she pointed back and forth between them, "then we both have to open the history books. Personal and professional."

"Deal," he said.

His hand slid over the center console, and brushed hers lightly, a touch so ephemeral it wasn't certain that he'd made contact at all.

Twenty-Eight

THE TWO ROYAL captains looked through each other across the table at the Italian place near their hotel. Mike toyed with his napkin, ripping it into strips. When the waitress put down his beer, his fingers went to work separating the label from the sweaty bottle.

Finally, he cracked his knuckles and nodded, just slightly, just enough to let Tris know he was ready. "All right. You've asked me about my past, about Legacy. I'm going to tell you. It's not a big deal. But first, you need to know. What happened at Legacy had to do with my marriage."

"Right. And?"

He nodded for several seconds before he spoke again. "Tris, I was married for about five years. I got the job at Legacy while we were still married."

For the first time Tris held back; it would be unkind to push. Anxious for any little nugget of information, wanting to yank the words out of his throat so she could *know*, finally, she resigned herself to let him tell the story at his own pace.

Quietly, Mike rolled his right sleeve up to his shoulder, so that it looked like a rubber tube circling his bicep. He gently lifted the cap of his white short-sleeved undershirt. There was a small tattoo. How had she missed it? But in bed with him, in the dark, she had been focused on other things.

It was a tiny heart with the name "Kick" scrawled inside.

Just then, a waiter appeared with their food.

"Looks great," Mike said, focused intently on his plate of baked ziti after quickly rolling down his sleeve. Tris had seen what he meant to show her.

"Sure does." Tris had her favorite—a meatball calzone. She cut a third of it off, picked it up and bit. It took the edge off. She pried a meatball from the crusty layers and snagged a piece of it with her fork.

Mike lifted a fork full of pasta to his lips, chewed and swallowed.

"I met Tina, oh, maybe ten years ago. I was thirty, she was thirty-two. She was from Massachusetts and looked so much like one of those Kennedy sisters, the royal one, who they called 'Kick?' Ever heard of her?"

"Of course," Tris mumbled.

"She was impossible not to love. So pretty, so kind." He shook his head at the memory. "And all she wanted to do was be with me. You know how it is at the beginning, right?"

She did indeed. The story Mike told of his life with Kick was one of young love, lots of sex, and his wife's waning patience. The more he traveled, the less she tolerated him being away. Tris had heard this tale before. The calzone sat untouched since that first bite.

"It was hard on her. Her father was a pilot, and he was gone all the time. I guess when I was flight instructing and was, you know, home every night it was different. Even flying charter, I was only gone a night or two at a time. But then I got on with Legacy. A dream come true—I thought—for both of us. But Kick took the week-long separations hard."

He described his first months on reserve, never knowing his schedule. His wife's frustration intensified in lockstep with his panic.

"I swear, I didn't know what to do. She was so upset all the time. When I was home, I did everything she asked. Went to every one of her work functions, did things around the house. I was like her slave toward the end." His voice held no rancor, only regret.

"Finally, I surrendered. I told her, okay, I'll leave Legacy. What the hell, there are other ways to have a flying career, right?" Resentment finally crept into his voice.

"But then I learned she was cheating on me with some guy she'd met at a seminar out of town. She moved out without telling me while I was on the road." At Tris's gasp, he nodded. "Yup, I came home from a trip one day, and everything of hers was gone. Everything she'd brought to the marriage—furniture, books, even the silverware." His shoulders tensed, but his tone never changed. "She didn't leave me as much as a spoon." Mike stabbed at the stubby round noodles on his plate.

"I'm sorry Mike. I really am."

"Thanks. I took it hard, I'm not gonna lie. I couldn't deal with . . . with things for a while. I quit Legacy, Tris. They didn't chase me out. No drummed-up training failures to get rid of me, you know, like the airlines do. Nothing like that. I left." He swallowed and wiped his mouth with the strings of paper that had once been his napkin. "And that's it" He dug back into his dinner as though the conversation had made him ravenous.

They ate quietly for a while. Tris liberated another meatball from her calzone.

When their silence became awkward, Tris forced herself to speak, to say something, anything, to help Mike go deeper, tell her more. "Sounds like leaving Legacy wasn't enough to turn things around," she said, against the lively beat of utensils clinking and diners chatting.

"It wasn't." He wiped his mouth again, this time with a napkin from a fresh stack their waiter had surreptitiously dropped on the table and placed his utensils in the empty bowl. "But that's over, Tris. It's all over." He lifted his chin and looked over her shoulder, through the open floor-to-ceiling glass window of the restaurant, toward either his future or his past.

They walked back to the hotel hand-in-hand. Tris sensed longing in his touch. And returned it with her own.

Mike had opened the door into his history, and by doing so, he'd shown her how to tell him about Bron. In the safe space he created for the two rookie lovers to relive the shame, conspiracies, and emotional damage of the past, Tris saw the possibility of love without blame, the chance to speak truth without pretense. She could share the guilt over Bron's death that she'd borne for so long, and how much she not only still loved him, but missed him.

So she did.

In the dark hotel room, they lay on their backs, side-by-side on crisp white sheets, their heads nestled in down pillows.

"I loved him. Despite the age difference, despite the fact that he was so *positive* all the time. I mean, how could anybody really be like that? But he was. That was Bron." Tris tried to keep her emotions in check, but by the time she spoke about the end it was no use.

Crying openly, she told Mike about the last night of Bron's life, how there in her apartment she set the events in motion that led to his death. "I told him no. That I wasn't ready for him to move in. To this day, I don't know why. And so, instead of staying over, he decided to go to the crash pad. He kissed me goodbye. He said he loved me. And you know the rest."

Mike spoke not a word as Tris relayed her last moments with Bron. She'd invited him into her grief and appreciated the reverence he'd shown by just listening.

Finally, he spoke, his words and tone brimming with compassion. "If he were here today, he'd forgive you. And he'd love you even more."

Twenty-Nine

THAT NIGHT IN Burbank, after Tris and Mike opened their hearts, their bodies came together. A toss of her hair, a rub of his beard, were all the invitation each needed to settle into heightened intimacy. Once she knew she wanted Mike, once her anger switch had flipped off, once she'd told him about Bron, it was easy to move their relationship forward. She was grateful at how easy it seemed.

"I need to see you. All of you," he said. He stood at his full height, fit, lean, with the heart tattoo bearing his ex-wife's name etched onto his shoulder.

"Can you turn the lights out first?"

"No." He smiled kindly, almost apologetically.

Her pulse quickened. Doubts battled attraction, and she wondered if this was such a good idea after all. It had been so long, and there was nowhere she could run to if she had second thoughts.

No, this was Mike. She didn't want to stop.

"Okay." She slowly lowered the thin sheet, exposing her skinny, straight body, breasts large, round, still firm. More than a handful and a mouthful, Bron always joked.

Mike's expression didn't change. His eyes didn't widen. He took her in, clinically, like he'd review a chart in the airplane. Ever a pilot, his finely-honed ability to maintain the majestic calm masked any emotions underneath. He could have been uncertain. Or nervous. Or frightened out of his mind. In this moment, she truly admired that skill, one that was part of her own expertise.

When he joined her in bed, his physical excitement betrayed the calm exterior.

"You first," he said, as he positioned himself in exactly the right place. Bron's memory shared the bed with them at first, then mercifully faded into the night. Tris settled into a bliss she'd almost forgotten, from a love that lived long ago.

She was thrilled to return the favor.

When they were done, Mike groaned a bit while turning on his side to face her. He rubbed his beard and scratched his neck, wearing the smile of a man who'd delivered a gift that he knew the recipient desperately wanted, and received the same in return. He closed his eyes for a few seconds. His crow's feet deepened, and his lips moved in silence. A prayer? Maybe it was just his way. A gesture of appreciation for such a fine, fine evening.

He was still there in the morning.

The piercing beeps of a pager caused both pilots to bolt upright in bed. When her eyes cracked open, Tris noticed that they'd fallen back asleep for an hour after some early-morning satisfaction. Mike yawned, she jumped up to check the page.

It was the office. 9-1-1.

"Something's up at the home store. I'm calling Phyll," Tris said after Mike rolled out of bed, patted her butt, and headed to the bathroom.

"When do we launch again?" He called over the sound of relieving himself behind the partially closed door.

"Nine-thirty. The same three back to Exeter." Tris flipped open her mobile phone and pressed number 1 for the office.

"Tris? Where are you?" It was Phyll and she sounded desperate.

"At the hotel. Where else?"

She heard Phyll call, "still at the hotel," to someone.

"Tris?" It was Woody. "What the hell? Our passengers are waiting for you at the airport. Where are you?"

Frantic, Tris pounded the pillows that obscured the alarm clock.

"It's only seven-thirty. We're going to grab the van in a half hour. What's the problem?"

"Did you read the paperwork, Tris? All times were in *Central*. You are scheduled to launch at nine-thirty *Central*. I'm looking right at the manifest. It's pretty clear."

Damn damn damn. Tris scrambled for the paperwork. The minute she picked it up, she saw it, in large block letters: "ALL TIMES CENTRAL." It wasn't unusual, since sometimes the Royal traversed numerous times zones in a day; they kept everything consistent that way.

"Woody, we're on our way. We'll be there in no time. I'll call ahead and get the airplane fueled. I'll fix this."

Woody's voice was ghostly calm. "You know I'm going to have to refund part of their fee for this mistake. See ya." He slammed the phone down.

"Mike, hurry. We've gotta get going." He was in the shower and hadn't heard her. She jumped in with him.

"Hey. Nice," he said, turning toward her with the soap.

"It's not. We're late. I screwed up. I didn't read the manifest correctly. We're so *fucking* late."

Mike was confused. "Huh?"

"*Central* time. Damn it." She grabbed a washcloth and began scrubbing. There was a shower cap next to the sink, but she didn't notice it. Her hair got soaked. She'd have to towel-dry it.

They were in the elevator within fifteen minutes, at the airport in forty. She sent Mike out to pre-flight while she apologized to their passengers.

The Royal's wheels left the pavement of Burbank's Runway Three-Three at nine-thirty a.m. local time, two hours late. Their passengers munched happily on gourmet sandwiches from an upscale local caterer. By some incredible miracle, a Citation Jet's trip had cancelled, and the crew generously donated their passenger's sandwich platter. Tris took the names and email addresses of the two pilots, vowing to make it up to them.

Stiff and edgy, Tris forced her focus onto the flight home, trying desperately not to imagine the conversation she expected to have with Woody when they landed.

In the right seat, Mike calmly performed his duties as co-pilot, speaking expertly to ATC and making sure their navigation was updated with route changes. On those rare occasions when she caught his eye, he smiled warmly.

"It's fine. It'll be fine," he said at one point, but his voice lacked conviction.

A heavy jet passed them in the opposite direction, contrails coiling behind it for miles. In this peaceful place, in the environment she loved beyond explanation, Mike had pulled ahead in the race for the Chief Pilot job.

Her jealousy flared. She tried to tamp it down with logic—she had made a mistake, yes, but no one got hurt. It might cost financially, but all of her loyal service had to count for *something*, right?

She ignored Dr. C's advice to let negative feelings "float by in her mind," as envy consumed her. This time, her error could cost her something concrete, something she counted on, earned and needed.

Something she deserved.

Woody was standing by the open hangar door when the Royal pulled up to the ramp in Exeter. He escorted the passengers to their cars, all smiles, probably hoping he would not have to give out an "inconvenience refund."

Then he'd deal with Tris.

Woody ushered Tris into his office and closed the door.

"You think this is easy for me?" His low, carefully enunciated monotone scared her. "To have to choose between someone who has been with me as long as you have, and some new guy? Well, not new, of course I've known him for years, but he wasn't here with me at the beginning. But Tris *you* can't seem to keep it together. Lemaster. Burbank. And those trips where you say Bruce let you down? Man, I gotta wonder now, maybe he wasn't getting the right signals."

Tris almost jumped out of her chair. "Woody, I'm sorry, but you've got it wrong. These occurrences are not related. Bruce's performance issues have not been exaggerated. Have you asked him about Jackson Hole? He'll tell you himself."

Woody's mouth opened in surprise, then snapped shut. "You think so? I'm not so sure," he said, distracted by a note on his desk.

"What do you mean? Not so sure about what?" Her pulse raced.

Had Bruce pleaded his case directly with Woody? Or worse, had he done it through Mike? Had Mike repeated something to Woody?

Woody picked up the receiver on his desk phone. "That's all. Thanks for coming in, Tris." He pressed some buttons and turned his back to her.

When Tris opened Woody's office door, she caught a glimpse of Bruce, but he scurried off as though she might explode.

Mike stood by the Bunn. He'd waited for her.

"What's Bruce doing here?" she asked, looking around.

"He and I have a trip in a couple of days. He's getting a jump on things, to make sure everything's perfect. He even reviewed the freight manifest and checked the load. Acting just like a pilot who wants to upgrade."

Anxiety swirled, starting in her stomach, it rose through her chest, and lodged in its usual spot in her throat.

Mike never seemed to lack, or desire, information. Tris was out of the loop on Bruce—she knew it, and she didn't like it.

But that could change. "Keep an eye on him, Mike. In the cockpit," she said carefully, lowering her voice. "I'm not sure what he's told you, or what Woody has. But a couple of times when I put Bruce in the left seat, he had a hard time flying the airplane. A really hard time."

Mike's shrugged. "I don't plan to put him in the left seat, except on the ground, to see him taxi, until his checkout on the angel flight. If he can fly it from the right, he can fly it from the left. You know that."

"I know that's true of most pilots. I'm not sure it's true of Bruce."

The entrance door to the hangar opened then shut.

"Hey, you two. What trouble are you cooking up?" Bruce said as he went to grab some papers from his cubby on his way home.

"Oh, trying to stay out of trouble as usual, Bruce," she said. "Seems like you have everything ready for your next trip. Good work."

Bruce smiled. "Thanks, Cap," he said as the door shut behind him.

Tris beat some dust off her uniform pants and grabbed her coat. Mike now had the angel flight file open in front of him. He stared at the dummy flight details they'd put together to estimate potential fuel loads.

"Do you want to see the passenger information? It's in a separate folder. The one you have is just the flight planning information." Tris asked.

Mike rubbed his beard. "No need, is there? You've got that covered, right?"

"I do."

"So. See you when I get home?" he asked, with a big grin. They'd promised each other the night before that whatever choice Woody made, their competition would be left in the hangar.

It took every ounce of energy she had to smile back. "Sure. See you," she said, and scurried away.

Thirty

THE LIGHT AT the entrance to Dr. C's door stayed red for what seemed like an hour. When Tris checked her watch, though, only a few minutes had passed.

She'd brought along the angel flight passenger's dossier to pass the time, including some new material that Phyll had picked up yesterday from Tetrix. Phyll was quite put out by having to go all the way over there to grab, "a couple of strips from their local rag."

On top of the file were copies of two new articles from the *Nunatsiaq News*, and the latest medical brief. There were no changes to Christine's condition, at least none that was relevant to the flight.

The first article was titled "Grief Counselor's March to Beyond." It was a Q & A with a local reporter, dated a week ago. Tris skipped to the interview portion. Christine was an expert in grief, and years after Bron's death, Tris still looked for answers anywhere she could find them.

Q: Dr. Edgemon, you've helped so many local Inuit understand and deal with the death of loved ones.

Now that you are dealing with a life-threatening illness, does all the therapy you've given actually help you?

A: The process of death isn't what people think. Yes, death is the end of physical life. But, mostly, the course of death, the path of it, is a project to be managed, a stage of life to be planned for, approached, experienced, and assessed. That's what I try to teach my patients, try to pull them in to understanding that this is a very unhappy, distressing time. But the more predictable, the more regular they can make it, the easier it will be on them and their families.

Q: Is that how you feel about your own situation? That your illness, your ALS, is something you need to stay organized for? To plan for?

A: That's exactly how I feel about it. I remember when my father died, oh, I was about seven years old. He committed suicide, so we weren't expecting it. My mother just got on the phone, calling all the people who needed to know, the mortuary, the cemetery, everyone. She gave my brothers and me duties to perform. She managed the process. That's how we got through it. There was no time for her to fall apart. She had three children.

Q: What about the famous Kübler-Ross model—the five stages of grief. Do you subscribe to that model?

A: Of course. But those are internal reactions. What I'm talking about are external actions we use to accept the grief. Feelings, well, no one can truly control them. All we can ever control are our actions.

Q: Are you grieving your own death?

A: My husband Erik and I have the luxury—and I feel

that way about it—of being able to make decisions now. So that when I'm gone, Erik can truly grieve, can feel the loss, can process it and, I hope, move on.

Death is a project to be managed.

Tris dropped the article in her lap and closed her eyes. Step by step, putting together a death plan, making your wishes known. If she'd only known Bron would die that night. If he'd known. What more might they have accomplished in their time together?

"Hell, no," Tris whispered, and shoved the article back in her folder. "I'd have stopped him."

The red light went off, and Tris popped out of her chair, pacing a few steps in each direction before Dr. C appeared and invited her in.

"So," Dr. C said, after opening pleasantries. "What do you have to share today?"

It all came racing out. Mike, their relationship, having sex with him for the first time, his background, his marriage. Bron—the unexpected guilt she'd experienced, mostly in her dreams, as she emotionally pulled away from him. And work, the incredibly stupid mistake she made in Burbank.

"Why are you so upset about that trip, Tris? It seemed like all that really happened was that you got home a little late. Is there more?"

Dr. C just didn't understand.

"No, it's critical that these trips leave on time. Our passengers pay ridiculous amounts of money to leave when *they* want. Not when it's convenient for us. Woody is furious about it."

"How do you know? Is that what he said?"

"Yes. He suggested without actually saying that I might not be—that I might not be ready for . . . that I might not *get* the Chief

Pilot job." Tris looked for something to dig her fingernails into other than her palms. She forced her hands to grip the arms of the upholstered chair she sat on.

"You're making yourself upset by anticipating something that hasn't happened yet. Why do that, Tris?"

Sometimes she just wanted Dr. C to slide down the rabbit hole with her.

"Because it was a bad mistake. And I'm still competing for the Chief Pilot job. I mean, he hasn't made a decision, but this really puts me behind Mike. And Mike . . ."

Dr. C had been making notes, and when she finished, took a moment before she spoke. "Is there something more about Mike's involvement here?"

"It's not Mike, it's me. No, it's not Mike."

"Sounds like you may be trying to convince yourself of something. What's going on with Mike, Tris?"

Pilots are trained to handle distractions and pride themselves on that skill. Mike's background, his first wife, Legacy. Why didn't she check the paperwork before going to bed? She'd done it hundreds of times before. But her mind had been full of Mike—his issues, and her need for him. Her *want.*

"It was nothing he did. It's that he was *there* in the first place. Or not. I don't know."

Dr. C waited while Tris gathered her thoughts.

"It's like I let everything else go because of him. He told me about his past, things I wanted to know, answered the questions I'd been asking him—about his ex-wife, for example. And then we made love. And I wanted so much to stay in that space, that moment. I ignored my responsibilities. I wasn't on vacation, a trip out of the city for fun. I was supposed to be *working.*" Tris swallowed her own self-disgust. It burned.

"I mean, how can I expect Woody to trust me with operational authority, *Chief Pilot authority,* if I can't keep my eye on the ball? Stupid, stupid, stupid." She rose from her chair, and went to look out the window, at the parking lot. She started to catalog the people she saw: *Nope. Don't know him. Or him. And, uh . . . nope, not her either.*

"Tris, can you please sit down?" Dr. C's patient voice implored. "You know, we've talked about this. How you'll take an event and start tying it to a series of dreadful outcomes that haven't happened. Imagining everything that might go wrong, almost like it's pre-ordained, like you deserve the trouble. Is that what you're thinking now?"

Tris was steadfast. "No. I'm not. But I will admit, sometimes I can't get a break."

Dr. C made a note, nodding the whole time. "I understand that. You've been made to bear quite a bit. But the important question here is how do you wish to move forward?"

Tris's eyes closed. She visualized calmly explaining to Woody earlier that she had made a mistake, and the steps she took to correct it. *If you fuck up, fess up, and fix it.* That was one of Bron's sayings.

"Well, I guess I'll have to respect Woody's faith in me. If he still has any."

"Has he given you any indication he's lost that faith?"

"You mean other than hiring Mike and having me compete with him for the top job? Other than questioning my—my *fitness*?" Her anxiety spiraled again, and Tris couldn't figure out how to stop it. Breathe? Punch a wall? Neither seemed helpful.

Dr. C turned and put her pad and pen on the desk behind her. "Of course, that upsets you. Understandably. And your relationship with Mike creates different feelings. Can you share what you're feeling about Mike in all this?"

"Jealous. He's had a relationship with Woody for years, so that could give him a leg-up on the Chief Pilot job. And I'm jealous of his love for his wife. Someone he cared about enough to sacrifice his career for."

"Is there something else, Tris?" Dr. C asked.

Tris nodded sharply. Her right knee bobbed up and down from her anxious leg bounce. "Well, the thing is . . . I'm falling in love with him."

Thirty-One

THE COROLLA'S TRUNK banged shut, and soon Diana was in the passenger seat. She looked way better than she had the last time. She'd put on weight and was back to wearing a thick coat of foundation on her face. Tris noticed a few tiny pimples on her chin.

This time, Tris was the one struggling to explain her new situation as they drove back to her apartment.

Diana was riveted by the story of the Chief Pilot competition. She sat back and shook her head at the end. "Woody hired that guy? Was it already in the works when you started dating?"

"Was it? He might have been talking to Mike behind my back for weeks. I have no idea. Maybe. Woody didn't discuss it with me. Neither did Mike. Not until it was a done deal."

"Fuck Mike. Fuck Woody. Fuck 'em all," Diana spat. "None of these guys is worth the breath we use to say their names."

Diana's brash reply made Tris consider her next words carefully. "You know, Di, this is the guy I'm involved with."

Diana looked away. "Fishin' in the company pond again, eh?

How did that work out the last time? He died, right?"

Diana usually went out of her way to be polite even when she had to deliver a critique. Tris had copied the technique from her as a flight instructor. No, the woman in her car looked healthier than she had last time. But it wasn't the Diana she knew.

Tris pulled over to the side of the road, pressed her foot on the brake and glared at her friend. "Bron and I weren't finished. We would have gotten back together except—"

Diana looked horror-stricken. "I'm sorry, I get it. But at work. Can you really trust anyone you work with in this business?"

"Come on, Di, where else am I going to meet people? All I do is work, and when I'm off, I'm generally on call so I can't even go over to O'Slattery's and have a beer."

"I know. I know. Not sure what got into me there." The two women were silent for the rest of the short drive. When they arrived, Diana settled on the couch and rubbed Orion's belly. He purred like a motorboat.

"How long have you got, Di? When do you need to catch your flight?"

Diana pulled a flight manifest out of her purse. "I've got two hours, and then you can drop me back." She gave the walls of the living room a full-circle review. Gray silhouettes surrounded geometric shapes where photos used to hang.

"You ever gonna put anything up on those walls?"

"Haven't gotten around to it, I guess," Tris said.

"You mean you haven't gotten over him."

Another zinger from her old friend. Maybe it was the jet lag. Flying all over Europe and then back to the US was exhausting. Every day for Diana was a Ball Buster, the nickname Tetrix pilots gave to their annual ten-day, fourteen-city trip to Europe. Tris had only needed to fly it once to experience its debilitating effects.

Regardless, there was truth to her barb. "No. I took all the pictures of Bron and me down. I have nothing to replace them with. That's all."

Tris went to get a beer and motioned to Diana who waved her off. Diana was jump seating—technically that meant she was an active crew member and couldn't drink.

"Hey, Tris," Diana called from the living room, "so about that guy at work you're sleeping with. Or just seeing—sheesh, sorry."

"It's fine."

"So. Your guy. Does he respect you?"

On this point, Tris was resolute. "He does."

"And in bed?" Diana knew her better than Tris realized.

Tris blushed. "He's a pretty stellar performer there, too." She walked back to the couch with her beer. "He's a new captain, so I have to train him."

"In the cockpit or in bed?" Diana sparred. Both pilots laughed at that.

"Just on *company* procedures. I'll be giving him an internal check on those in a week or so. But otherwise, we're essentially equals."

Diana sighed. "No, you're not."

"Huh? Woody said we were."

"But he's a guy. It's different, as you well know. Once a woman has the power to affect a man's flying career, it's *way* different. Tris, you may think this Chief Pilot thing is only going to be a moment in time in your relationship. But it's not. So, this, uh, relationship. Only casual?"

"I don't think so, Di. My heart tells me it's more. But who knows? Maybe that's just because I want it to be."

Her instincts had let her down so many times of late, she had lost confidence in her ability to read any situation. The uncertainly around her relationship with Mike frightened her. She'd botched things with Bron. All indications were that she'd misjudged Bruce. Floating around her consciousness was a warning: *if I make another big mistake, I might not recover.*

Diana's hard line softened. "Man, I am a jerk today. I am happy for you if you really like him," she said, and looked it. "But the competition between you . . ." Diana's voice trailed off. "How do you deal with it?"

"We try really hard not to talk about it. We both want the job."

"Do you want the position bad enough to choose it over your relationship? If it came to that?"

Her first instinct was to respond *of course.* But doubt immediately set in. She hadn't considered whether the Chief Pilot position was more important than Mike. It'd never occurred to her that she'd have to choose. How naïve.

"At this point, I swear I don't know."

Thirty-Two

TRIS AND MIKE lay side by side on the futon in his bedroom.

"So, what was it like to be married?"

Mike groaned a little and twisted his body to change position. "My arm's falling asleep. Let me up." He pushed against her and rose from the bed.

Tris followed him out of the bedroom. When she rounded the entryway into the kitchen, Mike had his mouth under the running faucet. Tris loved to watch him drink water. Her grandfather used to do the same thing. She grabbed a cold slice of pizza from the box on the counter and wandered back to the bedroom. He still hadn't answered her.

"So. Marriage. Yay or nay?" she asked again.

Nothing.

She'd found a painting of a New England landscape to go over his dresser: a gorgeous Cape Cod home, its wraparound porch dusted with snow, frozen lake in the background. It was the first gift she'd bought him, and they had just finished hanging it. Mike loved it and referred to it as their "someday."

Tris could see them there. She could actually see it.

The new artwork looked at home among the few photos Mike displayed. They were of his family, his youth growing up in Alabama, and one vintage shot of his grandparents' wedding.

Mike's southern upbringing was rarely evident, other than the Southern accent he occasionally put on as a joke. But his mother was what he called a quintessential Southern Belle, a woman who "wouldn't check the mailbox unless her hair was freshly fixed and she was fully dressed, heels and all."

Tris had picked up his ringing landline one day to find her on the other end, and that's exactly how she sounded. "Well, hello, Tris. Now that's Patricia, right? This is Jeanne, Jeanne Mahhhshall," she drawled. "And how are you today?"

It was Mike who suggested that they meet each other's parents. Tris avoided the subject with a joke about having to have her hair teased and get a string of pearls in order to meet Jeanne. She was in no hurry to have Mike meet her mother and stepfather. She hadn't told them about Mike yet.

Mike had returned from the kitchen and leaned against the bedroom doorframe. "I heard you, you know."

"Then tell me about it. Good. Bad. I mean, other than at the end. I know that was hard for you."

He stroked his beard, deep in thought. Words would come eventually.

Mike threw a question back at her. "Do you want to get married, Tris?"

"Uh . . . wait. Married? To you? Or just, you know, generally?"

He laughed. "I gotta do some laundry. Want to throw anything in?"

"No. And, as to marriage, maybe. Someday. Now I've answered your question, you answer mine."

"I will. Another time, though. I have to do laundry. And clean the kitchen. You relax," he said, and started collecting dirty clothes, bath towels, and soiled kitchen items. He threw them into a laundry basket he'd tucked under his arm.

Tris followed him. It was a simple question. Tris had never been married and really wanted to know what it was like.

Mike had grabbed the key to the building's laundry room and a bunch of quarters. "Last call."

"Nothing. I have to do laundry when I get home, anyhow."

Mike stood in front of her, mere inches separating them. "Sounds like wasted effort to me."

"Oh, yeah," she chided. "You want to come over and share folding duties with me?" Folding was her least favorite household chore.

He put his arms around her and kissed the top of her head. "Maybe that's not all we could share," he said softly.

A flash of déjà vu caused a moment of panic which quickly gave way to calm. She'd been here before and gotten it wrong. Dead wrong. Right here, right now, was her second chance.

"So, you're saying you want to do all my household chores along with your own? Clean up after the cat?"

The corners of Mike's eyes crinkled in a way that left no question about his sentiment, or intentions. He had never said those three words, and Tris hadn't either. Neither wanted to be the first—another competition between them, this one to see who could hold back the longest from admitting the feelings that lived inside them both.

He smiled down at her and ran the back of his hand lightly across her cheek. "Maybe," he said. "Maybe we'd share them. If we lived together."

She pulled away slightly, but still faced him. "Well, offers to clean the litter box don't come along that often. Hard to resist."

"Then don't."

Tris considered this kind, loving, gentle man. She didn't have the right words, not yet, and desperately did not want to say the wrong ones again. So, she said nothing, and simply held him. It was the best she could do.

She and Mike were quiet for a long time. When he spoke, his tone was soothing, almost reverential. "Tris, look. We can talk about this. Discuss it. I'm not going to walk away." He paused. "And I'm not going to die."

"Thank you," was all she could muster.

He wriggled out of her grasp. "Still got laundry to do," he said. There was no hint of disappointment or hurt in his voice. No, she hadn't screwed this up. They'd revisit the issue, she was sure. And soon.

"Seriously, though. Now that we're talking about taking a step forward, I really do want to know. What was marriage like?"

His body tensed. "Oh, it's the best. Right up until your wife starts sleeping with someone else."

CHRISTINE

Since they convicted Kevorkian, and I don't have access to a prescription pad as a Ph.D., I had to figure out another, better way. I simply could not have you find me at home. In my work, I've learned that finding a loved one . . . like that . . . is the hardest part for people to overcome. I would never do that to you.

So, I stopped down by Pete's place. He didn't even flinch when I asked to borrow his .22. Why would he? I told him ours was jammed and no one around here—no one—is without a working handgun.

Remember living our high-end, judgmental, socially conscious lives in the liberal suburbs of Exeter? How morally reprehensible we found people who "needed" guns in one of the safest neighborhoods in the country? Right up until Warren crept back into our lives: skulking in the bushes, pretending to run into us at the grocery store. And then the phone calls, the hang-ups, the noises in the backyard in the middle of the night.

That fear became a part of my being. Just as

Warren followed me around Exeter, my fear followed me here. How long was it, Erik, before I stopped expecting him to appear? How many times did I lie to our neighbors, to my own parents, about why we had so many locks on our front door?

And even now . . . I'm still afraid Warren will show up and poison this place too.

Thirty-Three

ON AN UNSEASONABLY warm night, Tris and Mike sat on her patio, each reading in the light of a spare standing lamp she'd brought outside. At around nine o'clock, both of their pagers went off, each with Woody's mobile and the numbers 4-1-1. Tris returned the call first.

"Woody. Tris. You paged?"

Classical music played in the background, which meant Woody was at home. "Yes. Hey. Just a head's up. I want to meet with you and Mike after you get back from Teterboro. I asked Phyll to bring in lunch."

Given the expense, there had to be a good reason. "No problem. What's the occasion?"

"I'm naming the new Chief Pilot. I want you both there."

"I'll be there. Bye."

Tris told Mike that Woody had made a decision, and that he'd announce it in two days after her trip to the east coast. Mike called Woody himself a few minutes later and had the same conversation.

The two of them went straight to bed, but Tris couldn't sleep. She always tossed and turned before really early wakeups, and Woody's call didn't help. Mike snored softly into her shoulder as she stared at the ceiling.

Tired from fitful sleep, darkness greeted Tris at the airport way too early the next morning. Woody hadn't put a light near the dumpster where the employees parked, so she swung the driver's door open. The low-watt interior light barely illuminated the area around the car.

She crept quietly toward the hangar door so she didn't wake the usual suspects. Their breath rose in puffs from under piles of ripped, soiled blankets and newspapers.

It was 4:00 a.m. In a little while she'd be off to New Jersey and the craziness of Teterboro Airport. She hated that airport, so she'd let Bruce fly the leg out.

Lately, Bruce's flying had been solid. With every trip, she questioned her decision to pull support for his upgrade. Turned out the evaluation had had worse consequences for her than for Bruce—his upgrade was still on track, with Mike doing his training, and she was out of favor with Woody. And then there was Burbank.

"Hey," Bruce said, startling her. She had no idea he was there until he walked into the hangar from the office area.

"Hey. Where'd you park?"

"I didn't. Heather's car is in the shop, so I took a cab and left her mine."

"Getting close, eh?" Tris said, referring to the baby.

"Yup. So," Bruce said changing the subject, "who takes it out?"

"You can."

Bruce's eyes narrowed into a slight scowl. But he nodded.

She was not in the mood for attitude. "Don't you want to fly, Bruce?"

He turned on her so quickly she stepped back. "Why wouldn't I? Don't think I can handle it?"

"Oh, come on Bruce. Knock it off." She raised both her hands in surrender. "Look, we're all on edge. Woody's picking the Chief tomorrow and the angel flight is right around the corner. Let's just calm down and get through this trip."

The rampers assembled to pull the airplane out for fueling. Tris had the truck put on 150 pounds more than they needed and went to get the catering.

When she fished around in her cubby for messages, she found a thick fax. The cover sheet had a familiar logo—the Tetrix crane—and was addressed to "Captain Miles." A handwritten note, scratched in Zorn's familiar handwriting, said, "About your passenger. Husband dropped it off. BZ."

The next page was a photocopy of a note from a pad inscribed, "FROM THE DESK OF ERIK HUDSON." which read, "Hi Brian, here's some more info about Christie for your flight. We're so grateful. Thanks. EH."

Tris thumbed through the stack and found a newspaper article from the *Exeter Tribune* dated just days before titled, "Exeter Native Prepares For Her Own Long Journey."

The article included a photo of Christine sitting at a desk. Diplomas hung on the wall behind her, blond hair loose but pushed behind her ears, hands grasping the sides of the desk. Tris sensed tension, uncertainty.

Weeks ago, Tris had read the brief about ALS included in the file. Christine's prognosis was grim. Tris wondered, not for the first time, if there was a return trip to Iqaluit scheduled. Christine had been diagnosed almost a year ago. The brief was clear: ALS patients had a two to five-year life expectancy.

Death is a project to be managed.

Tris understood completely. Just like Christine, her own father's death had come out of nowhere. One day, he was sitting at dinner teasing his only child about the size of her hair bow. The next day, her mother sat at the same chipped Formica kitchen table, smoking, calling everyone they knew and choosing a casket. Their normally quiet house teemed with people for days—most of whom Tris had never seen before. She'd overheard discussions about cemetery plots and casseroles.

Project management.

The woman in the picture looked somber but determined. Exactly like Tris would expect someone managing the process of her own death to look.

Thirty-Four

DANNY WAS ASLEEP on the couch in the Legacy crew room when someone dug an elbow into his side.

"Huh? What?" He mumbled, still half asleep.

"Danny, get your ass off the couch. Pilots who are awake need to sit here." Danny could barely see but recognized the voice as someone he was in new-hire training with.

"Mmm-hmm. Uh, gimme a second."

He had no idea how long he'd slept. Danny was on ready reserve, which meant he had to be in the airport at 4:30 a.m., even though he had no trip to fly, so he could be crewed on short notice. At least the Legacy crew room's couch didn't smell like spilled coffee and late-night sex, like the one at Clear Sky. Back then, he'd hunt down the most comfortable chair somewhere in the terminal. Or curl up in a corner like a stray dog.

That's exactly how he felt right now. Alone, hungry, tired and extremely uncomfortable. That couch was awfully soft. His back and shoulders were sore from sleeping in a weird position, and not being able to stretch out his six-foot frame. Napping out in the open like that, where any crew member could come in and see him, Danny didn't even want to take his shoes off.

Still battling his way out of sleep, Danny thought he heard a name he recognized in a conversation taking place about five feet away, near the crew check-in desk.

He sat up, still groggy, and rubbed his eyes with closed fists.

They were discussing Mike Marshall.

"Yeah, I heard he went bat-shit crazy."

"She had to get a restraining order."

"Oh, yeah. He tried to kill her, *I* heard."

"Nah, I don't think it was that bad."

One pilot took a sip of his coffee. "Please don't ever let me get that pussy-whipped. If you see it, man, fucking shoot me."

"Me, too." The other pilot nodded. He was a captain Danny had flown with about a month ago. It was a good time to say hello.

"Hey, man," Danny approached the Legacy captain and the two men shook hands.

"Ready reserve, eh?" The captain smiled. Danny glimpsed himself in the mirror: tie askew, bedhead, and one pant leg hung up on a sock. He didn't even try to smooth himself out. Let the guys get a good laugh. He'd be able to ask a few more questions that way. Although pilots didn't need much encouragement to gossip.

"Hey. I heard you guys talking about Mike Marshall. I remember him a little. We used to flight instruct in the same circles. Is he here?" Danny already knew the answer.

"Nah, he was here for almost a year. Good guy to fly with. I did a couple long-haul trips with him."

Then the first officer chimed in. "Yeah. I remember him from new-hire training. There was something off about him." Danny figured this guy was the type who needed to one-up people. Some of the guys at Legacy were like that.

"Like what?" Danny asked, as he finger-combed his hair.

"Oh, it had to do with his wife. She wanted out of the relationship, I guess. And he lost it."

Danny shrugged, as though he wasn't sure what the big deal was. Lots of guys got ridiculously upset when their relationships ended. Little-known fact about men. He could think of a time or two that he had taken a break-up harder than the woman did.

"No, no, this wasn't like, 'Oh man I really loved her, this sucks,' kind of thing. I heard he went *crazy*." The first officer seemed more interested in the sound of his own voice than in relaying any facts. If he actually had any.

But he had Danny's full attention. "So, like how crazy?"

At this point, the captain shook his head, to discourage further conversation. "Hey, the guy's still flying. Maybe best not to talk about this."

The first officer rolled his eyes and turned away.

Danny agreed. There had to be more to the story, but the conversation was over for the time being. He'd hit up the captain for information a little later, when his know-it-all flying partner went out to pre-flight. Captains always had a few extra minutes to shoot the shit in the crew room.

Danny headed off to the men's room to make himself presentable. He grabbed a razor from his overnight bag and tried to figure out how to cup enough water in his hands to keep his face moist and not cut it to shreds while he shaved.

In the middle of this operation, the captain walked in. He gave a curt nod as he passed by Danny to do his business, but eventually they ended up next to each other at the sinks.

"So," Danny started casually, "what do you know about Mike Marshall? I ask because a friend of mine is dating him."

The captain's eyes widened, and his brows rose in a high arch.

"Really? Oh, well, she might want to think about that. Anyway, I can't really discuss it." He turned to leave.

Danny pressed. "This is one of my best friends. If she's in the trick bag with this guy I want to know about him."

The captain stopped and looked around before he spoke again. "Look, please keep this confidential." He checked the area one more time, as if he might have missed another adult-sized man in uniform there in the crew's men's room. "When I say Marshall lost it, I mean for real. I was on the union committee that reviewed his 'situation.' He showed up for work one day, checked in, did his pre-flight, walked on the plane and was met by local police. They said he violated a restraining order, got too close to his ex-wife, something like that. He got really agitated and started removing his clothes. And, man, I don't mean he took his jacket off because it was hot. I mean he started with his shoes, then his socks, pants, *fucking underwear,* and on and on. His, uh, *package* was hanging out for all the world to see."

Danny's curiosity piqued. But even this bizarre story, well, everyone had a bad day. "And then what? I mean, did someone snap him out of it? Was he arrested?"

Even though no one had entered the men's room, the captain hesitated. He rubbed his hands and shook his head slightly from side to side. It took a few seconds before a resigned look on his face indicated he'd say more.

He patted Danny on the shoulder, and gestured over to a corner of the room, between the last stall and the urinals. Standing there, he spoke in a hushed tone.

"He had to be removed from the plane. Buck-naked. They drag him off, and take him to the, uh, hospital. He stays there a day, then they release him." The captain stopped and searched his surroundings again. The look on his face made it seem like he'd endure physical pain if he continued speaking, but continue he did, his head bowed as he looked directly down at the subway patterned black and white tile, edged in grout that was either gray in color or hadn't been scrubbed in a very long time. "He'd showed up at her place every night for a month, violating the restraining order. She was scared to death of him. At least that's what the police report said."

Blood pumped so quickly to his heart Danny felt his arteries expand. He stood very still, at great effort. "And then?"

Now the captain shrugged. "Well, of course we all liked the guy and wanted to do right by him. I mean, under the union contract, technically there was no reason to fire him. Out of uniform, I guess." He chuckled but stopped when Danny gave him a hard look. "Uh, I guess they could have invalidated his medical, and sure as shit he wouldn't have gotten another one. We let him resign."

The captain checked his watch. "Damn. I gotta go. Taking a full boat to Charleston. See ya," he said, and he was gone.

Danny remained glued against the grimy tile wall. Tris had never mentioned this to him. Either she wanted to keep Mike's secrets, or she had no idea.

And if she didn't know, he had to tell her.

Now.

Thirty-Five

TRIS WAS STUCK in a three-way conversation none of the participants wanted to have; yet each wanted it over with.

"Let's eat." Woody said solemnly and pulled a chair around the small card table. Phyll had carried out a sandwich tray after the Royal returned from Teterboro. It was crowded in next to the flight-planning computer. The Bunn had been moved to the floor to make room.

Tris was still in her uniform. Mike wore a button-down shirt and jeans.

Mike stepped between Tris and Woody to grab a sandwich, and shot her a quick smile, which she did not return. She pushed potato salad around her plate next to a croissant stuffed with rubbery roast beef.

Woody took an enormous bite of his turkey club, chewed for what seemed like forever, and swallowed. "You're both an integral part of what we're building here," he began, and took another bite. "We're growing," he said with his mouth full, then swallowed abruptly. "Jimbo and I are close to signing the deal for that second aircraft. You're both smart pilots, hard workers, and there's no way we could—no way we'd want to—do this business without either of you. And," he nodded toward Tris, "you're loyal—loyal to me, loyal to my business. I know that."

The phone rang. Phyll was in the ladies' room. Both men looked at Tris. Annoyed, but smiling, she picked up the phone.

"Hello. Westin Charter. May I help you?"

"Yes," a man's voice said. "I need to speak to Woody."

She recognized the voice. Brian Zorn.

"Who?" Woody mouthed.

"And who may I say is calling?"

"This is Brian Zorn, the Chief Pilot at Tetrix, Inc. I need to talk to him about that angel flight he's doing for us."

Tris hesitated.

"Hello? Who is this? Is Woody there?" He asked again, impatiently. She could almost see him tapping his fingers on the desk.

She exhaled the breath she'd been holding. "Hi, Brian. It's Tris Miles. Woody's right here. Hold on." She heard him say "Tris," as though he'd hoped to chat with her, but Woody had already grabbed the cordless phone and taken it into his office.

Tris waited for her pulse to return to normal as Mike munched on a bag of Lays.

Woody returned, and without a word downed the rest of his turkey club in two bites. "Mmm, so, the angel flight launches in ten days. What's the flight planning status?"

Tris was prepared. "Well, I called our international flight-planning service—we're using Universal this time—and brought them on board as soon as I found out about the trip. Before you were hired." She motioned to Mike.

Mike nodded. "Well, you're all over it, then." He smiled appreciatively, without a hint of scorn or rancor.

Woody took a long swig of coffee. "Sounds good."

She filled them in on the details of the flight plan as Mike listened in silence, and Woody ate a brownie. Tris grabbed a chocolate chip cookie from a dessert tray but had no interest in eating it. The two pilots didn't look at one another.

Woody polished off his coffee. "Okay. We've gotta get going on this. Tris, good job—you're my senior captain. Congratulations, Mike. You're the Chief Pilot of Westin Charter."

The two men clasped hands, and then both ceremoniously extended theirs to Tris.

"Congratulations, Mike." She pressed each hand hard enough to send the message that they hadn't beaten her.

But they had.

"Mike, it's your show. Tris, you continue to organize the passenger details. I'll leave it to you both." With that, Woody wiped his mouth, balled his napkin and threw it on his plate for someone else to clean up, and was gone.

Just like that, Tris was subordinate again—this time to someone she couldn't ignore or dismiss. She now reported to a man who wanted to share his life with her.

Mike moved his chair next to Tris, lightly touching her thigh. "Bruce already pulled sample flight plans from Universal. He's studied the charts, the itinerary. We have everything set other than the final passenger manifest. Tris, you'll fly as captain, of course, but in the right seat as support for Bruce. I need to see him make command decisions."

"Have you checked him out there yet on any of your flights?" Tris asked cautiously.

Mike rubbed his chin. "Nope."

"That's where he's had issues, remember? Mike, you'll want to test him in the left seat before we go to Canada."

Mike shrugged. "Honestly, Tris, I don't see the need. He flies great from the right seat. A captain has to swap seats all the time. You and I do it regularly."

She shook her head. "This is different, Mike. I'm telling you; Bruce is different."

He took a deep breath and let it out slowly. "I don't think it is—that *he* is. So, about the angel flight. You'll continue to coordinate with the team at Tetrix and get all the passenger data and information you can. Any special requirements, whether our passenger will need a wheelchair, special pick-up, etc. If our passenger doesn't need anything special, then you and I can discuss any details the day before we launch."

"I can delegate most of that to Phyll. She normally handles passenger info."

He shook his head. "No. This is too important to the company. I get why you don't want to do it, Tris. But you need to."

She'd told him everything about Tetrix, things she hadn't even told Dr. C. When the memories made her tremble, Mike held her. When she teared up, he did too. He'd processed every horrific detail, his emotions mirroring her own.

They'd ordered Chinese afterward. Celebrated how she'd risen from those defeats, clinked their chopsticks over Beef Lo Mein and bit opposite ends of a shared egg roll. Those culinary rituals cemented their relationship as the fresh start both so desperately wanted.

"Sure. Whatever you say, Chief." She laid her napkin on top of her uneaten food, tossed the whole mess into the trash, swung her coat on and headed toward the door. She left Woody and Mike's trash right where it was.

"Hey," he called after her. She didn't stop. "*Hey.*"

Tris had already stepped outside, but she raised the heel of her right foot behind her to stop the door from closing and considered her partner.

His shoulders sagged, the edges of his almond-shaped eyes turned down, lips parted. Both arms were extended, his right hand reaching toward her, fingers beckoning her to grab them. "Tris please. Don't run away from me again. Please. Come on Tris. Don't do this. See you later, all right? Your place? You know I have a trip tomorrow. Let's be together before I leave. Say yes. *Please.*"

Oh, how she wanted to. To smile at him. Maybe even press her lips together slightly in the promise of a kiss.

Instead, she uttered a humorless laugh, raised her foot and let the door click shut behind her.

PART III:
THE ANGEL FLIGHT

April 2000

Exeter, Illinois
Iqaluit, Nunavut, Canada
Bangor, Maine

Thirty-Six

DANNY'S HOTEL ROOM in Little Rock looked out on City Hall. Its tall, narrow windows reminded him of a prison he used to fly over as a flight instructor.

Everything reminded him of a prison lately. He had called Tris on her mobile at least ten times. It kept going to voice mail. He truly was trapped—between wanting to tell her what he'd learned and knowing he should stay out of it. Leave her alone. Just let it be.

Then he'd remember how hurt she was when Bron died. No, this wasn't the same thing. But she could still be hurt.

Maybe Mike had already told her about his abrupt departure from Legacy, about the restraining order, the police. Everybody had secrets and each couple revealed them—or not—when the time was right.

It drove him crazy, not knowing if she knew. Tris would have said something, would have told him about this, wouldn't she? Or maybe she'd keep Mike's secrets.

Danny was about to call her again when his pager buzzed. It was an Exeter number he didn't recognize.

He entered the number on the keypad of his mobile phone. "Hello. This is Danny Terry. Is someone paging me?"

"Hang on. Hang on..." he heard someone say in the background. Tris.

"Tris. Where are you?"

"The Westin hangar. But I'm using the mechanics line. There's a bunch of people around. So, you've been calling. Sorry it took me a while to get back. What's up?"

After two days of rehearsing what he'd say, how he'd tell her, now he was tongue-tied. How do you tell someone their boyfriend is a stalker?

"Hey, Tris. Well, you know how you asked me a while back why Mike left Legacy. Did he ever tell you?"

"He quit to save his marriage. So sad—it didn't work. What's going on? I'm doing an equipment check for the angel flight."

Danny talked faster. Nerves. "Yeah, well, a guy I ran into in the crew lounge seemed to know Mike's situation here pretty well. There's way more to it."

"Can you tell me quickly? If not, can we meet up when I get back?"

He finally had her attention. He hated gossip. But this was Tris.

"Tris, the word on the street is that she dumped him, and he lost it. Lost his cool."

"What? How?"

He couldn't stand it anymore.

"He showed up to the airplane for work one day and the police were there to detain him. And... well... they say he stripped off all his clothes."

Tris busted out laughing. He had to move the receiver away from his ear.

"That's the craziest thing I've ever heard. Mike? He's one of the most mellow, easygoing people I've ever met. He flew the 76 all over the world with Legacy. And, by the way, he just beat me out for the Chief Pilot job. Nah. You got that wrong."

And now he wondered himself. Did he, indeed, have it wrong? Was he trying to pry them apart? *Wait. Did she just say she didn't get the Chief Pilot job?*

In the desk chair in his hotel room with his feet up on the air conditioner, Danny pushed himself so far back he almost fell over. "You didn't get Chief Pilot? Man, that sucks. So, Mike's the Chief?"

"He is. As of a few days ago."

"Well, then you've *gotta* hear this, Tris. The guy I talked to, a captain at Legacy, said he was one of the people who handled Mike's case with the union. They let him resign to—I don't know—help him out. And now he's your *Chief?*"

"*The* Chief Pilot, Danny. Not mine. For the company. I'm still senior captain. Anyway, I think this may be another example of 'air phone'," she said, using the bastardization of the game "telephone" as a placeholder for the fantastic transformation pilot chatter underwent as it was passed on.

He squeezed a plastic water bottle and watched the clear liquid rise to the top before it spilled over. "Yeah, maybe you're right. This guy was probably exaggerating." But Danny believed every word that captain had told him. Too much cloak and dagger around the conversation for it to be bullshit. If someone made stuff up, they'd usually start laughing in the middle of the story, or at least at the end. This was real.

He had to tell her all of it.

"Look, I know this all sounds nuts. But let me tell you the rest."

"There's more? You're kidding."

Danny heard a compressor start up in the background. He hesitated, but only for a second. "I am serious, and so was the captain who told me this story. After their divorce, Mike wouldn't leave his ex-wife alone. He stalked her. The cops were called."

This time, Tris hesitated, just a beat. "That's crazy," she finally said. "If all this happened, why didn't Emily or Heather ever mention it to you? Or to Bruce? Because I'm telling you, I have not seen anything or heard a word to indicate that is the type of thing Mike did, could, or would have done. No kidding."

Now it was Danny's turn to sound unsure. "I asked Em. She said she had no idea. But, then, you know, Mike's parents aren't super-close to Em's and . . ."

"Danny, I know you're only looking out for me. Come on, buddy. If what that captain you talked to said happened actually did, there'd be some story following Mike around. You know how it is in aviation—a story like that? And, yet, there's nothing. Woody's known him for years. If this was in his background, you think he'd have gotten the CP job?"

"Tris, don't you think you should at least ask him? Maybe ask Woody if he's heard anything?" He'd gone this far, why not go all the way?

"No way Woody'd hire someone with a criminal record. Look, thanks for having my back. Let's get together at our donut place soon. After the angel flight, okay?"

The longing Danny held in check finally seeped out. His words were choked, guttural. "All right, then. Bye, Flygirl."

"Bye, buddy. See you."

Thirty-Seven

AS DEPARTURE DAY approached, Zorn summoned a representative of the angel flight crew to the Tetrix hangar. As much as it grated on her, Tris had to go.

She elected to take the long way around the perimeter of the airport, instead of a more direct route. With temperatures in the high forties and bright sunshine, it would be an easy mile walk.

After last week's Chief Pilot decision, she and Mike hadn't spent a night together, although they talked on the phone every day. The Royal had four days of roundtrips to Miami in a row, and Woody wanted Bruce to fly with Mike as much as possible before his big day.

Mike had caught a bad cold going back and forth between winter and summer, so both he and Tris agreed it was best to sleep in their own apartments.

Their physical separation gave Tris time for her disappointment to thaw. The letdown over losing the promotion was still palpable but dissipated a little bit each day.

Mike hadn't taken the promotion from her. *She'd* lost it. *She'd* made the wrong call on Bruce. *She'd* been late in Burbank. She could play the victim if she wanted to, a role she'd been forced into before. But that uniform no longer fit her.

"I can come over and bring cough drops and Nyquil. And wear a mask," she'd joked on the phone with Mike the night before.

In a voice that sounded even scratchier and sexier than usual, if a little nasal, he said, "Nah. I have everything I need. Except you. I surely do want you."

Those words, the memory of them, warmed her during her walk. Finally at the Tetrix hangar, Tris pressed the familiar buzzer.

This time, a man's voice answered. "Yeah. What?"

"It's Tris Miles from Westin Charter."

The door buzzed open. And there stood Ed Deter.

Still bald and plump, with rimless glasses perched on his craggy nose and small, round eyes focused on her, Deter looked like he hadn't aged since she last saw him on her final day at Tetrix. He hovered behind the reception desk with a Styrofoam cup of coffee in his hand.

Tris resisted the urge to ask if he'd been demoted.

"Well, Miss Miles. Long time." Deter stuck his hand out. She had no trouble grasping it. Despite their differences, they'd made a form of peace.

"Ed. Hello. I'm here about . . ."

"The angel flight. Yes, I know. Everyone else is flying, so Zorn asked me to meet with you. You flying it?" He focused intently on the captain's bars on her uniform jacket, visible since she removed her coat.

"I'll be in the right seat. We're checking out a new captain."

Deter's lips opened in surprise. "You're a check pilot now?"

"I'm a senior captain at Westin. *So.* The passenger details?"

But Deter was not to be rushed. While he rummaged on the desk for something, Tris heard Dicky Lord's voice coming from the hangar. Tetrix had hired Dicky as a captain, bypassing Tris. A bad taste materialized on her tongue. Tris was sweating, so she took off her uniform jacket and cooled off in her short-sleeved pilot shirt.

She needed to get out of there, and fast.

"Here's a copy of the internal flight request," Deter said. "It has some details about your passenger you may not have seen yet." As Tris was about to take the document, Deter flipped it toward her on the desk. Then he asked her to wait.

"What? Is there more?" she said, one foot toward the exit.

The entrance doorbell rang again. "I think you'll want to stick around for this." Deter buzzed someone in.

A tall, slender man with a severe receding hairline walked in, wearing a Burberry coat and black-framed glasses. Tris recognized him but couldn't recall from where. He was probably one of the Tetrix passengers she used to fly.

The man walked up to the desk, looked at Tris and then asked Deter, "Is Brian Zorn here?"

"No, I'm sorry. I'm Ed Deter." Deter shook the man's extended hand. "But I think you'll want to meet this woman." He pointed at Tris. "Captain Tris Miles," he said, matter-of-factly.

The man turned, and again stuck out his hand. "Hello. I'm Erik Hudson."

Christine's husband. Tris took his hand in both of hers and squeezed it. "Mr. Hudson. I'm honored. I'll be the captain flying your wife, Chris—uh, Dr. Edgemon, to Exeter."

Hudson beamed. "A lady pilot. Christie will love it. I can't wait to tell her." He considered Tris, his eyes filling with tears. "Thank you. For everything. For going to get my wife and bringing her here. I don't know what I'd do . . ."

Hudson pulled a handkerchief out of his pocket and wiped his nose and eyes. "She's losing faith, losing hope. Who can blame her?" He spoke quietly, almost to himself. "This is Christie's only chance. Our last chance."

Deter's eyes had closed, his head bowed. He mumbled something under his breath—a prayer? In that instant, the shadow of her awful experience at Tetrix—the internal saga that had strangled her for so long—disappeared in the wake of their responsibility to this desperate man and his sick wife.

Awash in visceral currents of hope and hopelessness, Tris understood how their mission had gotten its name.

Thirty-Eight

IT WAS A REGULAR two-day trip. Another two-day trip, like he'd done hundreds of times before. Bruce repeated this mantra over and over. Just a typical flight. Everything was the same. *Except it wasn't.*

"Where's my socks? Heather?" He called from the bedroom, a bit too loudly, since Heather stood no more than two feet away pulling laundry out of the dryer.

No response. He'd have to grab them himself. Bruce couldn't finish packing until he got those damn socks. Packing was a process; do it the same way every time, nothing gets forgotten. Socks next, then underwear, then shirts, then pants.

He punched his fist into his palm, shook his head, and marched into the hallway. Heather stood by the dryer folding a pair of socks.

"Here you go, honey."

Bruce yanked the still-warm socks out of her hand, strode back to the bedroom, threw them in his bag and proceeded with his internal checklist. He wouldn't take a pair of jeans. He wasn't going out. He'd have room service, if anything. It was expensive, but the

217

last thing he wanted to do was go out with the happy couple on their overnight.

It wasn't like Tris had been jerking Mike off in the cockpit. No, nothing like that. But they were close, he could tell. Wonder what Danny's opinion was about them? Everyone behaved like Danny was so in love with Em. Bruce knew better.

After this flight he'd be able to run his own show. Woody said that the second airplane would be on line in a couple of weeks.

Once his upgrade was done, Mike promised that Bruce could help choose a new first officer. Someone *he* wanted to fly with. That girl who he'd instructed with at the flight school came to mind. She was gorgeous, and a pretty good stick. He'd get a resume from her after he upgraded. She'd be grateful for the opportunity, just like he'd been back in the day. They'd have a blast going on overnights together, hanging out—especially after the baby was born, when he'd probably need a little bit of fun.

Suddenly, the sheer weight of his love for Heather overwhelmed him. *What am I thinking?*

Bruce sat next to his partially packed suitcase and folded his hands in his lap. Then he fished his pager out of his pocket. The red light wasn't flashing. No new pages. But he pressed the display button, again and again, at least ten times before he threw the thing against the wall.

"Did you drop something, baby?" Heather called.

Say nothing. Say nothing. He picked up the pager and finished packing. He zipped up the Purdy Neat and rolled it over to the door with the handle raised so he could grab it as he walked out.

Bruce bent over, breathing heavily, in and out, eyes shut, hands balled into fists in his pockets for he had no idea how long. His pulse had been steadily increasing, to the point where his skin flushed.

What the fuck is wrong with me?

Nerves, it had to be nerves. Tomorrow was a big day. He'd confirmed that there would be no freight aboard, at least out of Exeter. And, really, who would want anything carried to the middle of East Bumfuck, Canada?

If there was no freight, there could be no HAZMAT. There couldn't be another Lemaster.

"Hey, did you call that therapist whose number I gave you?"

Bruce swallowed hard. "I have an appointment for after the angel flight. But, Heather, really, you know the risk . . ."

"Didn't Mike tell you pilots see shrinks all the time? And just don't report it?"

Bruce shoved his hands back into his pockets so hard, the waistband of his jeans slipped down to his thighs. *When did my pants get so loose*? "Do you think he did? Saw someone? After the divorce?"

"He should have—he was wrecked," Heather replied. "Ask my parents. If anyone knows, it's them."

Bruce realized he didn't want to know. Their home phone rang. Probably a telemarketer. Heather waddled over to answer it.

"Hey, Heather," he called a few minutes later in what he hoped she'd recognize as a normal tone of voice.

"Mmm?"

"Hon?"

He heard her mumble something, and then call back to him. "Bruce, I'm on the phone. Give me a minute." More mumbling, then the sound of the cordless phone settling back in its cradle.

"Who was that?" he asked as he walked into the living room.

Heather's eyes were rimmed red and she repeatedly raked her hair back with her fingertips. Not a good sign.

"What's wrong? Is it the baby?"

Heather sniffed and shook her head. "No, the baby's fine. I was just talking to Em. She's pretty upset."

Em was always upset. She was a very unhappy girl. Was he the only one who knew that? "What is it this time?"

"You know, Bruce, she's your sister-in-law. Why don't you care about her?" This again.

"I do. I *do*. What's wrong?"

"Danny is able to hold a line at Legacy—actually have a schedule—if he agrees to switch his crew base to Boston." Bruce could not believe the lingo Heather used to talk about airline schedules. Em must have schooled her. Em was sharp. His wife was the pretty sister.

"And?" Lord, she drew out a story.

"He wants to keep his Denver base. He doesn't want to commute from Exeter to the east coast."

Neither would Bruce. But he did not want to wade hip-deep into this conflict. If Danny held a line, even in Boston, he'd be home more. And his schedule would be more predictable; he wouldn't be able to fudge it. Even though Bruce hadn't flown for an airline, he was super-savvy about the tricks of the trade. Being on reserve was perfect for those pilots who didn't want to spend a lot of time at home.

"Well, that makes sense, hon. If he can get a schedule in Boston, he's probably not far away from it in Denver." That was a total lie, and Bruce felt guilty about it. Denver was Legacy's most senior base. Danny could probably upgrade to captain anywhere else before he'd hold a line as a first officer in Denver.

"You always take Danny's side."

"What the *hell* are you talking about?" He barked. "That's *bullshit*, Heather, and you know it!" His shout startled her, and she instantly sobbed. Bruce sat down next to her, took her hand, and gently moved an errant strand of hair behind her ears.

Who was this man, the one who made his beautiful, loving,

pregnant wife cry? Bruce didn't know him, not at all.

Bruce apologized, kissed Heather on top of her head, and went to check his packing job.

Thirty-Nine

WHEN HER LAND line rang, Tris was momentarily annoyed. The angel flight launched the next day, and she had so much to do. But then she saw "Unknown" on the caller ID. *Please let it be Di.*

"Hey Tris, how's it going?" *Thank goodness.*

"Di, so much has happened. Let me tell you—"

"I wanted you to be the first to know—I'm headed back to Brussels," Diana said, talking over Tris.

"Wow, that was fast. How? I mean, it sounded like they were intent on keeping you here in the US for a bit."

"Well, my doctor was able to get to the heart of my issues. They were all interrelated. And it's physical."

"What is it, Di?"

"My mother was the same age as me when she went through it. She died so long ago I never had a chance to ask her. I'm in early menopause."

"Wait. This is all *hormonal*? Seriously? Well, what do you have to take to fix it? Is it on the AME's approved list?"

Diana paused. "There's no precedent for this with the FAA, I'm told. Think about it, Tris. How many women do you know that stay in our career long enough for this to be an issue? Even if they do, would they dare bring it up to an AME? I mean, they're all men, right? Naturally, there's no one here to ask. The union guys are all men, too."

Diana was right. So many women quit flying before menopause. And who could women possibly talk to about it at work?

"Well, but, you have to do a First Class medical every six months. And random whiz quizzes. Aren't you concerned?"

"My doc said what I'm taking is a natural hormone, so it's not exactly a drug. Supposedly, it doesn't show up as anything the FAA is looking for. The feds want to make sure I'm not drunk or snorting coke or something. No chance of that."

To keep flying, Tris would have to take an EKG every year once she turned forty; another potential obstacle to clear. Now she had this to worry about. Every woman went through it, and Tris would get her turn. At only thirty-eight, it still seemed far away.

"What kind of doctor diagnosed this so quick? That was a crazy-fast turnaround."

"My Ob-Gyn. You don't think I was going to talk to my regular doc about this? No way. No, my gynie sent me to one of those natural supplement places, you know, with all the vitamins? And she introduced me to a friend of a friend, who gave me some natural energy boosters. I've been taking them since before I saw you last. I'm good to go."

"So what are you going to tell the company?"

Diana didn't hesitate. "Vitamin deficiency."

"Seriously? Di . . ." Tris didn't want to come right out and challenge Diana. "Aren't you concerned that—"

The elder pilot picked up on the thread. "I know. But it isn't *exactly* untrue. Who among these guys would know the difference between a hormone and a vitamin anyway?" She had a point. Maybe it was best left unexplained—one more quiet, unobtrusive way women learned to care for themselves in this crazy career.

Tris shook off the thought. "And you convinced them to send you back to Europe?"

"I told them I was fine. They whiz-quizzed me, which I expected. Of course I passed. Then they put me in the simulator. And I killed it."

Tris smiled. "Naturally." Diana's piloting ability was unassailable.

"Hey, so Di, Woody's made the Chief Pilot decision, and that angel flight is coming up..." There was a loud bang in the background, like someone had dropped something heavy.

"Sorry, Tris? What was that?"

Tris continued. "The Chief Pilot job... I didn't get it. He chose Mike."

Another bang. "Oh, no. I'm so sorry, Tris. Can we talk later? Damn, I gotta go." Diana talked away from the receiver, asking if something broke.

"When can we talk? I really need to—" Tris sounded desperate but didn't care.

Diana seemed not to hear. "Right. Thanks, Tris. Bye."

Tris heard the dial tone but held the phone a while longer, still hoping for her friend's attention.

Forty

"THE ANGEL FLIGHT leaves tomorrow. I'll be glad when it's over."

"I know you haven't been looking forward to it. Is it the trip itself?" Dr. C asked.

"No. Not exactly." How could she say it? Tris could barely admit it to herself. "I didn't get the Chief Pilot job. Woody gave it to Mike. And I was pissed—so pissed, so disappointed. But then . . ."

"What?" Dr. C asked, still scribbling on her notepad.

Tris grappled for the right words, the ones that would precisely define her feelings. Like a spinning wheel, letters turned in her mind until, finally, the right ones lined up. "Then I met the husband of the woman we're flying—Christine, the one with ALS. And, this flight . . . well, it could really be life or death. It could extend her life, this treatment." Her fingers were interlaced, flexing back and forth like a fluttering bird. "And Deter was there."

"Deter? Where? Did you two speak?"

Tris put both of her hands behind her head and looked up at

the ceiling. "We did. And it was . . . normal. I was at Tetrix, picking up some information about Christine. And there he was. Deter. But . . ." Her voice trailed off.

"What?" Dr. C had moved forward in her chair.

"He wasn't a monster. He was just a guy. A guy from my past. Not what he was to me back then. And he was . . . what's the word? He had compassion. The husband came over to thank me for flying his wife. He started to cry, and I think Deter did, too."

"Were you surprised?"

"About Deter? Maybe, a little. It was like he was a human being. I didn't expect to see him that way. I wasn't used to it."

"Being around him was not upsetting?"

Tris flipped her left wrist and checked her watch. She had to meet Mike and Bruce at Westin later on.

"No. After all this time, and all the anticipation about 'what if I run into him,' there he was, and it was a non-event. He seemed happy to see me."

Dr. C smiled. "Maybe he was."

"And I was, too. Not happy, exactly but relieved." Tris explained to her how the history that had been strangling her for so long seemed to miraculously lift away in those few moments.

"Have you talked with Mike about this?"

Tris took a deep breath and looked down. "Mike and I haven't been spending much time together. Since he got chosen for the Chief Pilot job, I've pushed him away a little. It wasn't his fault, really, but maybe I'm still blaming him."

The nails of both hands dug into their respective palms. Dr. C waited patiently.

"Mike never . . . Ugh. Look. Even while we were competing, I felt so . . . good with him. So connected. Us being together just seemed *right*," she whispered. "But then . . . Well, I've asked him to tell me more about his marriage, and he never does. So, I asked him about marriage in general—you know, what's it like? Nothing. And then Danny said something that—I don't know. There are clearly things that Mike's not telling me."

Dr. C. squinted. "Every person opens up in their own time, Tris. Has Mike given you reason to be distrustful?"

"I don't know. The angel flight. Not getting the promotion. I think it all needs to settle a bit. That's why I can't wait for this trip to be over."

Dr. C nodded and seemed lost in thought. Then she returned to what they'd been working on for the last few sessions.

"So, Tris, when the trip is over. When things return to 'normal.' What does that look like for you? At work? And in your private life?"

"You mean me and Mike moving forward?"

"Yes, that. But your job at Westin as well. Circumstances have changed. Your reality is not how you expected it to be, is it?"

Outside the office window a backing truck beeped, followed by the crash of a dumpster being emptied.

Tris twisted in her club chair, as if trying to put distance between the present and the past. "Things change. Circumstances change. People change. And everything I have, well, it can be gone in an instant. If I've learned anything from what happened with Bron, it's that. I can't push Mike away. I have to stay with this. He wants to live together."

"Is that so? Did he actually ask you?"

Tris nodded. "He did."

Dr. C smiled. "And what did you say?"

"Well, I didn't say no. Not this time," Tris replied. "We'll hash it out after the angel flight. This *flight*. Ugh. It's like a huge 'pause' button. Everything is in a holding pattern until it's over."

Dr. C closed her notebook. "So it is. I hope it goes well." She glanced at the clock. "That's it for today."

They scheduled Tris's next session for two days after she returned from Canada, then Tris grabbed her keys and quickly left. The elevator was right there, and she slid in before she'd even heard the familiar click of Dr. C's office door closing.

Forty-One

TRIS CHASTISED HERSELF during the entire drive home from Dr. C's. Mike had treated her like a peer, an equal; he'd invited her into every decision about the angel flight and kept her solely responsible for passenger details and planning. What in the world had made her want to distance herself from this man?

Whatever it was, whatever she'd needed time apart for, had passed.

"Hello?" Mike answered on the third ring.

"It's me. I'm so sorry. I miss you," she said, barely above a whisper.

"I miss you too. Tonight? Your place? After our meeting? We can pick up Chinese."

She chuckled. "Sure. But only if *you* pick it up."

"You got it. Kung Pao chicken and egg rolls."

Her favorite. "Sure. See you later. Hey, your voice sounds better. How are you feeling?"

He cleared his throat. "Fully recovered. And since you called, better than I have in a while."

"Okay, baby. See you soon," Tris said, and hung up. She smiled at Orion, smiled at the phone, smiled at the stack of mail she'd ignored even longer than she had Mike.

She went to her purse and pulled out the new set of apartment keys she'd had cut for Mike. Tris slid them onto the heart-shaped keychain she'd bought.

Tonight, she'd tell him: her answer was yes.

The crew of the angel flight assembled at a spare buffet table usually kept folded away in a storage room. The trip paperwork, including the passenger manifest, actual flight plans, and weather was spread out in front of them.

Bruce stood and addressed the two captains. His posture erect, he spoke confidently. "Tomorrow, April 11th, the crew will position the plane in Iqaluit, Nunavut, Canada. We will meet our passenger on Wednesday, April 12th for the trip through Bangor, back to Exeter. We are filed as a CMF—Compassion Medical Flight. On the radio, our call sign will be Compassion Royal Four-Five-Quebec, not our typical Westin Charter One."

Mike and Tris looked at each other with eyebrows raised, impressed. "Great catch Bruce. Thanks for that. 'Compassion Royal Four-Five-Quebec.' Sounds appropriate," Tris said.

"Nice Bruce," Mike echoed. "Hey, can you work on some fuel-load estimates based on the current forecast winds aloft? I need a sec to go over some equipment in the aircraft with Tris. We'll be out in the hangar." Mike motioned for Tris to follow him.

Once the door between the office and the hangar shut, Mike turned and gently pressed Tris against the wall.

"Mike. Come on. Not here." She wasn't exactly trapped but she didn't really want to move. He leaned in and kissed her, deeply, while one hand touched her cheek.

"I really missed you."

"I can see that. So, am *I* the equipment you needed to check?"

Mike put his hands in the air, an act of surrender. "I confess. You got me, Captain Miles." As usual, his eyes spoke the three words of devotion he never had.

She gently pushed him away. "C'mon. We need to go back in." He let her lead the way. Tris opened up the now-thick manila folder with all the details Christine's husband and the medical team had shared.

Mike poured some coffee from a pot on the Bunn's lower burner. "Go ahead, Tris," he said. Bruce sat poised to take notes.

"Thanks. Tomorrow, we leave on Westin Charter's first angel flight—uh, can we still call it that, Bruce?"

"Yup. That's never been the official name anyway. Aviation slang."

"Great. We'll fly empty to Bangor, Maine, pick up fuel, and then continue empty to Iqaluit, in the Nunavut Territory of Canada."

Bruce pretended to shiver. "It's friggin' cold up there. Have you seen the last week's temps? It's still in the twenties."

Tris rolled her eyes. "What did it hit here last week? The sixties? Can't wait to plunge back into winter again," she joked.

"Anyway," she returned to her presentation, "since I'm the one who has been handling the passenger information, let me bring you two up to speed. The requesting party for this trip is Erik Hudson, a Tetrix project manager. His wife, Christine Edgemon..." Tris nearly choked up, cleared her throat, and continued. "His wife Christine has ALS. We are picking her up to bring her back to Exeter for treatment at Exeter Medical Center."

Mike popped up from his chair, shoulders almost touching his ears, and paced. He'd moved so abruptly, Tris stopped speaking. Bruce just looked confused.

"What?" Mike snapped. "So, this passenger, this sick woman, does she need services? Wheelchair?" His eyes had narrowed until they looked like shards of flint, and his voice and expression were callous. The Mike she'd necked with a few minutes before had disappeared.

"I'm getting to that," Tris said, looking down at her notes. "She doesn't need anything. She can still walk and breathe on her own. We're good there. Now, the catering . . ."

Tris reviewed the orders the team had made for food, fuel, an overnight hangar in Iqaluit due to the cold temperature, and hotel rooms. And all the while, Mike stood by the reliable old Bunn, silent, arms crossed, eyes focused on a point somewhere outside the window.

Unnerved, Tris quickly finished the briefing.

"We good?" Bruce asked when she finally closed the folder.

"I think so. Good luck tomorrow, Bruce." Tris nodded toward her co-pilot. "Hope the check-out goes well. I'll support you in any way I can."

Bruce hesitated, then offered his hand. "Thanks, Tris. It's all good."

They shook. "How about you, Mike?"

But Mike wasn't listening. "Mike?" Bruce tried again. "Hey, earth to Mike. Looking forward to my upgrade flight tomorrow?"

Without a word, the Chief Pilot of Westin Charter grabbed his flight bag and practically ran out the door.

Forty-Two

"SORRY, 'RION. YOU can't join me on this one." Tris liberated the meowing little monster from her overnight bag. Not delighted with his new position on the floor, he jumped right back up on the bed and curled himself into a ball in her suitcase.

"That's the way it's gonna be, eh? Okay. I'll work around you."

The first two pairs of underwear she grabbed from the drawer would do. Then she yanked a clean shirt off a hanger. Jeans next. On the nightstand beside her bed was her diaphragm. Take it? Leave it?

She'd pop it in her bag, just in case. After she and Mike celebrated, of course. The heart-shaped key ring she'd present to him tonight was in her jeans pocket.

As if on cue, Mike walked in through the slider she'd left unlocked. He held two bags of Chinese food.

"Hey," she said as he breezed past her into the kitchen. The refrigerator door opened and closed, followed by the sound of a beer cap twisting off.

"Why'd you run out so fast earlier?" She stood in the kitchen doorway with her hands on her hips, smiling at the tall redheaded man.

"I don't know," he said and took a long drink. Pushing by her, he went straight to the couch and picked up the *TV Guide*.

"Hey, I taped the last episode of *The West Wing*. You know that's what I want to watch." No response. Good grief. What now?

"I'll watch *The West Wing* with you. I like it too, you know." He threw his words at her, along with a withering look. Mike's hair was windblown, like he'd ridden a motorcycle without a helmet.

"Mike, what's going on?" He disclosed personal details like a mother doling out candy to her children—one piece, enough to satisfy their cravings, and that was all. *Exactly like I do.*

Mike rhythmically rubbed his beard, scratching at its shaved edges. "Yeah," he said to the air. "Well, no, but I think I should leave."

"What? What are you talking about?" Exasperated, she motioned toward the kitchen. "You just got here. We have Chinese."

"Fine." He stomped into the kitchen. The silverware drawer slammed, and knives, forks and spoons created a metallic cacophony.

Diverted from packing, Tris followed him. "Hey, baby. What is going on? Come on. We've both got a big day tomorrow."

Orion must have relinquished his post in the suitcase since he zipped by her toward the inviting smell.

"C'mon. Let's eat," Mike said, carrying two plates of food into the living room.

"You go ahead and start. I'll be right there," she said, and turned on the kitchen faucet to wash her hands.

Mike tossed his napkin on top of his plate. "You know, honestly, I'm not hungry." He walked over to the slider and parted the vertical blinds.

"What? What's happening here? You barreled in here, wanted to have dinner, and now you're looking for . . . what are you looking for?"

"You got a problem with me looking out the window?" His eyes were dark.

"In fact, I do. Whatever's up your ass tonight, talk about it or don't. That's fine. But please don't take any emotional baggage on the angel flight that you can talk through now. Here. With me."

Mike side-eyed her. "Or what? You gonna ground me?"

Tris blew out a breath of frustration. "Please. Don't be an asshole. Mike, maybe you *should* go home. Have you even packed?"

"Yup. Go bag's in the car."

Tris touched the keychain with her fingertips. This crazy argument, this ridiculous test—no, it wasn't the right time. She pushed it down into her pocket as far as it would go without tearing the fabric.

"Baby, I want to hang out with you. I really missed you. But I don't know what's happening here. My mind's on the angel flight. Let's call it a night," she finally said.

Mike's stiff posture softened, as if his behavior over the last ten minutes never happened. "I'm sorry. I really am. I'm stressed, I think. I don't know why."

She didn't believe him. "Okay."

Mike stuck both hands in the back pockets of his jeans. "This wasn't the evening I'd hoped for," he said, and leaned down to kiss her on the cheek.

Tris accepted the kiss coolly. "The prep for the angel flight has been hard on all of us. Not to mention our passenger. I know we always have it in the back of our minds that our work is 'life and death.' And things rarely go wrong, but the stakes for Christine— Mike, this is the most important mission I've ever flown." She pictured Erik Hudson, felt the pleading grasp of his hand in hers, his desperation as he spoke of his wife.

Mike pulled away, looking grim.

Tris went on. "This time, it really *is* a life we may be saving."

Mike strode to the balcony doors and slid them open. "I get it. See you tomorrow," he said, and walked out into the starless night.

Shaken, Tris paced between her living room and kitchen. Mike had his oddities for sure. But the events of the last half hour were strange, even for him.

A breeze blew in from the patio. Mike had left the slider slightly open in his haste to leave. Tris moved to close it and noticed a folded piece of paper on the floor—it was a copy of one of the news articles in Christine's file. The headline read, "Iqaluit Therapist Serves Community."

Tris remembered this article. There was a picture of Christine in what looked like a gymnasium talking to folks dressed in faded jeans, sweatpants, and sleeveless puffy vests that hung open over turtlenecks. The caption read, "Dr. Christine Edgemon donates her time to the Tukisigiarvik Society."

A small water stain spread in the upper right-hand corner. The folds in the paper appeared to have been worked extensively. Tris had a fortune cookie slip like that, which read, "You have the ability to excel in untried areas." She'd kept it in her wallet for years.

It must have fallen out of Mike's pocket when he reached for his keys. Tris refolded the page and put it into her trip folder, alongside her passport, flight plan data, and weather package.

The smell of Chinese food was irresistible. She dug into the Kung Pao chicken and, a few seconds later, considered the clipping again. Today's meeting was the first time Mike was briefed about their passenger. Maybe he pulled the clip from the file to study up.

Orion strolled into the living room. She scooped him up and plopped him in her lap while considering multiple explanations for Mike's odd behavior. She'd ask him about it tomorrow. Hopefully by then he'd have calmed down. She absent-mindedly ran one hand down the feline's soft black and white fur and held an egg roll with the other.

The spare set of keys in her pocket dug into her thigh. She'd present her gift to him tomorrow night in Iqaluit, when they'd both be more relaxed.

Tris pressed her palm over the heart-shaped promise.

CHRISTINE

*My heart breaks every time you say we'll get
through this. I can't follow the path I've
been assigned to its horrible, predictable
end, and I'll use every ounce of strength I
have left to make sure you won't, either.*

Erik, dear, let me explain.

*Remember our flight to the states last year,
when Tetrix sent its corporate jet to bring us
to Exeter for your dad's funeral? After the
call that he'd taken a turn, you were almost
catatonic. So, I made the plans.*

*It was February, freezing, snow everywhere.
Our flight was delayed due to extreme cold. As
the last few hours of your dad's life ticked
by with us thousands of miles away, you were
losing it: snapping at the woman behind the
desk in the private terminal, practically
charging the pilot when he came out of the
men's room, spouting nonsense, scaring me and
everyone else within earshot.*

You were already grieving, my love.

*When I said, "His dad is dying, and we can't
get there," you melted, landed in the closest*

seat you could find, and wept.

The only other time I've seen you so sad was when we got my diagnosis. Because we both knew that soon, you'd be saying goodbye to me.

I tried to blot that experience out of my mind. But some things I recalled. Like how lax security was in that private terminal. No cops, no guns, nothing but a security guard who looked like Humpty Dumpty and only carried a nightstick.

How easy it will be. I'll be up in the air, far from land, far from any place or person who can save me.

Forty-Three

TRIS WOKE TO find the t-shirt she'd worn to bed wound around her waist. She'd barely slept. That ridiculous argument with Mike had put concerns in her head she couldn't shake.

Was some of what Danny told her true?

Or was she spinning a confusing story out of her own insecurities; connecting unrelated events, sprinkling them with salacious details that were likely untrue, all to manufacture a scenario that existed only in her imagination? Was she simply doing what she'd always done—conjuring a reason to walk away?

She dragged herself out of bed. There was no time to dwell on it. She dressed quickly and packed a few final items in her overnight bag. The keychain lay in her purse.

Trip paperwork listed her as pilot-in-command. During the angel flight, she'd support Bruce. But she'd also have her eye on Mike.

Once at the airport, Tris walked quickly into the hangar. The huge, chilly open space was quiet. Tris hugged herself, pulling the lined uniform overcoat she wore tightly around her.

Then a door slammed, the sound reverberating throughout the hangar. Bruce had arrived, one hand wrapped around the handle of his overnight bag, the other holding a cake.

"Hey. Heather had yet another shower this weekend. We had this cake left over. She didn't want it, so I brought it in."

"Well, this is a first. I've never had anyone bring a cake to an overnight before." Tris laughed and went to take it from Bruce. Looked like chocolate with coconut on it. Right up her alley. "My favorite. You got candles too?"

Bruce laughed. "After Lemaster? Uh, no, I do not." He looked around. "Where's Mike?"

"Around here somewhere, I guess. His car's outside. So, Captain," Tris said in a solicitous tone, smiling brightly, "may I stow your overnight bag?"

"Ha. Nah. I've got it, Tris. I've got to check something inside the airplane anyway." Bruce smiled, nodded, and walked over to review some weather reports that were posted on a nearby whiteboard.

Tris took her measure of the tall, lean man who might well be pilot-in-command in two days' time. She was proud of him, but still wary; she'd test him a bit. "And what would that be?"

He played along. "Well, we're over water, remember? Just making sure all the life vests are in place. We don't need a raft, thank goodness."

Bruce seemed fine. Yet, her emotions slid up and down like fingers on the neck of a guitar. Tris pushed them aside and focused on her last-minute flight preparations. She heard Bruce greeting Mike as he walked aboard the aircraft. Step by step, the three pilots got the trip ready. Why was she so rattled?

The ramps and runways at Exeter International were clear of any snow or ice, and the winds were calm. The pale morning sky was dotted only by fair-weather cumulus clouds that looked like the crumbled topping of a coffee cake. The crew of the angel flight could not have asked for better weather.

Mike sat behind them in the jump seat as Bruce prepared to command the Royal.

"Before takeoff checklist complete," Tris responded after Bruce confirmed that the last item had been checked. "You ready to go, Bruce?"

"Yes," he said, in a clipped, professional tone. "Tell Tower we're ready."

Tris clicked the microphone. "Exeter Tower, Compassion Royal Four-Five-Quebec ready for takeoff, Runway Four Left."

"Roger, Compassion Royal Four-Five-Quebec. Fly heading zero-four-zero, Runway Four Left, cleared for takeoff."

Bruce rolled the turboprop onto the runway, gave it full power and in no time, they'd levelled off at four thousand feet.

"Nice departure," Mike mumbled. He was hooked into the pilot's intercom through a spare jack behind the right seat. Crew communication under ten thousand feet was limited to items essential to flight, so he didn't elaborate.

The climb to their final altitude of thirty-five thousand feet was nothing short of glorious. Tris never tired of crossing Lake Michigan headed east. She scanned the beaches on the Michigan shore, deserted this time of year. In just a few months, they'd be packed with vacationers lounging under colorful umbrellas.

Tris preferred the cool, stark beauty of winter, which was best appreciated from inside the Royal's warm cockpit. What she loved was not so much what she saw, but the *way* she saw it: up high, with a view so wide she could follow the twisty road connecting the many small beachfront towns that sprouted up along the shore.

Bruce had configured the airplane perfectly for cruise flight, and the peace of the stable cockpit was disturbed only by the occasional call from ATC.

Tris was vaguely aware of Mike and Bruce discussing a point of procedure when Mike's voice rose. It vibrated in her ear, disturbing her reverie. He'd begun flipping through the pages of the Practical Test Standards, then fired a question at Bruce.

"Bruce. If you do well today, and I approve you as captain, what will your takeoff minimums be?"

"Sorry, Mike," Bruce replied diplomatically. "What do you need?"

Mike repeated his question, this time more slowly.

The captain-to-be in the left seat looked both startled and confused. "Uh, we finished my oral exam, didn't we Mike? I mean . . ." Tris shook her head as imperceptibly as she could, imploring Bruce to just answer him.

Luckily, Bruce caught on. "I'll be a high mins captain, Mike. That means I'll need to check visibility and cloud cover."

With no further discussion, Mike stood up, moved out of the cockpit and took a seat behind them in the cabin. Bruce shrugged, rolled his eyes, and continued to monitor the instruments. The autopilot was on, and they were cleared direct to Bangor.

Just like that, the numb hum of an uneventful flight returned.

Forty-Four

"HEY, MIKE," **BRUCE** called, after he moved his microphone away from his mouth so he didn't blow out Tris's eardrums. They were back in the air after fueling up in Bangor. Thirty-five thousand feet below them, Northeast Canada provided a view of snow, frozen water, and microscopic towns.

Within seconds, Mike stood behind them. "Yeah? I was catching up with the news," he said, waving a *USA TODAY*.

"Hey, man, so, I wanted to ask. You know, I have an interview with Legacy coming up in about two weeks."

"I remember. Good luck."

"If this ride goes well, would you mind writing me a letter of recommendation?" Bruce didn't hinge his request on their family connection. Tris admired that.

Mike's pause exceeded a comfortable length. "Bruce, look, I get where you're coming from. The more letters you have, the better. But I'm not sure, uh, that I'm the person you want."

"Yeah, but I figured you quit on good terms. Didn't you?"

Mike snorted. "Yes, I guess you'd say that. I don't think I have any enemies there. But I did leave. I'm not sure I'm the person you want to write a letter. I'm going to decline. Ask Danny." As he walked back to the cabin, he called to Bruce over his shoulder, "But you're doing great today."

"What was that about?" Bruce whispered to Tris over the intercom when he was sure Mike couldn't hear.

"Well, I—" Tris stopped. Danny's tale wasn't the type of thing she'd repeat, certainly not without confirmation. "My advice is to leave it alone."

"You don't know?"

Tris deflected the question. "Well, don't you? He's family, right?"

"Not close," Bruce replied immediately.

"So, what was he doing at your anniversary party?"

Bruce chuckled. "I think he only wrangled an invitation when he heard you might be there. At least that's what Heather said." Tris smiled serenely and let her concerns from the previous night slip away, just a little.

Bruce lifted the thick folder Tris had put together with the details about Christine. "So, let's talk about our passenger for a few minutes. Her husband arranged the trip, right? But we're not carrying him?"

"The husband goes back and forth frequently. He's already in Exeter."

"Good. Man, I read some stuff about her disease on the internet. Brutal." Bruce shook his head.

"What's this?" Both pilots were startled when Mike appeared behind them, this time holding an open plastic bag with a familiar yellow item inside.

"Huh? Is this a trick question?" Bruce tried not to sound sarcastic.

"Why isn't this pouch sealed? Westin Charter Operating Specifications require that life vests be in a plastic pouch, sealed, with the seal not broken."

Bruce looked over at Tris, who shrugged. Perhaps. But still . . .

"I get it. I'll check it out when we land in Canada and see if I need to get a replacement. No biggie. There are four more aboard. I put an extra one on," Bruce replied evenly.

Mike huffed and returned to his seat in the cabin.

"What the fuck?" Bruce looked over at Tris, who could only shrug.

The Royal descended on final approach into the wide-open landscape of Iqaluit. Visibility was low. Bruce rhythmically scanned the flight instruments as Tris talked to ATC. She'd shifted as far forward in her seat as possible but hadn't made visual contact with the ground. Finally, the tiny town popped out in relief against towering banks of snow, seeming like an intruder in this area surrounded by miles of wilderness.

Mike sat in the jump seat watching Bruce's approach and landing. Tris resisted the urge to coach Bruce, who, as it turned out, needed no help. With the wind gusting to twenty knots, Bruce had only a few seconds to straighten the airplane's nose and set the Royal down straight on the wide asphalt runway, which he did expertly.

"Nice job," Tris whispered between responses to ground control at Iqaluit and completing landing checklist items at Bruce's command. Mike said nothing, just grunted and took a seat in the cabin as soon as they were on the ground.

Bruce steered the Royal to the ramp like an experienced captain.

Her face twisted into an expression of mild surprise mixed with pride. Bruce was kicking ass—he was prepared, left nothing to chance, and had the aircraft, procedures, and paperwork precisely put together. Most gratifying to Tris, he'd incorporated advice she'd given him in the past about how to command an aircraft.

The Iqaluit ramp sported a few airplanes, two helicopters, and a yellow fire truck. A small building with the letters "FBO" perched on top sat next to an odd-looking sallow structure: the Iqaluit Airport commercial terminal that locals called the "Yellow Submarine."

The crew quickly secured the airplane and left it to ground handlers to tug into the hangar overnight. They hustled out of the cold into the tiny executive terminal, that sported an imposing mounted moose head. A large polar bear pelt hung on the wall.

A dark-haired woman in a puffy coat sat at a desk. Bruce asked where he could check radar and followed the finger she pointed to an anteroom with a flight-planning computer. Once he was done, the three pilots requested a ride to their hotel.

"Sure," the woman smiled. "Would you prefer van or snow-mobile?"

Everyone laughed.

"I think van," Mike said, smiling. "With the bags and all."

"Right away, captains," the woman replied.

Bruce stood a little bit taller.

At the hotel's check-in desk, each crew member was presented with an actual metal key to their room. They giggled over the antique conventions of this small, out-of-the-way town while the clerk confirmed their one-night stay.

Bruce took the lead. "So, tomorrow, let's head to the airport at five a.m. I'll arrange our ride. I've gotta run to my room and call Heather. See you tomorrow." He waved and rolled his bag down the hallway.

Tris and Mike stood near the elevators, under a painting of what looked like a local warrior holding a spear. The tension of the previous night ran between them like electric current.

Mike considered his feet. "I may just meet you guys at the airport tomorrow."

"Mike, please. There's no reason for you not to ride with us. That's silly. Let's just relax tonight. Let's talk. Something's bothering you, that's obvious."

He rubbed his beard and looked away. "Well, I'm not sure I'll be going to the airport directly from the hotel." With that, Mike grabbed his go bag and marched to the open elevator.

He's running away from me.

"Wait. What?" Tris tried to catch up with him but got to the elevator as the doors shut. For a split second, she could see Mike inside, his head hanging.

Mike was part of the crew, and while Bruce was handling captain duties, Tris was still PIC. She needed to know where her crew could be reached. As soon as she got to her room, coat still on, she called Mike.

"Hello. Mike Marshall." He answered as though he was expecting someone he didn't know.

"Mike. Hey, it's me." No response. "So, I need to know what your plan is, and where you'll be coming from tomorrow."

"Why? I have my pager in case you need me. I have an old friend here in town."

"In *this* town? You've got to be kidding. You haven't mentioned it once the entire time you've known about this trip." After a long stretch of dead air, she continued. "Mike? Come on, what's happening here?"

He sighed. "I didn't realize until yesterday that someone I used to know lives here. I haven't reached out yet, but if I can get in touch, I'll probably want to hang out tonight. I don't mean to be obtuse. I'll tell you more about it tomorrow on the way home." His voice simply sounded sad. "I . . . I . . . Goodnight, Tris," he finally said, and hung up.

Tris held the receiver for a second before placing it back in the cradle. His tone signaled the promise of truth, like maybe he'd finally explain things to her. Should she tell Bruce what was going on?

The shrill ring of the phone startled her.

"Yes? Hello?"

A beat passed. "Hi, Tris." Mike had called back.

"Yes? What?"

"I'm so sorry. I'm being such a dick."

"Okay, so come to my room for a little while. Whatever's on your mind, you know you can tell me." She'd persuade him to relax. She'd give him the keys. They'd forget the weirdness of the last twenty-four hours and enjoy the evening together.

Mike was silent for an uncomfortably long time.

"Hey? Mike?"

"Tris, look, I should have told you."

"Dammit, Mike, told me *what?*"

"There's always a few loose ends in people's lives. You know that, right? I've got one. Here in Iqaluit, incredibly. I need to tie it up."

"You're scaring me."

Another long pause.

"I know. And I am so, so sorry."

CHRISTINE

Erik, I love you. There is no doubt in my mind that you are the one, the right one, the only one. After how things ended with Warren, I wasn't sure I'd ever be with someone again. I wish I could hang around, and we could live the life we planned in this land beyond our past.

I can't do it, baby.

Now, it's time for the most important thing— telling you everything I love about you. The big and little things, the everyday things, the once-in-a-lifetime things. How when we're sleeping, even if we're both exhausted, you make sure that some part of you touches some part of me. Even if it's just toe to toe, finger to knee, or hand to hand. You make the coffee, every morning, even if we're fighting, and you bring some to me. Sometimes you carry our mugs into the shower with you, and we both laugh as we try to drink it without getting water in it—and fail every time.

Erik, baby, I am always going to be with you. I'll be there when the wind blows. When a snowflake hits your cheek, in that second before it melts, I am there. In the first warm rays of sunshine after the endless winter finally breaks, I am there.

It's basic physics, baby. That which exists, which has existed, never ends. It never dies.

I'll always be there.

With love, devotion and everything else,

Your Christie

Forty-Five

AT FIVE A.M. in Iqaluit, Tris stood in the lobby of the crew's hotel with the house phone's receiver to her ear.

"He's still not answering," she said to Bruce.

He checked his watch and exhaled slowly through puffed cheeks. "We can't wait any longer. Where *is* he?"

Tris shrugged.

Bruce called over to the front desk, "We're ready. Let's go."

Their transportation was unique to say the least. Tris and Bruce huddled on the front bench seat of an enormous pickup truck with a snowplow attached to its grille. They'd tossed their bags into the flat bed and had to dig them out from the pile of tools, tarps, and empty coffee cups when they arrived at the airport.

There, in the waiting area they'd left only hours before, Mike lay snoring on a couch under the open mouth of the pelted polar bear. The same woman was behind the front desk. A uniformed security guard carrying a walkie-talkie read the local paper.

Mike had on his pilot shirt with the tie loosened, captain's jacket draped over his body—and his untied tennis shoes dangled from his feet. Gritting her teeth, Tris resisted the urge to shake him and demand to know where he'd been last night. Instead, she stepped over and got a cup of coffee. A box of donuts sat on the coffee table. One of Mike's feet rested close to the tip of the coconut-covered one Tris had her eye on.

Bruce sidled up to her and gestured toward Mike. "Whaddaya want to do with him?"

"Let's get ready to go. We can wake him in a little while."

He hesitated. "He's supposed to be observing me."

Tris picked up on Bruce's disappointment right away. "Bruce, I'm pilot-in-command of this flight and a captain at Westin Charter. If you handle yourself as one, I'll personally recommend to Woody that he upgrade you."

Bruce nodded, grabbed their overnight bags, and walked out to the ramp. The cold rush of air from the open door caused Mike to shudder. He opened his eyes, spotted her, and rolled into a sitting position on the couch.

"Hey. What time is it?" Mike checked the wall clock. "Oh good. Plenty of time."

"How long have you been here? Did you sleep here all night?" Tris stood next to him, arms folded.

"Nope. I got here a couple of hours ago. I stayed at the hotel after all."

"So, did you accomplish what you needed to?"

Mike's eyes went vacant. He stood, and robotically smoothed his clothes. "Nope. I never found her. It's okay. I'll see her soon."

Goosebumps rose on Tris's arms in the overheated lounge. "Who?" she replied anxiously.

The door to the building opened, and a tall blond woman

slowly walked in. She shouldered a tote and leaned heavily on the handle of her roller bag. With every pair of forward steps, her left foot landed at an odd angle, causing her to zigzag.

"Hello?" The woman called.

Mike's mouth dropped open and his body bent backward, as if he'd been pushed. After a couple of seconds, recognition swept over Dr. Christine Edgemon. She raised a hand in front of her eyes, like someone blinded by what she saw.

"Warren?" she asked, in the small, scared voice of a child.

Mike straightened up. "Hello, Kick," he said, his tone as neutral as his expression.

Warren? Kick?

"Is he the pilot today? Is he flying the plane? He can't be here." She took two awkward steps toward the exit.

Tris shot a sidelong glance at Mike as she shepherded her passenger to the small room Bruce had used for flight planning. Christine lowered herself onto a plastic-covered metal chair and ran both hands through her hair.

"Ma'am, let me introduce myself. I'm Captain Tris Miles. Mike, Captain Marshall, is an observer on this trip. Is that a problem?"

Christine held her head in both hands and squeezed. "He can't be here."

"Can you please tell me why?"

Christine took a deep breath. "I need to call my husband. I need to call Erik. Is there a pay phone? My mobile phone. I . . . I don't have . . . I didn't . . ."

"I can help you reach him. But first, can you tell me what's wrong?" Tris reached for Christine's shoulder, to reassure her.

Christine recoiled, jabbing her thumb in Mike's direction. "It's *him*. He's *here.*" Her voice shook with fear.

Tris leaned around the door frame and glanced into the waiting area. Mike was crouched against the wall next to the polar bear. His mouth was frozen in an "O" shape, eyes fixed on the floor where his wallet now lay, surrounded by credit cards splayed near a few errant bills and some pennies.

"Ma'am, what is it about Captain Marshall? Do you know him?"

Christine whimpered. "Warren is here. Oh, God he's *here*."

She called him Warren again.

Recollection hardened inside Tris like ice.

Calmly, deliberately, Tris said, "Ma'am, please just sit here and relax. I'll be right back."

In the waiting area, Mike held something the size and shape of a credit card. She took it from him and turned it over in her hand.

It was his pilot certificate.

She'd reviewed it once before—at Lemaster, to make sure he was qualified to fly the Royal.

UNITED STATES OF AMERICA
DEPARTMENT OF TRANSPORTATION
•
FEDERAL AVIATION ADMINISTRATION
IV NAME
WARREN MICHAEL MARSHALL

"Mike," Tris spoke softly, pressing the sharp edge of the laminated card into her palm, willing her hand to stop shaking. "Do you know our passenger?"

Mike's chin hit his chest. "She's my wife."

Neither had seen Christine limp up, slightly hunched, gripping her shoulder bag so tightly her knuckles were white.

"*Ex*-wife," she announced.

The three stood motionless in the stifling room. Errant sounds of flight prep—computer paper spilling from the printer, a ringing phone, trucks traversing the ramp—were all drowned out by the internal alarm that blasted Tris from head to toe.

He lied to me ran like a ticker tape in her brain.

Mike hadn't moved. The front desk phone rang on, but the clerk ignored it.

"I can't—I can't stay here," Christine whispered, and moved in rigid, jerky steps toward the exit, using the handle of her suitcase like a cane.

Tris summoned the composed countenance she'd long cultivated and called on before in critical situations. And made a command decision.

"Dr. Edgemon, wait. Let me take you to a private room," Tris offered. Christine nodded, and within minutes, she was sitting in an empty office away from the waiting area.

"Please try and relax. You'll be safe here. No one will disturb you; I promise. Here," she said pointing to a desk phone, "use this to call your husband. Just dial '1' before the number. I'll be right back."

Tris found Bruce in the flight-planning room. "We have some unexpected, uh, challenges on this trip. I'm going to need to call Woody, but in the meantime, can you please keep Mike—" She caught herself. "*Mr. Marshall* right where he is. Don't let him on the airplane and do not, under any circumstance, let him get anywhere near Christine."

"Huh? Why? Tris, who is she?"

"Mike's former wife. Very much alive and our angel flight passenger."

Forty-Six

TRIS STRUGGLED TO make Woody understand the mystifying circumstances that threatened the progress of the angel flight. She barely comprehended them herself.

Make this about the mission. Focus on Christine.

"Woody, there's not much time. All of our flight planning hinges on us launching in the next half hour. The airplane is ready. I can get our passenger aboard as long as Mike," the name caught in her throat, "uh, your *Chief Pilot* doesn't come along."

She felt Woody shaking his head forcefully almost two thousand miles away. "Are you kidding? Leave him there? Fuck. How am I gonna get him home? Do you have any idea how much an airline ticket costs from there?"

"I'm not comfortable carrying them both. She's *terrified* of him."

"Tris, we have no choice. Our reputation depends on completing the angel flight. It's your call, but Mike—Warren, whatever . . . Tell me, in your judgment, is he—how should I say?—a danger to her? To the aircraft? Right now?"

Tris was grateful for the implicit understanding between her and Woody—as pilot-in-command, she had the final authority over the safe operation of the flight.

"I don't think so, no," she said. While Tris wanted nothing more than to leave Mike right where he was, the company was obligated to get him back to Exeter.

"I have an idea. We'll keep Mike in the jump seat, away from her, and close the curtain behind him. It's just a few feet of separation, but I think we can chance it. Arrange an airline ticket for him from Bangor." After seconds passed, she prodded him. "Did you hear me?"

Relief bracketed Woody's words. "Yeah. Sounds like you've got it covered. He's off the trip in Bangor. Get the airplane home safe, and we'll sort the rest of the crap out when you get here."

Bruce entered the room with a "what's going on?" look.

Tris held up a finger.

"Will do, Woody. We're on our way. See you later today." Tris snapped the flip phone closed.

"What's happening?" Bruce asked.

"Here's the plan. Mike's no longer evaluating you, Bruce. But he's still going to sit in the jump seat through Bangor, then he's airlining to Exeter. We have to keep him away from our passenger."

"Have you told him?"

"Not yet. Let's get our passenger aboard first. I'll handle him."

"Really? Isn't he our boss anymore?" The way Bruce asked the question was so innocent, so devoid of guile, Tris grinned.

"It's our show now, Bruce. Yours and mine, like it's been many times before. We're in charge of this flight and responsible for getting our passenger to treatment." Posture straight, hands on her hips, chin thrust forward, she considered Mike, still slumped against the wall. "And when we get there, I think we're going to need a new Chief Pilot. Okay. Let's put her on."

Together, Tris and Bruce walked Christine onto the Royal and got her settled.

"Are you all right here, ma'am?" Tris asked, while Bruce went to find some pillows for her.

Christine frantically surveyed the cabin. "Where is he? He's not coming with us, is he?"

"He'll be sitting in between Bruce and me. We'll close the curtain so you can't see him, and I'll make sure he doesn't bother you." She pointed toward the cockpit. "Will that work for you, ma'am?"

Christine's expression morphed from frightened to thoughtful and settled at purposeful. She sat up, raised her shoulders, and tightened her grip on the shoulder bag.

"That's fine," she replied. "That will do nicely."

Forty-Seven

"WHAT DID I DO? This makes no sense," Mike protested, moving a step closer to Tris. "I'd never hurt Kick."

What did you do indeed—you lied to me, lied to Woody, stalked your ex-wife. And lied. You lied.

Hurt and deceived, Tris fought the urge to run, to cry, to scream. But in this moment, she was not the woman he loved, or who might have loved him. She was commanding the angel flight.

"Warren, that woman is scared to death of you. And this mission is about *her.* You'll sit in the jump seat, with no operational authority over this flight. None. And you'll avoid our passenger. Tell me you understand."

"But I..." Mike pleaded, looking at Tris. But like gazing directly into a blazing sun, her resolve forced him to look away. "There's so much I want to say to you—"

She cut him off. "Not now. Please. Just do as I say. This is what Woody wants, and what our passenger *needs.* You're getting on a commercial flight in Bangor. We'll sort this out another time."

Mike followed Tris out to the Royal. Christine was safely belted into the seat where Tris had put her, reading *National Geographic*. With no further discussion, Tris led Mike to the cockpit, squeezed past him and drew the cockpit curtain tightly behind them. Tris fastened her belt and shoulder harness and confirmed that Mike was secure in the Royal's thin metal jump seat.

Bruce was already strapped into the left seat. For a moment, she considered switching seats with him, taking total command of the flight. But Bruce had performed admirably. He deserved a shot to finish his upgrade, and Tris would give it to him.

"Engine start checklist, please," he called, officially starting the series of events that would take the troubled group home.

The crew of Compassion Royal Four-Five-Quebec were soon climbing into the skies above Iqaluit, where Bruce pointed the airplane toward the US.

The angel flight had begun.

An hour out of Bangor, Tris allowed herself to relax. Mike leaned against the bulkhead, his eyes closed. Bruce had run the flight efficiently.

Tris got up once to check on their passenger, which required clunky choreography. Mike had to raise the jump seat and stand up, and the passageway between the cockpit and the cabin was so narrow, Tris couldn't help but come in physical contact with him. His hand grazed hers, and she pulled it away as though he'd tried to stab her. A flash of pain crossed his face.

In the cabin, Christine put down the magazine she'd been reading. Her hands clenched her shoulder bag so tightly they looked like part of the strap.

"Dr. Edgemon, do you need anything? Are you okay?" Tris asked.

Christine was quick to reply, "No, no. I'm fine. Fine," in a way that left no doubt that she wasn't at all fine. She looked out the window. "Doesn't seem to be anything down there. Are we close to any cities?"

"Not really. It's pretty sparse out here. We'll be in Bangor soon."

"How soon?" Christine abruptly sat up and hugged her shoulder bag to her chest.

"Less than an hour now. Ma'am, please, if there's anything you need, anything we can do, let me know. Things—" Tris looked toward where Mike sat on the other side of the cloth barrier, "things will be calmer on the way to Exeter. I promise." She couldn't wait to be on the ground in Bangor, offload Mike, and send him on his way.

Christine smiled awkwardly, maintaining her grip on the bag.

Just south of Mont Joli airport in southern Quebec, forty-five minutes from Bangor, Tris and Bruce began preparations for landing in the US. Tris pulled the appropriate charts, which were even more of a challenge to review with Mike crowding the cockpit space.

Tris accidentally poked him with her elbow, and he said, "Look. I've got to use the lav anyway. Let me get out of your hair for a few minutes while you guys set up the approach."

ATC had just given them instructions to start their descent, so Bruce was busy with the autopilot. "Fine, but hurry up. And do not speak to our passenger at all." Tris replied, uncertain about letting him go, but unwilling to refuse anyone a trip to the lav. She mentally crossed her fingers and returned to setting up the navigation computer and aircraft radios.

Then she heard Mike's voice, followed by Christine's, talking quietly.

Damn it. He needs to leave that woman alone.

Their voices stayed low and a glance through the curtain revealed that they were sitting across the aisle from each other, speaking calmly. She'd finish preparing for the landing, then get up and drag him back to the jump seat.

A screech obliterated the calm, business-like whir of the cockpit.

"*Noooo!*" Mike yelled.

Two loud *pops* followed, like someone stepped on bubble wrap.

Tris yanked the curtain aside. Just feet away, Mike's body was upright in his seat; his eyes open, head thrown back, the chest of his white pilot shirt stained red. Red drops were splattered on the airplane window next to him.

The Royal's familiar dust-and-metal smell mixed with the aroma of spent firecrackers. Smoke swirled in the air. It smelled like Lemaster. Tris gagged and swallowed several times to keep from vomiting.

Bruce's mouth was open, his eyes agape. A low moan escaped his lips.

Tris clicked off her shoulder harness to rush to Mike. Bruce grabbed her arm and pushed her back, hard, into her seat.

"Are you crazy? You can't go back there."

She gasped. "But Mike's hurt."

Bruce tightened his grip. "Stop. Tris. Stop."

Breathing hard, Tris took a moment to make sure she didn't hyperventilate. She whispered into her microphone. "Bruce, our passenger shot him."

Bruce's mouth moved—a pale slit surrounded by ghostly white skin. "Is there a gun? Do you see it?"

"I'm not sure—there has to be. The ... blood. That smell." She coughed. She willed herself to remain calm, but she was shaking, and her teeth chattered.

The airplane. Focus on the airplane. Aviate. Navigate. Communicate. Aviate.

"Bruce, keep your eyes straight ahead. Fly the plane. I'm going to change our transponder code."

Tris carefully twisted the knobs on the transponder until the numbers 7-7-0-0, the universal aircraft mayday code, appeared.

"Compassion Royal Four-Five-Quebec, Bangor Center. Verify squawking seventy-seven hundred. Say intentions."

"Center, Compassion Royal Four-Five-Quebec is declaring an emergency. One passenger may be armed, and another is hurt. He was shot. We—" Stress-induced tears welled in her eyes, and her voice was unsteady. "Our intentions are to land in Bangor, our destination, the closest airport. We have someone aboard with a gun ... someone's been ... shot ... and we don't ... we don't ... we can't lock ourselves in up here. It's just ... a curtain ... that's our only barrier. The crew is exposed."

"Compassion Royal Four-Five-Quebec, understood. Proceed direct Bangor. How many souls aboard?"

"Four," Tris replied quickly.

"Compassion Royal Four-Five-Quebec, roger. Can you tell us the amount of fuel you have in pounds, and the age and gender of the injured passenger?"

"What is going on Tris? I don't understand." Bruce hadn't panicked. He was intent on flying the airplane. In any emergency, the safety of flight came first.

She held up her hand toward Bruce and answered ATC. "Bangor, Compassion Four-Five-Quebec has one thousand pounds of fuel. The injured party," Tris took a break to steady herself, "the person with a gunshot wound is a forty-year-old male."

ATC responded immediately. "Compassion Royal Four-Five-Quebec, we copy. You mentioned a firearm. Is there someone on the airplane that is still armed? Is the crew in imminent danger?"

"Stand by," Tris said crisply.

Bruce was monitoring the gauges. He'd leaned as far away from the open space between the cockpit and the cabin as he possibly could.

"Bruce, you have a better view than I do from here," Tris said, regretting now that she was in the right seat. "Pretend you're looking at something on my side of the panel. Can you tell me what Christine is doing?"

Bruce shook his head. "I don't want to look. What if she shoots *me?* I can't . . ."

"I hear you, Bruce. I know. Please. Just turn your head a little. I can't see her clearly from this seat."

Reluctantly, Bruce lifted his right hand above his head, pretending to flip an overhead switch while he peeked in the back.

"Oh man, Tris. Geez. Oh man. Mike's slumped over." Bruce's voice had a touch of hysteria.

"Okay, Bruce. Take it easy. What's *Christine* doing?"

Bruce angled his head slightly. "There's a gun, Tris. Right on the seat next to her."

"But what's she doing? Is she holding it? God . . . is she pointing it?

"You're not going to believe this." Bruce's brows furrowed. He closed his eyes quickly, then opened them. "No. She's reading *National Geographic.*"

Tris and Bruce exchanged looks, and she keyed the mike. "Bangor, Compassion Royal Four-Five-Quebec. Our passenger is armed. And she appears to be reading a magazine."

Forty-Eight

BRUCE PUSHED THE engines to just below red-line power as the Royal sped to Bangor. Tris's hands had barely stopped shaking when they heard another *pop*.

"What was *that*?" Tris jumped up in her seat, straining at the belt and harness that she'd loosened. "Oh, shit. Look behind you, look behind you," she implored Bruce. "Oh, shit."

Bruce turned his head and immediately gagged. His hands tightened on the control column. Thankfully the autopilot was still on.

"I-I-I," Bruce stuttered, gulped, and tried again. "I think our passenger shot herself."

Tris couldn't make herself look. "How long to Bangor?"

"Fifteen minutes. Maybe less," Bruce answered.

"Bangor Approach, Compassion Royal Four-Five-Quebec."

"Four-Five-Quebec, Bangor. Go ahead."

"Both passengers are injured. I repeat, we have two wounded parties in the airplane." Tris checked the pressurization gauges to confirm that the shot hadn't pierced the fuselage.

"Understood Four-Five-Quebec. Age and sex of the second party? And is the airplane itself in distress?"

She choked back a sob. "Female, age 42. An ALS patient. The one we were flying to . . . to save," Tris could barely finish the sentence. She steeled herself to continue. "It appears that the airplane is not damaged."

A long pause. "We read you Four-Five-Quebec. Compassion Royal Four-Five-Quebec you are cleared to land, Bangor airport, any runway. Wind three-two-zero at ten knots."

Using Runway One-Five would get them on the ground the fastest. Tris didn't care that they'd have a ten-knot tailwind. One-Five was over 11,000 feet long, and they'd slam the plane on the ground and stand on the brakes. If either Mike or Christine were still breathing, she had to give them the best possible chance at survival.

"Bruce. Bruce. Do you have the airplane?"

Bruce responded to Tris as though she'd lost her mind. "Of course. Whaddaya think?"

This was a bad, bad sign. "I need you, Bruce. I need your help. Listen to me. Just put the airplane down. Land hard, don't goose it. Drop it and stop it as soon as you can. I don't know if they're alive back there."

"Roger, Tris. I've got it."

They were only twenty miles away. Bruce lined the aircraft up perfectly with Runway One-Five. "Gear down, before landing checklist," he ordered.

No way. It was too soon.

"Negative," Tris replied. "Maintain speed. We agreed. You need to chop and drop. For now, we go fast."

"Negative? Hey Tris. *I'm* flying here. *I* want the gear down." He looked at her wide-eyed, with his lips parted. His hands shook.

"No. Keep your speed up."

Bruce reached for the flap handle. Tris slapped it away. "We are way too fast for flaps, man. If you extend them now, they'll be ripped right off."

Bruce dropped his head and hunched over, his forehead practically touching the top of the instrument panel.

"One. Thousand," came roaring through the speaker.

"I don't know what to do," he said meekly.

This is it. "Bruce, I have the airplane." She took the yoke and pushed his hands from the power levers.

"Five. Hundred."

He straightened up. "What? No, you don't."

"Bruce! My airplane. Do you understand? Hands off the controls."

Bruce's hands flew back. "What the fuck?"

Tris flew as fast as she could for as long as she could, yanked the power back, lowered the flaps and gear.

"Fifty. Twenty. Ten."

She dumped the airplane on the runway. Her feet jammed on the brakes so hard her butt lifted off of the seat.

Stopped on the ground, Tris killed the engines and set the parking brake amid a kaleidoscope of flashing lights.

Bruce stared straight ahead as the door popped open and uniformed emergency crews rushed aboard.

Forty-Nine

"SHOW ME YOUR HANDS!"

"Come on, hands up. Show 'em to me!"

Two different voices shouted as uniformed Bangor SRT officers crashed into the Royal in full tactical gear with automatic weapons pointed upwards, searching for Christine's gun. Their padded vests, helmets, and visors made them look like aliens, but they were all too real.

"You two, show me your hands!" one of the officers said sharply to Tris and Bruce. Her arms shot up above her head, eyes wide, body frozen in terror. Bruce wore a blank expression, his translucent skin veiled by sweat. His hands stayed on his knees.

"Do you have any weapons on you, ma'am?"

"Nothing. No weapons," Tris whispered.

"I've got it," the other officer shouted, and gestured toward the cockpit with Christine's gun in his hand. "Looks like one of these two is the shooter. They're both unconscious."

"Get the medics up here."

With that, the officer who held Christine's gun walked off the airplane, and two people in identical uniforms came aboard.

"Ma'am and sir, we are EMTs," one of the new arrivals said to Tris and Bruce, although it wasn't clear if Bruce heard anything. "My partners are removing the passengers. Are you hurt? Are either of you hurt?"

"No. I'm not. We're not," she said, gesturing to Bruce. "Please. Help the passengers. Are they alive?"

"No way to know yet, ma'am. You two just sit here while we tend to them. Okay?"

Tris nodded and the commotion behind her increased steadily.

"Right here. No, *here.*"

"There's too much blood."

"Slowly. *Slowly.* Damn, this aisle is narrow!"

Shivering uncontrollably, Tris grabbed Mike's uniform jacket, hanging from a hook across from her seat. It smelled of black cherries. She buried her face in the sturdy blue garment and cried.

Then a new odor hit the cockpit. Bruce had wet his pants.

She wiped away her tears with the arm of Mike's jacket. "Bruce? Hey Bruce?" Tris put her hand on his shoulder as EMTs struggled to get a second gurney on the aircraft.

"This one first," someone yelled. "This one's alive."

Did that mean someone died? On my flight? Mike?

"Who's alive? Who's alive?" she yelled toward the EMTs. No one responded.

"Hey. Tris. How's it going?" Bruce licked his lips and moved to undo his seat belt and shoulder harness.

"Stay put, Bruce. Doctors are here for our passengers. They'll want to talk to you. And me, too."

"Me? I don't know anything."

"Right. Of course. But they'll want to talk to you about, you know, what happened and everything. A debrief. You know, like we always do."

A third EMT, who looked like a teenager, escorted Tris and Bruce from the cockpit. Outside, two ambulance sirens blared as they sped away with Mike and Christine. Tris stole a quick glance at the blood-soaked passenger cabin, the carnage her airplane had become; the grisly remains of the angel flight.

Tris followed the EMT, bowed under the weight of his heavy equipment bag, into a hastily-set-up tent. Blood pressure normal, eyes able to follow the tiny penlight, and no pain. She wasn't hurt. They let her go and turned to Bruce, sitting stunned.

Everyone was attending this party. Airport employees in yellow safety vests milled about. Forensic investigators snapped on gloves and slipped into Tyvek booties. Yellow police tape was everywhere. Beyond the security fence were so many news trucks and cameras, the lights blinded her.

Tris was drawn to the Royal. As she approached, Bangor police and crime scene techs shooed her away.

"Where's the captain? Is he around here somewhere?" someone called from near a wide tent the teams had set up right on the runway. It was easy to hear the voice. Then Tris realized there was only one runway in Bangor, and her airplane was on it. They'd shut down the whole airport.

"That's me," Tris said. A man with a clipboard wearing a gray-blue blazer and a tie that hung several inches above his belt did a double take when he saw her.

"Hi, uh, captain. I'm Detective Schirmer with the Bangor Police

Department." He grabbed her hand in a slack handshake.

"Okay. What do you need?"

"Well, you'll have to take a urine test. Procedure. And ma'am, of course we need to interview you."

His words floated around her like captions in a cartoon. Unreal. Nothing about this was real.

Tris pointed toward the Royal. "Can I go in? I'm the captain of this aircraft," she said softly. "I need to inspect the damage. To tell the owner."

"Sorry. No chance. We have to preserve the scene, ma'am. I'll take you to the station to be interviewed."

"Please. I won't touch anything."

He shook his head. "Out of the question. Ma'am, can you follow me please?"

"Wait. Where's my co-pilot? Where is he? Bruce? *Bruce?*" she cried out, frantically searching for him amid shouts of, "Hey, Captain," from the reporters beyond the fence.

"Ma'am, please," the detective said, and took her elbow. "I need you to come with me. Please, ma'am."

Tris yanked her elbow away. Surely this man meant her no harm. But, really, who and what could she trust anymore?

She was freezing. Time to put her jacket on. Then she realized she'd absent-mindedly carried Mike's jacket instead of her own off of the Royal. She threw it toward the detective as if it were radioactive. "Here. Take this." The man caught it in mid-air. "It belongs to one of the injured passengers."

Mike had lied. His wife was alive. Christine. And she had been petrified when she saw him.

Danny was right.

Fifty

THE SECURITY LINE at Denver International Airport was practically out the door. Danny cut to the front and flashed his crew badge. He was desperate.

Heather was in labor. Em said that they might have to do an emergency C-section. And no one could reach Bruce. All of Danny's attempts went to voice mail. Surely Bruce had checked his mobile phone by now. Where was he?

Constantly checking his watch, his phone, his pager, shifting from foot to foot, Danny waited for an international crew of flight attendants to clear security ahead of him. Those wide body crews were endless. He counted at least fifteen. He could say *his* wife was in labor, and he needed to cut the line. But he was just antsy, and it wouldn't help—the flight he was jump seating on didn't leave for another hour.

His mobile buzzed. Em's mom. "Elise? What's up?"

"Hello, there." His mother-in-law never said his name. Em said it was nothing personal, and to ignore it, but it still bothered him.

"We're at the hospital. Would you like to know what's going on?"

Is she fucking kidding me? "Of course, Elise. Tell me. Please."

"Well, Heather is in a room with her daddy and Sissy." Elise's baby talk was particularly annoying when Danny wanted information.

He couldn't be patient with her right now. "*Yes. And?* How's Heather? How's the baby?"

"Oh, she's fine. She's fine. They both are so far. Look, I don't know if they can wait to do the surgery for Bruce to get here. That's what Heather wanted me to tell you. She can't reach Bruce. Can you try?"

"I have. I will. Can you please put Em on the phone?"

"Em? You want to talk to Em?" Sometimes he truly wondered if the woman was all there.

"Yes. My *wife*. Please." Elise didn't respond, but he heard the click of her high heels. She always wore them, no matter what she was doing or where she was. Grocery store. Baseball game. Back yard. And, apparently, the hospital.

"Honey?" Em. Finally.

"Hey girl. What's going on?" He tried to sound light and encouraging, but concern seeped into his voice.

"Danny." That was all she said before she started to cry.

"Emily, baby, everything will be fine. I'm off reserve, the next flight to Exeter leaves in a little over an hour. Four hours and I'll be home. Hang in there."

Em sniffed loudly and then coughed. "I'm trying. Danny, I wish you were here. They're prepping her for surgery."

"They will do what they need to do. Are *you* all right?"

"I'm fine. I am. I miss you like crazy. Please promise me you'll be here soon."

Tears worked their way to the corners of his eyes. He blinked them back, but one fell toward his ear. Danny wiped it away, checked himself, and continued to inch forward in the security line.

"Sure baby. I'm on my way."

His pager buzzed in his pocket seconds after he heard a voice mail announcement on his mobile. Danny ignored them both. He had to get to the gate to have any chance of claiming the jump seat.

Once through security, he checked his phone and pager. Tris had called. She'd know where Bruce was.

Then his pager buzzed again. Tris's mobile number with "9-1-1" after it popped up. He leaned against one of the standing terminal diagrams. The tram to the gate was pulling in. He'd lose reception once he got inside, so he let it go by and pressed her number on the keypad.

"Danny." She sounded out of breath when she answered.

"Hey, listen, I don't have much ..."

She cut him off. "I'm in Bangor. Mike got shot on the trip from Iqaluit. And our passenger. Mike's in the hospital." Her voice trailed off.

Did she say shot?

"He *what*? What the hell happened? Where are you?"

Danny flashed back to a time when he'd have boarded a plane to wherever Tris was to meet her, be with her, calm her. "Heather's in early labor. I'm about to grab the jump seat back to Exeter. Look, I need to talk to Bruce."

"Wait. Danny. About Bruce. Look ..."

"Oh, no. Was he shot too?"

The sound of heaving breaths was all he heard for a few seconds. Finally, she blurted out, "No. But he almost ... in the cockpit ... Danny, I can't."

"Tris. Hey, calm down. Talk to me." It sounded like she was in the middle of a train station.

"Oh. Okay. I'll move," Tris said to someone other than him. "It's the police, Danny. I've got to go talk to them now."

"Where's Bruce? He's having a baby. I've gotta talk to him."

There was more commotion in the background. Someone yelled, "Over here with that. No, no, over *here*."

Fatigue coated her words. "You can't talk to him. No one can. He's on his way to the hospital. To the psychiatric ward."

Fifty-One

HOLED UP IN the airport administration building adjacent to the Executive Terminal, Tris was being questioned by two Bangor detectives. She wished these cops were like the ones she saw on TV, who moved swiftly through interrogations, with snappy segues and offers of coffee and sandwiches. But they were regular cops. People like her. Flawed, bored, always self-conscious, sometimes self-critical.

Tris wanted to know about Mike. Warren. Christine called him Warren. His wife called him Warren.

Who, exactly, *was* Mike?

"Let's back up a bit." One detective was bald, the other had a comb-over. This was from Comb-over. "When did you first realize there was a pre-existing relationship between your passenger and Mr. Marshall?"

When indeed. When had Mike first told her about his wife? Kick. Kick from Massachusetts. Or so he'd said. Tris had no idea what was true and what wasn't.

"Today. In Iqaluit."

"How much did you know about their, uh, prior relationship?" This one from Baldy. They'd already asked her if she knew about any of the twelve individual times that Warren Marshall had stalked his ex-wife, violating her restraining order.

Stalking. A restraining order. Just like Danny said.

"What did I know?" she practically spat the words. "He told me his ex-wife was dead. That she cheated on him, that she left him, that she died. That's what I knew before today. Before I learned that he lied." Tris curled both hands into fists, fingernails pressed firmly into her palms.

Baldy considered a file in front of him. For a moment, the only sound in the room besides breathing was the rustle of papers. They were fastened into a legal-sized folder at least an inch thick. He fanned the pages, and Tris saw flashes of photographs. She prayed they didn't ask her to look at photos of Christine and Mike together.

If she'd known—if she'd only known—she'd have told Woody, and Mike would have been out the door of Westin Charter.

But she had known. Danny told her.

Baldy spoke. "Sounds like he took the breakup of their marriage hard. Did you know about the law enforcement involvement?" His eyes narrowed and for a second he looked like he was going to reach across the table and grab her throat. Right out of a TV script. In fact, he was only reaching for his bottle of water.

Tris raised her arms in frustration. "I knew none of it. None. He told me she'd died." The last words were barely audible. Her head bobbed and she willed her eyes to stay open. She struggled not to simply curl up in the metal chair, like Orion. He could fold himself into a ball, and fall asleep anywhere, any time. Except dinner time. She was so hungry, she'd probably eat his cat food if they served it to her.

"Ma'am, do you have any idea how the gun got aboard? Did you put it there?"

"Me? No. That's crazy. I have no idea. Don't *you* know?"

The officers stared at her. She half expected them to blind her with a light bulb and order her to confess.

"Look, can you—can we do this later? Tomorrow? I've got to get to the hospital and check on my crew."

Her crew. Bruce. Mike.

One of the uniformed officers had said he'd drive her to the hospital. She had to make sure Bruce was all right. Did he know his child was coming?

She should call Diana. Or Danny. No, not Danny. He'd be at the hospital. With Em.

Who was there to talk to? Who would believe this story? This was not a crew room yarn, one of those "back in the day" conversations. People, real people, *crew members, passengers* were harmed on her watch.

"Please. Let me check on my crew, get some food, get some sleep. I'm sure I'll be a better witness in the morning." That wasn't protocol, she figured, and neither Baldy nor Comb-over seemed inclined to give her a break.

Then the door opened from outside, and a third officer came in. Also middle-aged, with a red rash rising over the tight collar of his shirt, he leaned in and whispered to the detectives. Comb-over and Baldy nodded.

Finally, Comb-over told Tris, "You're free to go now, ma'am. We're sorry to have kept you. We'll pick this up with you tomorrow. Thank you."

Confused and relieved, Tris got up, nodded to the triumvirate of police officers and headed out to the reception area to claim her stuff and get to the hospital.

Tris was almost out the door when Comb-over, whose name was MacAllister, she finally remembered, caught up with her.

"Miss Miles?"

"Yes?"

"One more question, if you don't mind. When did you first see the gun?"

Did she see the gun? Bruce had been flying the plane. Mike got up to use the lav. She'd heard the first two shots. Then a third.

When she finally spoke, the words came out slowly, deliberately, as though she'd only just learned how to say them.

"I first saw the gun after Warren Marshall was shot. She was holding it. Christine. My passengers? Are they alive?"

"Dr. Edgemon has passed. I'm so sorry."

Tris took a deep breath. "And Mike . . . uh, Warren Marshall?"

Comb-over nodded with a hint of a smile. "Last we heard he was in surgery."

Mike was alive. His ex-wife was dead. For real this time.

Fifty-Two

THE SCENT OF antiseptic mixed with urine assaulted Tris the moment the squad car pulled up to the entrance of the Emergency Room at Eastern Maine Medical Center. Shouting, crying, the rat-a-tat-tat of impatience, and the low moan of someone in real pain filled her ears as the automatic doors opened.

Tris avoided looking anywhere that she'd see her reflection and followed the uniformed officer to the lab to give them a urine sample. Her tongue slid over her teeth. Between interviews with the police and NTSB officials, calls to and from Exeter with Woody, trying to reach Diana, and leaving desperate messages for Dr. C, she'd had no time to brush her teeth.

It was twenty minutes until an officious nurse joined them to oversee the procedure. The transaction complete, Tris asked about Bruce. She would be able to see him soon, she was told.

"If you go sit in the waiting room," the nurse said. "We'll call you."

First, she trudged to the ladies' room. The image she saw looking back at her in the cloudy rectangular mirror that hung over a series of tiny sinks was worse than she expected. Her greasy hair clung together in clumps, exposing sections of her scalp. Her plans to wash it last night were forgotten after her last talk with Mike. She'd expected to be home by now, not spending the day being interrogated by law enforcement, or at a hospital a thousand miles away.

Paper towels coaxed from the wall dispenser helped Tris give herself an improvised sponge bath. She twisted her hair into a tight ponytail and scraped the bottom of her purse for a rubber band to tie it with. Her fingers brushed the keychain. Its heart shape now mocked her.

Luckily, she'd kept her paper coffee cup from the hours of police questioning. Habit. Pilots on a trip saved anything they could put to use later. She filled it with water after brushing and rinsed the toothpaste out of her mouth. Frothy residue rimmed the top of the cup, so she threw it out.

In a corner of the waiting room, toward the exit, Tris observed the parade of wounded and frightened people in and out. Busy day at the ER.

And there, all alone, with a series of extraordinary events to process, she wished she could reach over and hold Mike's hand.

W. Michael Marshall. Warren Michael Marshall. He'd mentioned his full name a couple of times, mostly as a joke. Pilots didn't have names like Warren. Just single syllable studly ones like Mike. Bron.

Bruce.

"Burkey? Bruce Burkey?" A plump nurse stood before the gallery of sick and exasperated, yelling Bruce's name.

Tris waved and caught the nurse's eye. She grabbed her overnight bag, hefted her purse onto her shoulder, and fell in behind the purple scrubs.

The nurse took Tris to an out-of-the-way reception area so they could speak privately. "He's in the psych ward right now. But he can have visitors. He's asked for you. Are you family?"

"No. A co-worker—wait, a friend. A good friend."

After a pause, then a nod, Tris followed her into Bruce's room. It had six beds, all separated by drawn curtains. When she slid in the indicated opening, Bruce lay facing away from her.

"Hey, Bruce." She stood at the foot of the bed.

"Tris. Hi. I have a son." His affect was flat.

"Congratulations. How do you feel?"

He snorted. "Well, I'm here, he's there, so not great. But he's fine. He's perfect, Heather says."

"What's his name?"

Bruce finally smiled. "My son's name is Jacob. Jacob Bruce Burkey."

Tris moved to him and touched his shoulder. "That's awesome. How's Heather?"

Bruce sat up. "She's really tired, but she's fine. How's Mike?"

She took his hand. "He was shot twice. The last I heard, he was alive. Our passenger is gone. Christine."

Neither pilot spoke for a while, their silence punctuated by beeping monitors and the low soothing voices of nurses.

"Mmm-hmm," Bruce said. "His ex-wife, eh? Damn. He said she was dead. I had no idea. Did you?"

"Nope."

Bruce looked his mentor up and down. "You look like shit. Uh, Captain." He gave her a half-assed salute with a flick of his wrist. They both grinned.

"Don't I know it? And look at you, lying around." A little laughter.

Bruce swung his legs over the side of the bed. "So, what's with all this? Do you know why I'm still here? I need to get home. To meet my son. And see Heather."

"Please don't worry, Bruce. I talked to Danny. He's on his way to Exeter, to the hospital. He and Em will be with Heather. And your mother-in-law." His expression soured at the mention of Elise, and she laughed. "Look, it's a good thing. Heather needs her mom."

"I guess." He paused, and then drew a couple of breaths, as though he were steeling himself. "Hey, Tris. Look, I have to tell you. I may have said some things to—to others . . . thought some things, damn it, *done* some things that I regret. You were right to pull my upgrade. Since Lemaster—"

"Bruce. Don't think about that now."

He came alive. "No, I have to apologize, Tris. The things I said—may have said—and did. Mike. The whole Chief Pilot thing. Oh, God, I'm so sorry."

Circumstances had brought them well past whatever Bruce had done, or how he may have harmed her. "Bruce, please. Come on. You know as well as I do that the crew that shovels together—"

"Stays together." He finished her sentence. "Tris, you've been nothing but fair to me. And I'm grateful."

They sat quietly for a few minutes. Tris's mind wandered. Phyll had booked her a hotel room for a few nights, and an open airline ticket for her flight back home to Exeter. The Royal was a crime scene. It wouldn't fly for a while. What crime, exactly, and against whom, no one knew yet.

Bruce said his working diagnosis, "whatever that means," was PTSD.

Of course it was.

"Have you seen Mike?" he asked.

Tris took a deep breath. "That's my next stop."

The two pilots hugged, and Tris went directly to the nurse's station. A male nurse wearing Mickey Mouse scrubs sat at a computer terminal.

"Sir," she began.

"One second," he cut her off, and continued typing. When he finished, he looked up. "Yes. May I help you?"

"Yes. Warren Marshall. What room is he in?" she asked.

He nodded, clutched the computer's mouse, clicked a few times, and looked up. "He's here. What is your relationship to him?"

Good question. Tris laughed, which, by the nurse's expression, he clearly misunderstood.

"Did I say something funny?"

Tris shook her head. "No. He was my passenger. You know, on that flight."

"Ah, yes. Ma'am, what is your name?"

"Miles. Tris—uh, Patricia Miles."

His expression tightened. "Ma'am, Mr. Marshall mentioned your name to us before he went into surgery. He *specifically* asked that you not be permitted to see him."

Iqaluit Therapist Dead on Life-Saving Medical Flight

BY NUNATSIAQ NEWS

IQALUIT—Christine Marie Edgemon, 42, a local psychologist specializing in grief counseling, and wife of Erik Hudson, the Director of Project Management at Tetrix Inc.'s Nunavut facility, died on a flight from Frobisher Bay Airport in Iqaluit to Bangor Maine on Wednesday from a gunshot wound. A pilot on the flight, Warren Michael Marshall, who is also her ex-husband, sustained two gunshot wounds.

Edgemon died of injuries inflicted by a single gunshot wound to the head. Marshall is in critical condition at Eastern Maine Medical Center in Bangor.

"Dr. Edgemon brought the gun that eventually killed her onto the flight. We are investigating her intentions—we don't know yet if she intended to take her own life, her ex-husband's life, both or neither," said Detective Chief Inspector Robert Gann of the Bangor Police Department. "Edgemon was reportedly depressed over her illness. And Marshall had not recovered emotionally from the dissolution of their marriage two years before. We also don't know whether Edgemon and/or Marshall planned to be together on this flight." When pressed for further details, DCI Gann said the matter was still "under investigation."

Dr. Edgemon suffered from Amyotrophic Lateral Sclerosis, or Lou Gehrig's Disease. The flight, commonly referred to in the aviation community as an "angel" flight, was arranged by Hudson's employer, Tetrix, Inc., to transport Edgemon to the United States to obtain an experimental treatment for her disease that was unavailable to her in Iqaluit. Hudson was waiting for his wife to arrive at Exeter International Airport, the "angel" flight's final destination.

The "angel" flight pilots made an emergency landing into Bangor International Airport when they realized a gun had been fired. The names of the two pilots have not yet been released.

"I knew there was something odd about those folks," said Birdie Cummings, an employee of Frobisher Bay Touchdown Services in Iqaluit, which serviced the airplane when it was parked overnight. "Before [Edgemon and the pilots] took off, there was some kind of argument. I couldn't tell what it was about."

The plane took off without incident, and there was no record of mechanical difficulties. The National Transportation Safety Board is also investigating.

Iqaluit police are investigating the security systems in place at the private terminal, which failed to detect that Edgemon brought a gun on the plane.

"It is customary for private jets to park away from commercial operators," said a source at the Government of Nunavut. "The private terminal is not equipped with the same level of security or number of metal detectors as the commercial area is."

Investigators learned that Edgemon and Hudson had flown back to Exeter International Airport the year before through the private terminal, so Edgemon may have known she would not be searched for firearms.

"Everyone associated with Iqaluit Airport is devastated by this event. We can assure the public that they are perfectly safe flying out of the airport. This incident, while tragic, is isolated. This security situation is under review, and we will do whatever is necessary to assure the safety of the flying public," said the same government official.

PART IV:
POST-FLIGHT

April 2000

Exeter, Illinois

Fifty-Three

SCREAMING? MAYBE HOWLING? Bruce couldn't come up with a word that accurately described the sound that child made. Bellowing? No, bellowing involved spoken words, right? Less than one week old was probably too soon for words.

The noise gave Bruce a newfound respect for his son. He marveled at how someone so small could make a ruckus so big. And Heather was so sleep-deprived she slept right through it.

Bruce scratched at the dried spit-up on the leg of his shorts. He'd lost count of the times little Jacob had puked on them. Time had little meaning since he got home from the angel flight. He'd walked out of one type of bedlam and entered another. His son had demolished the quiet, manageable lifestyle he and Heather had enjoyed.

He pushed the soft pink earplugs deep into his ears and went to get a moist cloth to wipe his pants. After digging through a jungle of plastic cups, tops, lids, and bottles, he found what he hoped was a clean washcloth. Apparently, it had already been used for—he couldn't tell. Something that smelled really bad.

Maybe he should wake Heather. She'd know where to find a clean towel, or she'd do some laundry. No, Bruce had promised to manage the baby while she napped. Heather barely got any sleep anymore between feeding him, changing him, and listening to him cry.

The joy of parenthood. He wasn't feeling it.

Before Bruce was released from the hospital, one of the social workers on staff had talked with him about "coping skills." The officious counselor suggested ways to think about stressful events that might come up until Bruce could see a regular therapist. But none of those skills prepared him for the onslaught of challenges that came along with having a baby.

The therapy he got in the hospital was so much bullshit anyway. Those people didn't know anything. How do you cope when your freight catches fire and explodes, just feet away from you? Repeat, "this too shall pass"? Just shrug your shoulders and get over it? What a crock of shit.

Bruce had put off calling the therapist. The FAA had already suspended his medical certificate, so he could see a shrink out in the open if he wanted to. But Post-Traumatic Stress Disorder? Didn't only soldiers get that?

Maybe he'd call tomorrow.

On the crowded dining room table, the ceramic bowl Heather bought to display a mound of fake plastic fruit was shoved aside to make room for piles of unopened mail, which formed barriers between crusted baby bottles. Most of the letters were medical bills. They only had the bare minimum health insurance. Heather had begged him to increase their coverage, pay a little bit more. "Just to be sure honey," she'd pleaded.

But they were young and healthy. And the extra money was needed to buy other things.

"Our insurance covers pregnancy and delivery. What more do we need?" he'd argued wearily.

The answer, it turned out, was plenty. He'd seriously misjudged the expense of having a child. The baby stretched their finances to the limit, and it would only get worse until Bruce could return to work.

Being grounded until the criminal and NTSB investigations concluded, he had no source of income. Far from stressing him further, he was secretly relieved. The last thing he wanted to do was walk onto an airplane.

In the fridge, Bruce spied two bottles of beer and a Diet Dr. Pepper. The microwave clock read 2:30 p.m. He reached for a beer, then stopped. No. Not yet. When Heather got up, maybe. When he woke her.

He popped the top of a soda and wandered around their living room. Photos of his parents, her parents, him, her, the two of them lined the walls and display cabinet shelves. Typical young-married-couple stuff. A photo of them on their honeymoon surrounded by something Heather had sewn that read, "Home Sweet Home" hung above their wall-mounted phone. Well, it used to be sweet.

His kid kept screaming, so Bruce went into the bedroom to see if he could persuade the little guy to stop. Heather was dead to the world, snoring, splayed out on their comforter and partially covered in laundry. Clean? Dirty? Bruce couldn't tell. He was jealous.

Jacob's little fists were balled up, eyes scrunched closed and toothless mouth open wide, his face crimson from effort. Maybe Bruce could give him a bottle. That was it, feed the little critter. His technique was improving, and now he felt more comfortable holding his son in his arms while offering him some expressed breast milk.

Expressed breast milk. Three words Bruce didn't ever expect to hear strung together in a sentence, let alone say.

Bruce scooped Jacob up, careful to support his head, which he wasn't even sure he had to do anymore, but, hey, for safety, why not? Heather hadn't provided him with the daily update on proper baby handling procedure. With all that had gone on in the last week, he cut her some slack. The baby, the angel flight with its honest-to-goodness life-threatening events. Combined with the chronic lack of sleep, it was just too much for her.

He held Jacob close. After only a few minutes, his touch seemed to lower the decibel level of Jacob's crying, so Bruce figured he was on to something. He rocked the little guy back and forth, like something out of a cartoon. Back and forth. Back and forth. The tighter he held his child, the quieter he got.

Bruce wasn't sure how long he'd been sitting on the edge of the bed with his baby when Heather grabbed him. She shouted, then began to shriek.

Jesus. More noise.

She yanked Jacob out of his arms.

"What have you done? Call an ambulance. Call it right now."

"What?"

She howled. "Bruce, what did you do? Call an *ambulance!*"

Bruce froze. Again. "What? Why?"

But Heather had pulled their son away and turned her back on him.

He punched 9-1-1 into his mobile phone. "Baby, what's the emergency?" he asked innocently.

Heather made a sound that he'd never heard before, like a warrior ready to attack. She ran back and forth with Jacob in her arms, looking out the window, like she was waiting for something.

"You could have killed him. You could have..." her voice caught, she choked once, and then sobbed, all the while stroking the almost hairless head of her newborn son, who again began to wail.

Bruce cancelled the call.

He'd gotten Jacob to finally stop crying, an almost magical feat. What was all the fuss about?

Fifty-Four

TRIS'S SMALL OVERNIGHT bag felt like it was filled with rocks. She lugged it into her apartment one slow step at a time. Every few seconds she'd stop and breathe. Each eye blink, swallow, inhale and exhale sapped her small reserve of energy. She was running on fumes.

When the door opened, there was Orion. The sight of the stout Tuxedo was the first thing that had made her smile in days. He rubbed his face against her shaky legs as she opened a can of food for him.

Bron's battered old sofa looked like a feather bed, and Tris didn't even take her shoes off before she sank into it. The couch smelled faintly of black cherries. The familiar scent, which would have soothed her days before, now pitched her anxiety. Her brain whirred like and old movie projector with scenes, past and present.

In a strange way, Mike and his ex-had gotten back together in her last moments, his blood and hers commingled on the interior surfaces of the Royal.

Mike was alive. One of the two bullets had lodged in his spine and was removed during surgery. His parents flew in from Birmingham to be with him, along with a sister Tris hadn't known about.

Another secret.

Tris was off work indefinitely. Neither Bangor police nor the NTSB had given Woody any idea when they would allow the Royal to be flown. Westin Charter's new airplane was coming on line in a couple of weeks, but it had to pass proving runs with the FAA before Woody could sell trips on it. Her mind raced to who might fly those trips. Bruce was grounded. Probably Woody and Tris, then. Hopefully, she wouldn't be pressed back into the cockpit too soon. The last place she wanted to be right now was on an airplane.

Orion jumped up on the couch, flopped over on his side, licked one of his paws, and went to sleep. Seemed like a pretty good idea. Tris pushed each shoe off with the opposite foot, curled up in a deep corner of the old couch, and was out in seconds

Her mobile phone woke her after only two hours. Not quite ready to get up, she pulled her phone from her pants pocket and flipped it open.

"Hello?"

"Hey, Tris? Di. What the heck happened? I got your message, and I'm hearing about your flight on the news." Diana sounded frantic.

It was unusually quiet in the background. "Hey, Di. Where are you?"

"The crash pad in Brussels. Please, fill me in."

Tris sluggishly sat up and rubbed her eyes.

"Hello? Tris? Are we still connected?"

Tris squeezed her eyes shut. "Yes. Right here. Sorry. My body is wiped. I swear I barely know where I am. I'm fine. But Di . . . everyone else . . . it was awful . . . surreal."

Diana responded as though she were thinking aloud. "Wow.

People shooting each other on airplanes. Next thing you know, they'll be shooting at *us.*" The idea of anyone trying to hurt a pilot in flight was so far-fetched even Tris had to chuckle.

Diana was silent as Tris related the details of the last few days to her. "Imagine my utter shock when we arrived in Iqaluit, of all places, and found Mike's ex-wife. The one he said he had a perfectly normal break-up with. The one he said was *dead.* Danny knew. He tried to warn me. If Woody had known—no way he'd have been hired. No way. And if *I* had known—"

"Did you want to know?" Diana had a way of slicing through the layers of an issue and piercing its heart.

"Yes. No. Damn, I don't know. That guy, he was so . . . *engaged.* Sat there with me at a restaurant in Burbank and told me the whole saga of his marriage. And listened to my stories about Tetrix, about Bron." She had to catch her breath before continuing. "Diana, I believed everything he told me. *Everything his touch told me. Everything his lovemaking told me. I believed it all.* And it was a lie. All of it."

"Are you sure, Tris? Are you sure what he felt for you was a lie?"

Was it?

"He wanted to move in together," she said softly. "He asked me before we left on that trip. I was going to say yes. I made him keys, Di."

Tris's pager beeped. All she saw were the numbers 9-1-1.

She wiped the tears from her face with her pilot shirt. It stank.

"Di, thanks for calling. I hate to do this, someone's paging me with an emergency. I've gotta go. I'll call you back."

Fifty-Five

EVERY FEW MINUTES, Tris got up, walked around a bit, then sat back down. Her palms were warm from rubbing them on her thighs, just to feel something, anything, besides the lump in her throat.

The coffee shop in a far corner of the mall, away from the steady stream of shoppers, was her favorite. Its worn leather club chairs looked so inviting, but Tris squirmed in the one she chose, and couldn't get comfortable. *Hearts in Atlantis* sat unopened on the chair's arm, its boarding pass bookmark peeking out the top.

She couldn't get Bruce out of her mind. Poor Bruce. Danny's emergency call was to tell her about something that happened with the baby. It wasn't clear what actually occurred. Maybe the baby stopped breathing, or Heather thought he had?

Turned out Jacob was fine. But the shock of it, another catastrophe on top of everything else Bruce and Heather had been through was unimaginable. When would it stop?

At least she'd had the chance to talk with Danny, someone who always understood her. She'd experienced the kind of terror no pilot she'd ever known had endured. But he was focused on Bruce and Heather. The couple were starting counseling together. He mentioned how hard it was for them to adjust to parenting. More than once during the call, Tris wondered if this was the kind of conversation Danny would best have with his wife. She'd listened, for Danny's sake, but could barely process his concerns through her own internal clamor.

She'd tried to reach Diana again, but her calls went to voice mail. Last night, she'd rifled through her address book, the small wire-bound volume with a picture of the sun on the cover that she'd bought in a souvenir shop in London, longing to see the name of someone she could talk to. Each entry had been painstakingly written in black pen—black pen only, for permanence, as though she were updating her logbook.

Yet the permanence never extended beyond the ink on the page, not to the friendships, the connections themselves. Reading name after name, then silently moving on to the next, hoping that she'd maintained some meaningful relationship with someone, one that would offer her comfort, or simply a non-judgmental ear.

Since she started flying, there was never enough time. "Sorry, I've got a trip," became her signature RSVP to every invitation. She'd done this. She was alone, and she'd done it to herself.

Tris tried to curl up in the chair and focus on her book one more time. Maybe she could force herself to relax. Yes. Right after one more check of her pager.

There were five missed pages. Woody had been trying to reach her. Damn. Why had she put the pager on vibrate and let it fall deep into her purse?

The book held her seat while she walked into the main mall to call Woody back.

"Westin Charter. This is Phyll." Phyll. Had anyone given her the low-down on what was happening?

"Hey, Phyll. It's Tris. Woody's been paging me?"

"Oh, quite."

"Been a helluva couple of weeks, eh?"

Phyll said something Tris couldn't make out, probably talking to someone else in the room.

"Sorry, love. Did you say something?"

"Can you give me some idea why Woody wants to talk to me?"

Phyll hesitated. "I wish I could. But the new airplane's coming on line next week. Lots of people in and out of here doing interviews."

"Pilots?" Tris tried to keep the alarm out of her voice.

"Yes, I believe so."

Woody didn't ask me to help with the interviews.

"Let me talk to him please."

"Right. But, Tris, how are you?"

Tris craved the moment she could give a real answer—freaked out, scared, exhausted. *And, for reasons passing understanding, I miss Mike.* But this was pro forma.

"Thanks Phyll. I'm all right. I'm fine. Tired. But fine."

Phyll must have pressed hold, because the recorded voice proclaiming the virtues of Westin Charter—in a speech Tris had memorized over the years—chirped away at her.

"Tris?"

"Woody. Hi."

"I'll get right down to it. I don't have a lotta time. So, I'm knee-deep in bullshit from, well, everyone ... the FAA, NTSB, police in Bangor. You name it. And your buddies at Tetrix call me every day asking me this or that. I guess their guy, the woman's husband, is raising a stink. Like we could have known anything."

Tris let Woody go on. He'd get to the point eventually.

"I've gotta talk to you. In person. Just me and you. Where we go from here."

Not at all unexpected. Woody had pretty much left her alone since she was home. But this was aviation. She was the only captain available to take responsibility for whatever Woody needed to offload.

"When?"

"Tomorrow. Nine a.m. See you then." He hung up.

Tris barely cleared the screen on her mobile phone when it rang again. There was no caller ID displayed, which usually meant Diana was calling from Europe.

"Di. Good. Thanks for calling me back. I just talked to Woody. He—"

Diana interrupted. "Look, I know this is a really bad time. But I could use your help."

Tris wasn't sure how much she could help anyone else right now. "Okay."

"Tris. I'm grounded," Diana announced.

"What? Why?"

The noise in the background got louder. People laughing and what must have been a juke box playing a song in French.

"Di, where are you?"

"Toulouse. I'm off the schedule. They sent my FO back to the barn, but they kept me here. To ice me. Probably while they figure out how to can me."

"Why this time? What's wrong with them?" Tris was flabbergasted.

Diana gulped so loudly Tris could hear it. "They have a good reason this time."

"Because?"

Diana breathed out noisily. "Because I struck my first officer. I hit him. When he didn't respond quickly enough to my request for a checklist. I actually hit him."

Did I hear her correctly?

"Di, start from the beginning, please. You know what I'm dealing with here. I want to help, but you gotta walk me through it."

And for the next few minutes, Diana led Tris on a harrowing tour of anger, frustration, and loss of control.

Tris listened, her own rage welling up. She hated flying, hated aviation and everything about it. For one thing, Diana was thousands of miles away. Even though they had a phone connection, for something like this, it wasn't enough. Definitely not enough.

"But why? This is incredible."

Diana didn't try to minimize her actions. "You know . . ." she paused, coughed, then continued. "If I had to guess, I think it might be some of those vitamins I'm taking. The ones I got at the gym. I don't think they were good for me, Tris."

"Were they actually vitamins?" Tris asked.

"We'll find out. The FAA medical team is doing a thorough screening. And then we'll see. They made me feel great—strong, energetic. But I think they . . . well, let's wait and see what the FAA says." Diana concluded.

Another float in the parade of horribles marching through Tris's world. Tris dug for anything she could say to comfort her friend. "They forced you into this position, Di. Made you get treatment. Now they're complaining about the effects of that treatment." But it was a weak defense. Because if Diana had done what she said—struck a crew member in the course of performing their duties—then it was indefensible.

"Can the union help?" Tris asked.

"How?" Diana's voice cracked. "I served my country. I served the company. I moved my life thousands of miles away—at their request—to act as a role model at this company, flying with kids who had, I don't know, 1000 hours of flight time. Barely."

"What's your end game?" Tris asked.

The question hung in the air. When Diana finally responded, the indignation from moments before was gone.

"I wish I knew. I've spent so many years here, built a solid reputation. A reputation I deserved. And now it's gone. Like that. Just *gone*. I can't get it back."

Tris blew out her breath. "Maybe it's time for you to come home. Wave the white flag. Find a job in the states. There's a pilot shortage—haven't you heard?"

Diana laughed. They'd been hearing about this 'pilot shortage' for years, as every pilot they knew competed for the few plum flying jobs out there. "So much seniority lost. Back to the bottom of the pile. And that's if I can even get a job." Now her friend was crying. Tris closed her eyes tightly, about to do the same. "I swear I don't even remember what he said or did. How could he make me do that? It's on the cockpit voice recorder, sure, but I can't *remember*. Did I black out? Thank God it didn't happen in flight. The only saving grace is that it didn't happen in flight."

Moments of silence were followed by the snap of a cigarette lighter, a whoosh of flame and the deep inhale that followed.

Diana's self-disgust was palpable. "Tris, I hit a guy. Stick a fork in me. I'm done."

Therapist Shoots Ex-Husband, then Kills Herself: Pilot and Passenger Embraced Before Shooting

BY NUNATSIAQ NEWS

Iqaluit—Christine Marie Edgemon, 42, the passenger on the deadly "angel" flight from Iqaluit to Bangor, Maine took her own life after shooting her ex-husband twice, according to the Bangor Medical Examiner's Office.

New evidence in the high-altitude airplane shootout was released by the Bangor Police Department and suggests that Warren Michael Marshall, a crew member on the "angel" flight, and Edgemon, his ex-wife, now deceased, may have embraced before any shots were fired.

"We've examined the trajectory of the bullets along with how we found the bodies. We've also reviewed preliminary investigative conclusions by the NTSB [National Transportation Safety Board]. Evidence strongly suggests physical contact between the two parties," said Detective Chief Inspector Robert Gann of the Bangor Police Department.

"We are still reviewing all the evidence. And we have yet to speak to Mr. Marshall, who is recovering from complex surgery at Eastern Maine Medical Center and only recently has been allowed visitors. As soon as his doctors clear us to interview him, we hope to have more information."

Marshall survived two gunshot wounds, which he received during the flight between Iqaluit and Bangor. The airplane, a Royal 350, was scheduled for a fuel stop in Bangor before continuing on to Exeter, Illinois, its final destination.

Patricia F. Miles and Bruce L. Burkey, the pilots of the catastrophic "angel" flight, so named because it was a non-profit flight taking Edgemon from remote Iqaluit to Exeter for specialized medical treatment, both escaped injuries. They are reportedly cooperating with Bangor police, NTSB, and Federal Aviation Administration (FAA) inquiries.

Miles and Burkey are being touted as heroes for landing the plane safely despite the discharge of a firearm only feet away from them. Neither pilot has commented. Woodrow Westin, of Westin Charter Company, who owns the airplane and employed both pilots said that Miles and Burkey, "value their privacy. But I'm sure proud as I can be to call them my employees, and my friends."

Edgemon and her husband, Tetrix Inc. project manager Erik Hudson, moved to the capital of Nunavut two years ago. Edgemon worked as a grief counselor serving the Inuit community of Iqaluit. In previous interviews, Edgemon, a licensed therapist, said she'd begun the work of helping people manage the deaths of loved ones and friends. Recently, she began counseling terminally ill patients to plan their own demise. According to sources close to Edgemon, she under-took that work to help heal the wounds she suffered from her father's suicide when she was seven years old.

Ironically, it was a single bullet to the head, fired by Edgemon herself, that ended her life.

Hudson has told police that his wife had recorded a suicide note addressed to him. He found it at their home. No portions of the tape have been released, but sources close to the investigation say that the tape left no doubt that Edgemon intended to commit suicide, and to do it on that flight.

Hudson could not be reached for comment.

No further details on the investigation into security at the private terminal in Iqaluit that permitted Edgemon to bring a gun aboard the "angel" flight have been released.

Fifty-Six

AS SOON AS a reporter told her that Mike was giving interviews, Tris called his hospital room in Bangor. For two days straight, she tried the number every hour. It rang and rang. No one ever answered.

Reporters loved to share the facts with Tris, each assuring her they had the best, most current information. Specifics of Mike and Christine's relationship—the marriage, breakup, divorce, and subsequent stalking—were splashed across the pages of the *Exeter Tribune.* The salacious details mercifully drowned out information about her and Bruce, for which she was grateful.

No one asked Tris whether her relationship with Mike was any more than professional. She silently thanked him for keeping that secret. "Angel Flight Love Triangle" was the last headline she wanted to see on CNN's news crawl.

Tris cried every time she stumbled upon one of the few things Mike had left in her apartment. A razor, which Mike only used to trim the edges of his full beard, a couple of t-shirts in the laundry. The worst breakdown came after she unscrewed the cap on his aftershave, the one that smelled like cherries. He rarely shaved but wore that scent whenever they were together. Each discovery reminded her of how close she came to a real relationship. And then she'd remember that he'd lied, and stop crying.

Tris gathered his belongings into a bag, dropped the red heart-shaped chain, now stripped of her apartment keys, to the bottom, and went to put it in the hall closet. On her way, Orion darted out in front of her. She stopped short, braced herself against the end table where her answering machine was set up, and accidentally hit the rewind button.

When it wound backward for a few seconds instead of quickly resetting, Tris took a seat on the couch next to Orion to hear the missed message. The bag lay crumpled at her feet.

The answering machine's recorded voice announced, "Message One received April 12th, 2000, at six-forty-six a.m." Just before the angel flight took off.

"Hi baby. It's me." Mike's voice filled the room. "I'm so sorry about last night. And the night before, and this morning. Well, about everything. All of it. All the things I didn't say, and especially about Kick, uh, Christine. Look, to me, she *was* dead. When she and I broke up, when our marriage ended, I couldn't accept it. I, I did some things I never should have done. Said some things. Said some things that weren't true. Did some things I'll be embarrassed about and regret until the end of my days.

"Yes, Christine Edgemon is my ex-wife. She is alive. She is our angel flight passenger. Baby, if I had realized that sooner, I would never have been here, never have been on this flight. And I would have told you. I didn't even think to read the passenger file until that meeting. I mean, you were so *on* it. And when I learned it was her, the day before the trip, I didn't know what to do. The angel flight, the whole Chief Pilot thing, the promotion getting between us, our future, then of all people we were picking up Kick, it was all too much. I figured we'd sort it out when I got home.

"And I still hope we will. But right now, you have to know how sorry I am. For lying to you. For not trusting you with the truth. You know how pilots are, right? I was afraid you'd think less of me, not respect me as much. Not love me.

"When this stupid flight is over, I'll tell you everything. The truth this time, all of it. And I pray that you'll still want me."

Tris sat completely still, listening as tears slid quietly down her cheeks. Orion had stopped purring.

"And to prove it, well, I guess I'll be the first to say it. Yeah. Here it goes." He cleared his throat and sniffed. His voice cracked slightly. "I love you. I do. I love you Tris. Good night, baby. See you later at home."

The answering machine clicked.

"End of new messages."

Fifty-Seven

TRIS PULLED INTO the parking lot of Dr. C's building the next day, and for the first time, she didn't care who saw her. Reading, sleeping, walking—none of that helped. The healing work done with the help of the woman in the string of pearls was the remedy she needed most. The Corolla swung into the first open spot, and Tris strode into the building.

Tris flung the door to the waiting area open and sat with her right leg bouncing like a jackhammer until the red light went off. Only seconds passed before Dr. C opened her office door.

"Hello Tris. Come in," she said, exactly as she had so many times before.

Once both of them were seated, Tris expected a barrage of questions from her therapist: about the angel flight, Bruce, Mike. But Dr. C observed Tris with her typical deadpan expression and simply said, "How are you?"

Tris parroted the question. "How am I? Honestly, I have no idea."

"I've heard what happened," Dr. C admitted. "It was hard not to read about that flight. Are you all right?"

"Physically, yes. But the trip—first, Mike lied to me about his ex-wife. The one he said was dead." Tris picked at a bandage on her right forearm, a remnant of the only physical injury she had sustained on the angel flight: a deep cut when one of the paramedics accidentally bumped her with their equipment. "But there she was. Alive. And planning to kill herself on my airplane."

She told Dr. C what she'd learned about Warren Michael Marshall, the man she'd welcomed into her past, her bed, and her life.

"Danny tried to warn me. He knew about Mike's past. He told me about it, and I ignored him."

"He did? And you didn't believe him? Why?"

Why, indeed. Her hands shot into the air, then slapped her thighs. "Because I thought he was jealous. How fucking arrogant. Why after so many years wouldn't I simply believe that one of my closest friends was telling me the truth?"

Dr. C frowned, clearly not satisfied. "Is there more to it, Tris?"

"I didn't want to believe it, I guess. Not then. It was spot on. But I..."

"Didn't you trust him?"

An involuntary laugh escaped her. "Danny? I did. I do. But..."

"But what?"

Tris stood up, stepped away. It was so hard to say it. "I wanted Mike. I wanted him to be the guy I believed he was. I miss him. Mike. Warren. I don't care what his name is. I *miss* him. The man I was with was *not that guy.*" Tris paced the room. Dr. C's eyes followed her, but she said nothing.

Church bells tolled faintly outside. For a moment, Tris wished she were in that church. Never religious, nor from a religious family, she was suddenly comforted by the repetitive sound, each toll the same. The bell rang at exactly the same time every day, day after day. Predictability. Certainty. Peace.

Those resonant chimes stirred up primal questions: Are our lives already mapped out? How much control do we have? Tris suspected—no, feared—she'd never find answers.

"What are you thinking about, Tris?"

"Something my mother used to say. 'People show you who they are.' That I should have faith in what I see, what people *do*. Not so much what people say."

Many hours had been spent in that room on the distant relationship between Tris and her mother. Both of their worlds fell apart when Tris was twelve, and her father died suddenly. Neither woman ever shared their grief. Tris was only a child. But well into adulthood, the pain over their mutual loss hovered between them.

Fear of abandonment was at the core of her underlying anxiety, Dr. C had said. And it was no wonder, as the only people she'd ever truly loved—her father, her grandfather, Bron—had deserted her. Now Mike was gone.

She was all alone.

Dr. C's lips parted, like she wanted to say something, then closed firmly. She leaned toward Tris. "Have you called your mother?"

Tris shook her head, feeling the now-daily prick of tears. "If it would help, I already would have."

Dr. C nodded. "You've talked to me about faith before, Tris. What is it you have faith in?"

She squeezed her eyes shut and the pent-up drops fell. "That I did the right things. Did the best I could with Bruce, *for* Bruce, *for* Mike, *for* Christine. But it wasn't enough. Nothing I did was enough." Her fists tightened and, this time, the fingernails pierced a layer of skin.

Dr. C waited for Tris to settle back in her seat. "Well, you know what I'd say to that." The therapist smiled.

Tris chuckled. "That I have to forgive—I shouldn't expect to forget, and I won't. That I have to forgive *myself*."

Fifty-Eight

THE KITCHEN TOOK on a sepia hue as the sun went down. The blinds were drawn, like someone had died.

Danny's beer was warm. Em had run into the bedroom crying. No matter how hard he tried, he couldn't always figure out the reasons Em got upset.

When she finally came out, she walked straight to the refrigerator without acknowledging him. Her face was swollen, her eyes red.

"Hey babe. Feeling any better?"

"A little. I think." The fridge door squeaked open, followed by the hum of the condenser. His hand relaxed its tight grip on the beer can. He could sense that the level of tension in the air was low and judged it safe to proceed.

"Good. I'm glad. Grab a drink, or a beer or something, and have a seat. Let's enjoy some quiet time, okay?"

She nodded her agreement, and a few seconds later popped open a Diet Pepsi and sat at their kitchen island.

Their house seemed like a museum, one of those staged rooms where the bedspread is never mussed. A book long forgotten sat at the same angle that it had for decades. Tenderly dusted, but never read. Not a pillow out of place, not a speck on the wide plank floors, not a drop of water on the tile in the kitchen. Faucets didn't drip. The trashcan didn't smell. Still, a musty, stale aroma hung in the room: the signature scent of their marriage.

He considered his wife, sitting quietly, sipping a can of soda. No surprises, but she was pleasant, honest, and had a good heart. Wasn't that everything he wanted in a woman?

As his heartbeat picked up speed, he reached the one inescapable conclusion, the one thing that no matter how hard she tried, his wife could not be. She could not be Tris.

He shook his head, tried to catapult the thought from his consciousness.

"What's wrong?" she asked.

"Nothing. Nothing. I can't believe everything that's happened." That much was completely true.

"Hmm. Yeah. It'll take a while for it all to sink in. So, have you talked to Bruce or Heather today?"

"Me? Em, you're the one they call." He caught himself starting to get testy. "But after our visit yesterday, seeing how we left them, I have a good feeling."

Em nodded as she swallowed a gulp of her soda. "Me, too."

"In a way, I kind of admire Bruce. I mean, it takes guts to admit that you've picked the wrong career, and walk away, just like that. After having a baby, too! Flying was something he'd said he'd always wanted, but he's realized it wasn't for him. Gotta give the guy credit. I'm glad they're going to counseling together. Bruce and Heather are gonna make it, for sure."

The air in the room took on a sharper smell. Em's shoulders now poked up toward her ears. His wife's apprehension destroyed the temporarily companionable atmosphere.

"It's not Bruce and Heather people have doubts about. It's us." Em leaned toward her husband. "Everyone does. Don't you?"

When Danny didn't answer, she went on. "What went wrong with Bruce? That story, about almost flying the airplane into a mountain. Or where he kind of spaced out on that insane angel flight. Has that ever happened to you?" She faced her husband, brows knit with concern.

Danny looked into his wife's eyes and patted her forearm for emphasis. "Em, listen to me. It never has, it never could. Bruce . . . well, I don't know, but according to Tris, what happened to him had been brewing for some time."

Em slid off the barstool and started to pace.

"Tris. Yes. His captain. His friend. Why didn't she do anything to help him? Where was she when her first officer needed her, huh? And Mike? Her *boyfriend*. Who knows if he'll ever recover? My brother-in-law and my cousin. Both . . . damaged. On *her* watch. Your precious Tris."

"That's crazy. C'mon. Be fair. Bruce froze at the controls. Mike got *shot*." And Tris could have died. She could be gone.

"Why didn't she take care of them?" Em cried, then sobbed, her body crumpling.

This was dangerous territory. If Danny jumped to defend Tris, which was his first instinct, the conversation would decay into their typical dispute about how he wasn't over her, on and on. He didn't have the strength for that today.

"Look, I know you're upset. Let's not talk about this right now. It's not productive."

"Well, that's a first," she shot back. "You not wanting to talk about Tris. That's never happened before." She flung the empty soda can into the recycling bin and stomped back to the bedroom. He heard the door slam shut.

Danny squeezed his empty beer can so hard the aluminum split on one side and cut his hand. He licked the blood off his palm before he pressed it into his jeans, staring at the jagged red dash still smeared on the side of the can.

Fifty-Nine

THE SIGHT OF the homeless guys milling about outside the Westin hangar comforted Tris. Billy-Bob had a cigarette in his mouth—unlit of course. He knew the rules.

"Hey girlie girl, where ya been?" he called. She shot him a quick wave as she walked by.

When the hangar door cracked open, Tris was assaulted by an unfamiliar and decidedly unpleasant smell, like industrial cleaning fluid. Maybe Woody had finally called a professional service to scrape the grime off the place.

When she saw the Royal perched in its usual spot on the concrete floor, the smell made more sense. What kind of solvent could erase the remnants of the horrendous events that occurred on board?

Tris stood at the bottom of the air stairs, took a step up, thought better of it, and stopped.

She wasn't ready to see the inside of the plane. Not yet. Someday, probably soon, she'd come in early for a trip and spend some time alone in the cabin; try to make a type of peace with what had happened there.

Phyll sat at the flight-planning desk, on the phone. Tris tapped her on the shoulder, and without interrupting what she was saying, Phyll exhaled like she'd been holding her breath, smiled up at her, and went back to consulting something on her computer screen.

The schedule was packed. A few trips were listed under an airplane tail number Tris wasn't familiar with. The second Royal?

"Hey Tris." Woody poked his head out of his office door and beckoned her inside. He walked out from behind an unruly stack of books and papers and hugged her. That was a first. "I'm so glad you're okay."

"Thanks, Woody. I don't even know where to start."

Woody looked her up and down, as if checking to make sure she was still in one piece. They'd spoken on the phone a few times but hadn't seen each other since before she left for Iqaluit. "I see you got the aircraft back. I haven't had a chance to look inside yet. Glad it's home."

Woody hesitated. "Me, too. The FAA won't stop sniffing around. They came down hard on me for not doing a better background check on Mike. If I'd have known . . . Geez, I'd known the guy for years, you know?"

The old boys network? Oh, I know.

"It's over, Woody."

"I sure hope so."

She could hardly fault Woody for not looking closely enough at Mike. After all, she didn't, either.

Tris shrugged. "Is that it?"

Woody raised his hand. "Tris, relax, okay? Just let me talk for a minute. Look, things are all over the place here. I can't begin to calculate the amount of money this whole disaster has cost us, and all at the exact same time Jimbo and I committed to buy that second airplane. I'm tapped. Completely tapped. And you can bet that after this, Tetrix isn't giving us any spillover flying."

"Have you talked to Zorn?"

"Practically every day," Woody replied wearily. "He's been involved in every detail of the investigation. He never misses a chance to point his finger, does he? 'Well, Woody,' he starts out really nice, '*you* were the one that chose Warren Marshall as your Chief Pilot. *You* put him in charge of that flight. You couldn't trust Tris Miles?' That guy's a piece of work."

Tris was all too familiar with her former boss's penchant for exaggerating to make a point. It was one of his many unattractive qualities.

"What about business? There are plenty of charter customers out there. What about the stuff you had on the schedule? Sounded like Phyll was booking a trip when I came in."

Woody smiled slyly. "So, like I said, things are disorganized, and I'm cash poor. But it turns out," he paused for effect, "that angel flight was a boon to our business after all, thanks to all the press our 'hero pilots' have gotten. I've been hiring rent-a-pilots left and right to fill in next to me while you've both been out, so I didn't have to cancel every single trip on the schedule. I'd forgotten how much hard work goes into these trips."

Tris gripped the metal sides of the guest chair. "Okay . . . ?"

Woody's fingers twitched at the edge of the desk. "Tris, I've got, well, I've learned something. I gotta hear it from you."

She was sure he could hear her heart pound. "Hear what?"

Woody paused, swallowed hard, and ran the palm of his hand against his forehead as he leaned into the desk.

"Are you seeing a shrink?"

He must already know, or he wouldn't have asked. Either way, she wouldn't lie to Woody.

"Yes. I am. I started seeing one after I left Tetrix. To get over my ex-boyfriend's death, and that horrible job experience. And it helped. It made me a better person. And a better pilot, Woody."

"Of course. You should talk to someone. But these guys, you know—" Woody raised both forearms in a gesture of surrender. "Tris, I don't care. Your personal business should be yours. Just know that it might not be as . . . as secret as you thought."

"Thanks. I appreciate that."

He continued. "With all the attention on us, maybe this isn't the right time for you—I mean, if someone gave you closer scrutiny . . . well, it's a risk. Crap on a cracker, Tris, you know the feds."

He didn't have to spell it out. If the government was investigating Westin Charter's hiring and training policies, surely someone would learn about her therapy.

She would politely resign and offer to help him hire a new Chief Pilot. Tris owed him that much.

Woody pushed up the bill of his Ridgid Tool baseball cap and scratched his forehead. Then he tented his hands in front of his eyes, which briefly shielded his face. When he looked up, his eyes were rimmed red. Tris had never, ever seen him like this.

"Right." Woody's voice broke, so he paused to collect himself. "Since the beginning, everything I ever asked you to do, you did." He put both of his forearms on the desk and leaned forward. Then, he stretched his arms out and pushed his chair all the way back into the bookcase, which wobbled. Luckily, nothing fell off and hit him in the head.

"I'd completely understand if you said no. But, please. Please be the Chief Pilot of Westin Charter. Make this company the way it should have been all along. I need you. And the risks . . . I'll take them if you will."

A barely perceptible nod passed between the two pilots. The industry signal of mutual respect.

"Of course I'll do it," she said.

"Thank you. I don't know what ... just thank you." Woody sniffed.

The two rose to shake hands, and as Tris took his, Woody awkwardly pulled her toward him and hugged her again.

"Good. All right. Good," he said, sat back in his chair, and grabbed a phone message.

There was one loose end nagging at her. "Hey, Woody, can I ask you something? How'd you find out? About the therapist?"

He exhaled. "Someone ... close to you saw you at your doctor's office. They put two and two together."

It could only be him, the person whose career she'd stalled, who went behind her back, who helped Mike get the Chief Pilot job. This must have been what he apologized for at the hospital.

"So, Bruce told you, eh?"

Woody's right eyebrow lifted. "Bruce? No, Mike. Mike told me."

Sixty

IT HAD BEEN so long since Tris bit into a toasted coconut donut, she'd forgotten how sweet they were. She blanched at the first explosion of sugar in her mouth but acclimated quickly. It got her wondering when she'd last eaten something for the pure enjoyment of it, and not solely to keep herself alive.

She picked a small flake of coconut off the cake underneath, so she could enjoy every bite, and then washed it down with a swallow of the delicious black coffee from the donut shop. Danny was a few yards away on his mobile phone talking to Em. He rarely walked away from Tris for privacy during calls, and she sensed that things were not going well at home.

Danny gestured constantly as he spoke, poking his free arm in the air. It made Tris sad. She really hoped that Em and Danny made it. But who ever knew about relationships? Only the people in them, and even then, who could ever really be sure?

Danny was frustrated. He grumbled that Em had become a different person since the fiasco with Bruce, Heather, and little Jacob.

Tris had finally met Jacob when she stopped by their house to drop off a baby gift. Bruce told her about his therapy sessions with Heather. Both pilots wished that he'd gone sooner.

Poor Bruce. He'd been percolating for the longest time. "My therapist said it was Lemaster," he told her. "Something about that fire raised issues—repressed memories that I'd buried since childhood. She said they'd lain dormant for years." Tris, having wrestled with her own demons, could only imagine his.

Yet when Bruce's issues erupted, they'd almost killed him and her—more than once. His decision to stop flying was the right one.

Danny slid his phone back in his pants pocket and joined Tris on the bench. There was no breeze, the high sun gave little heat, and the temperature was a perfect fifty-eight degrees. Diffuse sunlight poked through the full branches of the oak tree the two old friends sat under.

"So?" She ended the comfortable silence.

"Yeah, Em's pissed," he responded.

"Same stuff?"

"Some version of it, I guess. But it's weird, you know? I know why she's upset, and I really don't blame her. There's been so much stress lately. And, of course, she's still not pregnant."

Tris didn't look at him. "No? You guys still trying?"

"On and off. This is not a great time for us. But Heather and Bruce, they're doing great. He's so devoted to Jacob, and he really loves Heather. You know, Bruce's parents are coming out to stay with them for a while," he said between bites.

Bruce talked all the time about how much he disliked his parents. But Jacob was their grandchild. "Yeah. He told me. They sound like they're a piece of work. When I was a kid, I thought mine was the only screwed up family out there. It was isolating. And now, of course, I know better. I really feel for Bruce."

Danny nodded, finished off donut number one, and reached into the bag for the second. She admired his consistency. Two glazed, coffee light, no sugar. Every time.

"It'll work itself out. But what about you?" He hesitated. "Have you talked to Mike?"

She shook her head, and the two sat in silence.

Had Mike loved her? Was he even able to love anyone but Christine?

A whistling sound signaled that the wind had picked up. She pulled her jacket tight around her chest. "You tried to warn me. And I didn't listen. Didn't want to hear it, not a word. Dismissed it as crew-room gossip. But of course—"

"Gossip starts somewhere down the road as truth," he finished her sentence. "It's all right Tris. I understand. I'm just grateful you weren't hurt. That Bruce wasn't hurt."

Oh, but aviation claimed its casualties, and not just on the angel flight. Bruce, Diana. Mike. Their stories were the stuff of daytime television. *The Jerry Springer Show.* Not real life.

Danny changed the subject. "What happened at the meeting? With Woody?"

Tris turned to Danny, lips spread in a smile of pure joy and spoke the words that would move her forward.

"He made me Chief Pilot, Danny. I'm the Chief Pilot of Westin Charter."

Danny dropped the remains of his donut, stood and reached for her. She rose, and they came together in an embrace bonded by enduring friendship.

They'd shared hundreds of flight hours, a tragic loss, and a career that had both disappointed and delighted them. They held each other tightly.

There was no need for words. The past was behind them, the

future not assured. There was nothing but the present. No day but today.

June 3, 2000

THE MOVERS HAD filled their truck with Tris's belongings. She'd be in her new place this afternoon in time for them to be delivered.

Orion wandered around the empty apartment, standing on parts of the floor his paws had never touched. Surely, he must be thinking, "Where the heck is everything?" When the time came to leave, she left her apartment keys on the kitchen counter as she'd been instructed, scooped him up, scratched his belly, and plopped him in his carrier.

Soon, she and Orion would head to a new home, a fresh start away from blank walls which bore the shadowy outlines of her memories. But she had one stop to make first.

On this day, four years before, she'd gotten that early morning call from Danny, the one that told her Bron was gone. It was why she chose this day to move out and move on.

In a shady spot in the cemetery parking lot, Tris cracked open the Corolla's windows and put a light sheet over Orion's crate.

Turning away, she walked the familiar path to where Bron lay.

"Hey, baby," she greeted him, as she always did, before she sat down on the grass by his headstone. The gold-tinted paint that filled the etched letters of his name, dates of birth and death, and beloved status had started to chip a bit over the last year. Tris made a mental note to call the grounds keepers and let them know.

In the still afternoon, Tris silently carried on her conversation. Sometimes, she spoke to him out loud. Other times, her body language punctuated a point that she made only in her head. Eyes closed, she saw the two of them together. Then Mike popped into her mind, and her heart caught, just for a second. Bron wouldn't care. He'd have wanted her to be happy, and she almost was.

Almost. The only communication she'd had with Mike since the angel flight was through his mother, who'd left an answering machine message imploring Tris in her thick southern accent to stop calling. "Wahhhren doesn't want to speak to you," she drawled. She offered no update on his condition, no clue about the progress of his recovery. Just like that, Mike was gone.

All her life, Tris had believed in "the one." Mike was "the one." Before him, Bron was "the one." Tris had no future with either man.

What if there was no "one?" What if that was just something that existed on the Lifetime channel, or in greeting cards? Something conjured by advertisers to keep everyone searching, moving around and away, never settled or satisfied?

"Okay, baby, it's time for me to go," she finally said. "Just one more thing." She inhaled deeply and reached into her pocket. Her fingers easily found the folded piece of paper with the small metal lump inside.

She unwrapped the package and gently removed the Air Force wings that Diana had given her so long ago, a visible symbol of achievement the former military aviator had passed on to Tris to commemorate the end of her flight training.

Tris blinked back tears as she placed the tiny metal adornment at the base of his stone. Recognition for all that had been sacrificed. She kissed her fingertips and pressed them against his name.

Then she stood up and brushed the dirt from her jeans.

"See you," she whispered.

So much longing, so much loss. It was time to heal.

Without glancing back, Tris strode the sunlit path to her car, and toward her future.

Acknowledgments

ANGEL FLIGHT was inspired by a trip I flew as a pilot for Baxter International in the late '90's. Our crew was assigned to pick up a woman who had a severe spinal cord injury and bring her to treatment at the Mayo Clinic. She was the wife of a Baxter executive, and the company donated its jet and crew—at great expense—to transport her. She was immobile, and a medical transport would have been prohibitively expensive for the family.

I've never forgotten that flight which, to this day, is probably the most important I've ever flown. Our crew was comprised of a female captain and first officer. Our passengers included the injured woman's husband. I remember thinking how lucky I was to work for a company that would help this family, and knew I'd write about an angel flight someday.

While real-life experience provided the story seed, no novel enters the world as a published book without the help of many generous people.

First, the experts. Dr. Lawrence "Larry" Weinstein, a childhood friend, gave me expert insight into the workings of Aviation Medical Examiners. A number of people who I've never met also made substantial contributions to the authenticity of this story. Jennifer Pierce, an Air Traffic Control Specialist with the Houston ARTCC provided insight into what happens on the ATC side when a pilot declares an emergency—thankfully, something I never had to do. Author and retired Milwaukee Police Department Sergeant Patrick O'Donnell and Bangor Police Sergeant Wade Betters made sure I correctly described police procedure. Mary Jo Lagoski, MA, LPC answered all of my questions about therapy from a therapist's point of view. To all of you, my deepest gratitude.

Authors Marlene Wagman-Geller, Lori Oliver-Tierney, Gene Desrochers, Alexa Kingaard, and Mike Murphey were readers of early drafts. They had to muddle through a version of the story that wasn't quite there yet. Thanks to you five for taking the time to do that, and for your sincere praise.

Lori has been one of my major cheerleaders, which every writer needs whether they admit it or not. There were so many times when I was ready to say sayonara to this project, and Lori's encouragement and consistently positive attitude kept me moving. I'm grateful for your support and friendship, Lori.

Lori, Gene, Alexa, Mike and I are members of a small but fierce community of authors at Acorn Publishing, LLC. When I joined Acorn with FLYGIRL back in 2018, I had no idea I'd meet so many engaged authors. Thank you Holly Kammier and Jessica Therrien for inviting me once again to work with you and the talented cadre of writers at Acorn. And how do you two come up with those fantastic covers? Two gold medals in cover design from me.

San Diego Writers, Ink., is the cornerstone of the writing

community where I live. The six weeks I spent with Judy Reeves in a course based on her essential, "The Writers Book of Days," led to the first draft of this book. I was then privileged to be a member of two Read & Critique groups through SDWI, proctored by the one and only T. (Tammy) Greenwood, a constant supportive presence in my writing life, and author Mark A. Clements. Mark also performed a developmental edit at a critical transitional time for this manuscript. Thank you, Judy, Tammy and Mark for your advice and counsel.

The rubber meets the road, as it were, when a book-to-be is professionally edited at the story, structure and sentence levels. And for her efforts, I am beyond indebted to my editor Jennifer Silva Redmond. To paraphrase friend and author Eric Peterson, first, she made this book better—then she made it much better.

Hats off to the people who read and loved FLYGIRL, and who were willing to read pre-release versions of ANGEL FLIGHT. Thank you Amy Reder, Mimi Loucks, Theresa Freese, Sherrill Joseph, Robyn Muskat Frank, Karen Kirzner Adler and Mitchell Kardon for your interest in Tris's journey.

There is one person without whom ANGEL FLIGHT would never have existed in any form, let alone been published. From the last word of FLYGIRL through the crazy compilation that has become this book, my friend Barbara Shaw has provided counsel, critique and encouragement.

Barb read every version of this book, every alternate ending, reviewed every cover draft. She's evangelized my writing to anyone who would listen. Barb, who knew that a chance meeting on the courts at Balboa Tennis Club would lead to this? Sometimes, I get lucky. Thank you, Barb, for your friendship and tireless contributions to my writing journey.

ABOUT THE AUTHOR

Studio Bijou Photography

Robin D. "R.D." Kardon is a native New Yorker, educated in the New York City Public school system. She attended New York University where she earned a B.A. in Journalism and Sociology, magna cum laude, and was a member of Phi Beta Kappa. Robin graduated with a J.D. from the American University, Washington College of Law.

After ten years as a litigator, Robin began her professional flying career. She holds an FAA Airline Transport Pilot certificate with three captain qualifications and has flown all over the world in everything from single-engine Cessnas to the Boeing 737.

She currently resides in San Diego where she volunteers with local animal rescue organizations and dotes on her beloved rescue pets.

Follow Robin at
rdkardonauthor.com
@rdkardonauthor

Praise for FLYGIRL
Book #1 of The Flygirl Trilogy

by R. D. Kardon

"*Kardon's narrative is both thoughtful and gripping. She vividly portrays the fine line between respect and familiarity that women in nontraditional roles must walk to do their jobs well in the face of sexual harassment on one hand and antagonistic resistance on the other. Tris is an appealing and relatable character who struggles to keep both her self-respect and her ambition intact while negotiating the slippery morality of the corporate world.*" **—Kirkus Reviews**

"*[This] exciting, spirited debut follows a new female pilot as she vies to move up to the captain's seat . . . This soaring testament to the value of following one's dreams delivers the goods.*" **—Publishers Weekly**

"*Kardon creates a relatable heroine in Tris, a character who, along with her grit and determination to succeed, displays a range of authentic emotions and vulnerabilities . . . [I]interpersonal conflicts and the heroine's clear aspirations result in a satisfying narrative arc.*" **—The Booklife Prize**

"*A wonderful piece of writing with a bit of history and real-world issues laced throughout.*" **—The Indie Express**

"*Well written and interesting, [Kardon] tells the truth about those times.*" **—Texas Book Nook**

"*R. D. Kardon is such an imaginative and descriptive storyteller.*" **—On a Reading Bender**

CPSIA information can be obtained
at www.ICGtesting.com
Printed in the USA
BVHW032029250720
584663BV00003B/6/J

9 781947 392991